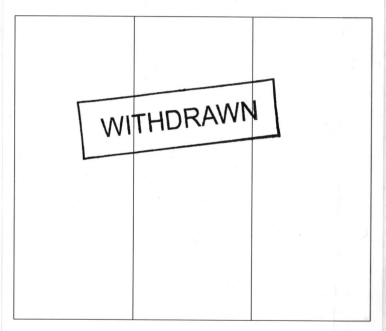

Also by Mandy Haggith

Fiction
The Walrus Mutterer
Bear Witness
The Last Bear

Poetry
Castings
letting light in
Into the forest

Non-fiction
*Paper Trails: From Trees to Trash,
the True Cost of Paper*

THE AMBER SEEKER

BOOK TWO OF
THE STONE STORIES

MANDY HAGGITH

Saraband

Published by Saraband,
Digital World Centre, 1 Lowry Plaza
The Quays, Salford, M50 3UB

and

Suite 202, 98 Woodlands Road,
Glasgow, G3 6HB
www.saraband.net

10 9 8 7 6 5 4 3 2 1

ISBN: 9781912235292
ISBNe: 9781912235308

Printed and bound in Great Britain by Clays Ltd, Elcograf SpA.

MIX
Paper from
responsible sources
FSC® C018072

CONTENTS

For Dad

TIN

SETTING OUT

SETTING OUT

MY PURPOSE

Laid out on my desk in front of me are three small tokens I wish you to have: a bronze owl, an amber bear and a walrus ivory dolphin. I don't yet know exactly how I'll get them to you, but I'll find a way. The owl is a symbol of Athena, the bear of Artemis, the dolphin of Apollo, but they mean far more to me than mere gestures to the gods. When you receive them, I hope that what I write below will help you to understand what they stand for.

What will this document be, exactly? A kind of letter? I suppose so. An epistle – the epistle of Pytheas has a ring to it, does it not? Perhaps it will be more than that. A testament? A kind of memoir? A confession? We'll see.

Where should I begin? With Rian, of course. She is the link between us. I bought her innocent and sold her world-wary. I have tried to pretend that what happened doesn't matter because she was a slave, but she was impossible to enslave, really. Some wild animals can't be tamed: otters, polecats, bears. Rian was like that. Ussa might have branded her, but her mind was always seeking freedom. When I bought her, I thought of her more as an adornment than a possession. She was an otter cub, and I wanted to pet her.

I first saw her on a stony beach in a strange northern region called Assynt. She stood out from everyone around her, even then. They were dark and swarthy, whereas she was small and her hair was amber, exactly the colour of the material I was seeking. It was like a flame coursing over her head and down her back. She never seemed to be aware of how striking it was, how beautiful it made her, and even though she tied it up, nothing could prevent it shining, gleaming, mesmerising everyone who looked at it.

I never learned her language, but I always make a point of knowing a few words in the tongue of every land I visit. I like to learn the word for beautiful, because it is often helpful to be able to show appreciation. I'd learned 'bóidheach' from the folk further south on the Winged Isle where we had been stormbound for a while, and when I spoke it there in Assynt, and touched her hair, some amber magic must have travelled between us, because somehow our fates became entangled.

Ussa had a lot to do with it, of course. She is the sorceress of entanglement. I know that clearly now and I had an inkling even then. I was under her spell, although perhaps not to the extent she wanted. I was already grasping the way her spells rebounded on her, the obsessive manner of her meddling. She took glamour to such an extreme it seemed sometimes like madness.

And Rian. Oh, Rian was a beam of innocence beside Ussa, a flower next to an eagle. You would have thought she wouldn't stand a chance against her, but of course if you pluck a flower, another will grow in its place. Purity can be crushed but it has a way of bouncing back. You can try to blot it out, smear it with dirt, but if it goes right to the core of someone it will resurface. Rian is delicate and Ussa thought she was weak. How wrong she was. She might not have been the quickest or smartest of people, but she was strong as rock.

4

What am I saying? I compare her to rock, otter and flower. She was all of these and none of them. She was unlike any other. You can tell already, of course; I fell in love with her.

I wasn't the only one flirting with her, but you know what? I think she was genuinely oblivious to us. She had that childlike innocence about her, like a shield. I think that was what made me feel so guilty about what happened.

I'll write more of Rian later, but first you need to understand the purpose of my journey. I went from here, Massalia, on the north shore of the Great Sea, in search of tin and amber and northern ivory. I hoped to identify resources in the north that are essential for our civilisation, and thereby find opportunities that would interest our emperor, Alexander. Yet whereas he took an army on his great venture east, I travelled alone. He sought to gain power, but I was seeking only knowledge. His life earned him grand statues and paintings adorning city walls, and although a few scratchings on parchment and papyrus will be all that's left to show of mine, I have what he has no longer. I live still, whereas the gods have allowed him to die. It gives me cause to ponder my fortune.

*

I am celebrated for my long voyage, but the inner journey I went on was longer and more dangerous, and the scars and souvenirs I have brought back to Massalia were mostly its result. I wrote about my physical journey in my book. I took a lot of pains over it. It is the only one I intend to publish, and I am proud of it. Even the title is good – *On the Ocean* – with its double meaning. On the one hand, it is a travelogue of my journey from home in Massalia to the mouth of the river Garonne and the rest of the way by sea, but on the other hand, it is also a treatise on the vast northern ocean, its people, its mysteries, its wonders. I ask myself why I bothered, sometimes, when people like Dicaearchus and

5

Mnason mock me for it, make me out to be some kind of fantasist. It all happened: there really is land that burns and melts, flaming, into the sea. And there really is, even further north, an end to the ocean where it freezes into slush and ice, so you can barely sail a boat through, where there is no land, nor sea nor air, but a mixture of these things, like a marine lung in which earth and water and all matter is in suspension.

They say I made it all up, these ignorant critics who have never stepped foot outside of their Akademie in Athens. Miserable old cynics they are. They doubt everything just for the sake of it. They even doubt the ocean giants, the living islands that lift to the surface and spout like smoke. The seafarers call them spirits; they revere them and sing to them. I have come to believe, with their knowledge of the vast ocean and how to survive on it, that those seamen have more wisdom than our great philosophers who, in their white robes and ivory towers, are only interested in the *idea* of the sea, not the taste of salt on their lips.

And as for the the walrus tusks from which the little dolphin is made, not a single person here will believe what I can tell about them. It was an old friend of my father's, a merchant and a devotee of Apollo, who offered me a generous reward if I could find out where the northern ivory originates. Even I struggled to believe half the stories from the Walrus Mutterer (no doubt you've heard them), but he swears they are true, and I have seen enough strange things to be credulous when an ocean farer tells me something, however far-fetched it might sound.

But if I start with the Mutterer and his stories I'll completely lose my thread. Although I intend this to be a personal story, a confessional, if you like, I suppose I should make an effort to make it logical.

OF BEARS

Please take particular care of the amber bear, for it is a thing of great significance and power. Consider it an amulet – but be wary of it.

I have always had a great interest in bears. The goddess of the oak groves and the hunt, Artemis takes the form of a bear at times and has the power to turn people into them. She does this so that we discover our true nature, for that is the magic of the bear. This is not necessarily pleasant, as I know only too well, but I was taught that the bear is a symbol of courage.

I encountered one early in my journey, not long after I left Massalia. It was very early in the year, around the time you call Imbolc, halfway between the winter and spring solstices. I headed west through the Midi, then up into the hills towards the head of the Garonne River. The sea route west out of our Great Sea – through the Pillars of Hercules and around Iberia – was of course out of the question. Apart from the fact that it is much further, I was not willing to risk travelling with Carthaginians, who control those waters and are by no means likely to grant a Greek safe passage. It seemed obvious to me to travel through Gaul. I speak Keltic fluently; my nurse made sure of that as she brought me up, and that made dealing with people easier everywhere I went.

So there I was, early in the morning, on my way in good time after spending the night in a shepherd's cottage. I had been walking through woods for perhaps half an hour, heading up a stream valley, and ahead of me I saw the pass, a narrow gap between the hills. In that gully I saw what I initially thought was a man standing, looking around and sniffing, and it was only when it dropped to four paws that I realised it was a bear. I feared I still had the smell of sheep on me from my stay the night before. It led off through the pass and I have to confess that this meant I

7

went on in great trepidation, wondering if it was lying in wait to ambush me.

I crept up to that pass with the hairs standing up on the back of my neck, padding as silently as I could. Before seeing the bear I had crunched along, striding and swinging my arms as if I was walking around a pleasure garden, but fear of meeting my end so early in my voyage in the jaws of a hungry carnivore meant that I approached the brow of the hill with great caution. I didn't see the animal again but it it had done me a great service in setting me on my guard. Peering out, I saw two men with horses down below me. My bear-induced fear prevented me from hailing them with a cheery good morning, which would have been my instinct. Instead I slunk into a gap between boulders, listening for their approach. From my hiding place, I watched. They were ugly bruisers, scarred and armed and undoubtedly dangerous. I let them pass without alerting them to my presence, more scared now of my fellow species than of the bear.

Instinct is a powerful force worth following. Take my advice and nurture it. This is the lesson of the bear. It was my fellow traveller throughout my journey, always reminding me to be alert to what might be over the brow of the next hill or hiding in the shadows. There are bears in the desert fringes of Afrika and bears even in the northernmost frozen wastes. Yes! There are white bears that live on the ice, huge and ferocious, they say – although I have only seen a mother with two cubs and she was solicitous of them, and gentle, and ran away from us humans to take her young to safety.

Bears have judged me, and found me wanting. But that comes later.

LE YAUDET

I first heard about ice bears from Ussa. It was early spring. The days were getting longer, and the weather was mild. I had been journeying for a couple of weeks and I was getting into my stride. I was becoming familiar with the ways of the ports and how to find boats that would be moving on up the coast, and I was learning how to persuade their captains to take me with them. Gold or silver wasn't always enough incentive. Every coastal community has a place where people gather for drink and stories and whatever follows from them, and so, when I reached Le Yaudet, that was where I headed.

Imagine the evening settling over the sea, lights on incoming boats dancing their ripple-dances on the water, and just back from the shore a cluster of stone buildings and timber barns where trade goods were stored. From the door of one building came the sound of a stringed instrument: a lyre. I can never resist music; it is like a lamp to a moth. I had already found a place to lodge for the night in a dingy fisherman's hut, but there were no other guests and the boat I had arrived on was returning westwards along the coast. I needed to find a vessel that would take me north to an island across the sea. I had heard several reports that this is where tin came from, although it was elusive. I had only seen ingots once so far, further south, in the hands of a trader who had bought them somewhere here, in this bustling place with its perfectly safe harbour.

So I was wandering, seeking, and the lyre pulled me in. I hung around until someone approaching asked me who I was. He was an enormously fat man with frog's eyes, carrying two big cod, and he said it was his house. I told him my story, and he invited me inside.

The building wasn't much to look at on the outside, but indoors it was splendid. Oak beams framed a long room, decorated with all manner of metal dishes and drinking vessels and brightly painted plates. The walls were plastered with murals of the sea; a monster of the deep with a huge winged tail reared up behind a raised dais on which the musician sat, playing his lyre and singing a song in the Keltic tongue. Another man was beside him with a big flat drum across his lap.

I was shown to a bench close to the musicians by a cheery girl, presumably the fat man's daughter. I felt all eyes upon me and once seated I looked around the other folk, most of whom were paying rapt attention to the singer. But there were several faces scrutinising me. A pair of hairy drinkers sat on stools close to our host, who stood beside the biggest barrel I have ever seen. In front of them, lounging at the head of the group nearest the dais, was the woman I now know as Ussa, but who then, as I set my eyes on her for the first time, was a regal vision. Her long, dark hair hung loose over a white fur coat. Her face was painted like a prostitute's, but her jewellery was startling: what a weight of gold chain hung around her neck. Her hands and arms carried a display of gemstone rings, torcs and bangles that caught every flicker of light from the lamps hanging from the rafters and the candles on the benches. All the light of the room seemed to converge on her and radiate out again. And this glittering, gleaming queen was staring straight at me. I felt as if she was examining goods for sale.

The girl brought a jug of ale and poured some for me. She mumbled something I didn't understand, but I assumed it must be a request for money so I gave her a gold coin. She examined it on both sides, put it in her mouth and bit it gently, frowning. Clearly satisfied, a broad grin broke across her face and she curtsied to me as if her thin shift was a courtier's dress, then trotted back to the corner where she handed the coin over to the frog-faced man. He repeated her scrutiny of it and gave a knowing nod of welcome as he caught my eye. There's nothing quite like gold to make a man feel appreciated in this world.

The white-coated woman had watched the transaction with interest. I wondered who she was, and made up my mind to engage her in conversation, if I could. Anyone wearing so much metalwork must have a good idea of where to acquire it, and probably knew a smith or two who might help me in my pursuit of tin. Not for the last time, as you'll find out, I underestimated her.

Seeing that some people were being given food, I waved to the girl and asked her if she would bring me dinner and offer the woman in the white coat a cup of whatever she would like to drink. I proffered another coin but she waved it away – my currency was clearly valuable enough in these parts. And so my relationship with Ussa began. She raised her eyebrows when the girl told her of my offer and when a goblet was given to her with something frothy in it, she raised it in a toast to me and smiled the kind of smile that makes the stallion in me want to ride (if you understand my meaning).

She had an entourage with her, mostly male. There was a foppish lad on her left hand, hanging on her every word or movement. She stroked him idly every now and again, as if he were a pet dog. Beside him, a thickset, ugly man with too many rings made conversation in what looked, even from my side of the room, to be a tiresome manner. I knew his type: they talk constantly about the costs of things and you know half of what they say is lies, but not which half. I have no time for them at all. Beside him was a beautiful man, I can describe him no other way: blond, lithe and dressed in a simple linen vest that revealed the lovely shape of his body. He made the others laugh, especially a burly threesome close by, and I could see Ussa touching him with her eyes and liking what she saw. Beside him was a similarly beautiful girl with a flute, his sister perhaps, who gazed at Ussa with what looked like awe.

Then there were three burly men dressed identically in hard brown tunics and leggings that looked as if they were made of sailcloth. Beside them was an older, leaner sailor, a shrimp beside seals. The big guys had tankards of ale, but the old fellow had just a little cup. The four of them reminded me of the bodyguards I have seen flanking our Emperor, Alexander; on a smaller scale, obviously, but it was the same idea. A cadaverous old man joined them, dragging a low stool over. He nestled beside the skinny sailor and the two of them were soon heads together in urgent conversation. I learned later that the big guys were Ussa's crew and the thin one was Toma, the skipper of her ship and one of the Northern Ocean's finest sailors. I don't think he ever really trusted me, but I respect few men more and even on that first sighting he stood out, for he was the only one in their group, in the whole room perhaps, who seemed immune to Ussa's charms.

Because she was, she is, voluptuous. She is a genius of seduction. I have honestly never met anyone like her.

The lyre player stopped and there were cheers and shouts for more music. Ussa turned her head to something the host said, and shrugged apparent agreement. She downed her drink and the fat man came and took her goblet. She pushed her bench back and joined the musician on the dais. She said something to the girl with the flute, who beamed and got up too. The beautiful youth, the rich man and the foppish lad all shifted around to watch the stage, where Ussa was making the musicians laugh. And then the drummer rolled his stick around the skin and Ussa finger-clicked them into a wickedly jaunty little song, simple as a child's ditty, but performed – oh, how can I help you to imagine it? Let me just say she made every word of the lyrics seem to smoulder with sex. Into the simplest phrases she squeezed innuendos I would never have imagined possible. It was enthralling and yet at the same time embarrassing. I found myself breaking out into sweat and finishing my drink much too quickly. She looked around the room, her gaze licking into the faces of any man she could make eye-contact with, but at the most lewd of the lines her gaze seemed invariably to be cast in my direction. When I felt it settle

12

on me, I experienced something I'd only ever heard and thought was just some cliché – that a look can make you feel as if you are being undressed. It was truly like that. Not so much her, as the way her lingering gaze on me made other people in the room turn their heads to see who it was that was getting so much of her attention. These smiles and envious glares were what made me feel naked and exposed. It was excruciating.

Yet, strangely, when she looked away and clicked her fingers, or swung her hips or tossed her hair behind her, I wanted her to look my way again. Like I said, she is some kind of sorceress.

I don't remember clearly what ensued. She sang. I think the girl played her flute while she writhed. I remember she took her coat off so we could all be in no doubt about her charms. Then she stopped and bowed to the cheers and shook her head to calls for more. After she had conspired with our host and swatted away a few admirers she came over to me and I found myself being seduced. As another younger, thinner and scantier-clad woman took the floor to whistles from the crowd, Ussa applied herself to conquering me.

To this day, she probably thinks she failed.

It was a game with her, I saw that immediately. I like games. I like to play cat and mouse and it isn't often that I get to be the mouse.

'I'll be completely honest,' she said to me. 'You're not the most handsome man in the room, but you have something about you that is intriguing to me.'

My gold perhaps. I liked the way she scrutinised me as if I was an object she was choosing for a collection.

'And who is more handsome?' I replied.

She chuckled. 'I do like men who are competitive.'

We bantered like this for a while before I asked her whether this was her home.

'I gave up the idea of home a long time ago. I am like a snail, only faster.' She waited for me to laugh at her double meaning. 'I carry my home with me. I wear it here, around my neck, on my hands.' She thrust her ring-laden fingers towards me, glittering.

'So you have no place of your own?'

'What use is a place? A woman in her place is nothing unless she can influence others and for that she needs this.' She tugged at her heaviest gold chain, pulling one strand so the other choked her neck and swinging the long loop like a weapon. I wondered then what cruelty she was capable of and I became a more cautious mouse.

'So you travel a lot?' I asked, with what I hoped was a voice of worship.

'I travel constantly.' She pulled the gold chain back to two even coils.

'Not only singing, I assume.'

'Not only singing, indeed. I supply people with the things they dream of and relieve them of their surpluses. I make everybody happy, most of all myself. And you? You travel too, clearly. You are most definitely not from these parts, not even known here. You look to me like a man on a journey.'

I nodded.

'And yet you speak our language. How is that?'

'It is not my mother tongue, but my nurse was a Keltic speaker, so I grew up with it.'

She touched my forearm with a finger. 'So, tell me your mission. Perhaps I can help you to find what you're dreaming for.'

There was a part of her, I could see, that genuinely wanted to please people. With her claws withdrawn, she was a beautiful creature, one any pleasure-seeking mouse could not help but be drawn towards. So I told her I was seeking the heavy stone from which the magic came to enable the smiths to smelt bronze. I didn't name it, because I know there can be taboos around such things.

'You're a seeker of magic.' She smiled at me with approval. 'How far will you go for it?'

'To the ends of the earth.' It sounded like a declaration and I knew as I said it that it was true. I am a scientist and I take my contributions to the Akademie seriously, but that is not to say I am not also romantic. I think many of us who strive for understanding and new knowledge are, at heart, adventurers. We are all mystics, one way or the other, delving into the mysteries at the edge of what is known, whether that is in the margins of mathematical treatises or on the fringes of our continents, or both.

'The end of the earth is a treacherous place.' She fingered her white coat, drawing my attention to it.

'Is that from there?'

She nodded. 'This is the ice-bear's coat. It is the most danger-ous animal on our earth. It knows no fear, not like the bears of the forests, which hide and run from men. The ice-bear is a demon. Its hunger knows no bounds.'

'And where does it live?'

'It rules the North. It can swim as fast as a boat and can run on the frozen sea. In its dominion there is perpetual winter.'

I pictured a frozen waste and wondered if that was my destina-tion. 'Is the heavy stone found there?'

'The tin stone? Cassiterite. You can use its name with me, I'm not scared of it.' She laughed at me. 'That stuff washes up on the beaches near where I grew up. I could take you there. I'm sure my aunt and my cousins would be very pleased to meet you. They'll sell you more cassiterite than you can carry. They'll weigh you down so you can't walk with all their heavy stones and fancy crystals.'

I couldn't believe what I was hearing. My quest had hardly begun and here she was suggesting it could be completed by a visit to some old relative of hers. I was sceptical. She must simply be stringing me along, trying to get me interested in her. She was succeeding, however, so I decided to humour her.

'And where is this place, where you grew up?'

'Belerion.' It wasn't a name I knew. She saw my blank look and gestured north 'It's over the Channel. They call it the Land of the Goddess, but it's too full of ghosts for my liking these days. However, if you're after tin, you must go there.'

'When you say over the Channel, where is that?'

'The sea,' she said, as if I was stupid. 'I'm from Alba, the big land to the north.'

'Alba,' I repeated. It was a name from a myth. 'So I am to visit Nesos Albionon, the island of Albion.' I felt a thumping of excitement inside. Now my adventure was really beginning. 'So it is not just a mythical place?'

She hooted with laughter. 'Pinch me!' She rolled up her sleeve and offered me her arm. 'Go on, sweetheart, press yourself to my flesh and verify that I am real! I'll show you just how real we people of Albion, as you so quaintly call it, can be.'

'And now I understand,' I said, stroking her rose-painted cheek, 'why the story calls you all Pretani, the painted people.'

Of course she wanted to seduce me, and I resisted. I was a cunning little mouse. Instinct told me that if I succumbed to her she would lose interest in me, so I held out, and in her desire to conquer me she did exactly what I wanted. She invited me to sail with her to Albion.

TO ALBION

I killed time until Ussa was ready to travel onwards, exploring the area around Le Yaudet. It was an interesting place, with many stone stellae, which people told me were erected by ancestors long dead. They revered them and left offerings of milk beside them, similar to the way we offer libations to our gods.

The weather was mild and I sauntered about. One man, seeing that I was interested in his stones, took me to see his house and an edifice underground that I now believe to have been some kind of sacred place. It was a kind of long, thin, corridor-cellar, and he pointed out where sacks of grain would be stored over winter. I mistakenly took it simply as a granary, dismissing his ramblings about ceremonies. I wish, given what I experienced later, that I had paid more attention to what he was trying to explain to me about how the people honour the spirits of the underworld in the season between one cycle of life and the next. That day, although the subterranean space was not damp, it was chilly and I wanted to be back out in the sunshine, watching people tending the fields where their grain was already sown, not wondering about how they made it through the winter.

We set off early in the morning, a couple of days later. Back home it would have felt like spring, but the mild spell had turned to something that still felt like winter, and a raw wet cold sucked at my bones, as it did so often in the north. I followed Ussa to the harbour and she led the way down the wooden jetty to where her boat, *Ròn*, lay. It was nothing like the elegant merchant ships I was used to from our sea, nor like the magnificent Armorican wooden vessels I had sailed north on. It was a rugged affair, consisting of a lattice of strong oak timbers over a hull of animal hide, mostly open to the elements except for a hide shelter at the prow. I have to tell you I was sceptical that it was sea-worthy. I was wrong, of course.

Ussa's three slaves were already on board, along with all of her cargo. I also recognised the old sailor from the tavern, who introduced himself as Toma and, by the way he showed me the boat, was clearly its skipper. The crew was completed by a boy, Callum, who looked like a miniature version of its captain and never took his eyes off him.

It was good sailing weather, Toma assured me. The wind was strong enough to make headway without being too wild, but it cuts through you. A wind on the open sea at those temperatures is life threatening. I had to put on all of my clothes and I swore that when I reached wherever we were going I was going to pay good gold for skin breeches like Toma's and for something warmer to

17

wear under my coat than the cloth garment I had brought with me. I saw even the slaves were dressed in woollen undershirts, with thick knitted tunics on top and skin coats with hoods over that. No slave in my experience had ever dressed so well, but this band of slaves Ussa travelled with, I came to realise, had to be able to withstand conditions the like of which, until that time, I had never even begun to imagine.

There is so much to tell you about the sailing but I devote a whole chapter to that in my book, so you can read it there if you want the details. What I really want to tell you about next is where Ussa took me, my first sight of Albion, and my welcome from the Pritanike, the painted people.

We sailed all day and I was a trembling shell of my usual self by the time we landed. I was soaked through: my fine leather coat was incapable of shielding me from the weather and the rain had penetrated to every inch of my skin. I was cold, miserable and barely able to take in what I was seeing, but I remember a pallid forest, hung with wispy lichens. It was dusk. Never have I been anywhere that conjured the atmosphere of Hades so well. Cloud billowed among the trees. Looking back out to sea, the sky merged into it in a swirl of grey, and out of the mist, beyond the beach, a hill rose up, conical. On it was a settlement they called Ictis.

We disembarked on the beach, and I don't know what they did with the boat. I was shivering and unhappy, and I had to endure some ridiculous process of questioning about what I was doing there by a woman in a long robe. All I wanted was dry clothes and warm food but her enquiries were about the purpose of my journey and the contents of my luggage. I don't know how rude I was to her but eventually I was taken to a hut and given hot soup and a bed.

I was ill for several days then, with a fever that was both awful and wonderful. I don't know if you have ever experienced it but there is a kind of euphoria that a high fever brings. I was well cared for, Ussa was attentive to me, and I will remain grateful to the people of Belerion forever. They could have robbed me of every coin that I was carrying, yet my stash of gold was perfectly intact when I recovered myself enough to seek it, and my box of instruments had not been tampered with.

Apart from their preliminary inquisition, they treated me with the utmost respect. They called themselves the Keepers and were mostly women, spiritual to the extreme I'd say, living a life of strange rituals governed by the moon and tides. It holds a special place in my memory, of course, for reasons I am sure you well understand. I wonder if Rian is still with them.

Anyway, those kind people nursed me back to health and then I spent a happy time among the tin workers, learning some of their secrets and customs and discovering their land. I'm sure I barely scratched the surface of their mysteries but I will tell you what I learned.

Tin, as you no doubt know, is needed for bronze, which is essential, on the one hand for the weaponry needed to conquer barbarian lands, and on the other for objects of beauty. If you have never seen its alchemy you should try to, although it is rare that you will find a smith who will share the secrets of his knowledge. Most will make out that there is only copper and magic involved. It is true that there is much that seems magical about it and so many arcane rituals that it has left me unsure whether it requires divine intervention, or whether in fact there is nothing else to it than the blending of two metals, no more magic than adding yeast to flour to make bread. Copper is the bulk, but tin is essential.

I have been lucky: I gained the confidence of a smith. He was a magician for sure, but he respected my scientific work and he showed me the smelting process. I swore myself to secrecy of course, so you will not find his methods in my book, although I allude to what I learned and give as much away as I dare without breaching a sacred promise. But for all I know he will be dead by the time you read this, and I think the spirits will not begrudge me passing on this knowledge.

A teardrop of shining tin will melt a whole heart of copper. You can stand a block of copper in the forge – the shape and size does not matter. It glows but does not melt. A dragon could breathe on it and it would not melt. It stands there as if fireproof, as if the crucible insulates it from the flames. Yet if you add a tiny drop of tin, what happens is extraordinary.

If you get a chance to watch the tin work its magic in a crucible, grab it. Smiths are chancy people, and secretive, quite rightly. Don't push them too far with your probing. And when they offer you the opportunity to see the alchemy, watch with both eyes wide, wide open, because it is one of nature's wonders.

The tin melts to a silvery drop in the base of the crucible and you can see it hungering for the other metal. The copper tries to resist, but the tin melts it from the bottom, as if it is sucking it down, sup, sup, sup, licking up the metal just above the surface of its pool, like a tide licking up the rocks on a shore. And the copper succumbs. It can resist the fire but it cannot resist the tin, just as a beating heart cannot resist the tears of a loved one. It melts down, it joins the tin, the tiny drop swallows the whole heart into itself and the result is bronze!

Tin is precious and rare, found nowhere on the shores of the Great Sea, so we must import it and its sources are beyond our control. The trade route to the east through Anatolia originates high in the mountains of Balkh. It used to be secure but there are conflicts in that land and sometimes the supply dries up, as it did for the years before my journey. Smiths get nervous then, the price of tin rockets and even broken bits of old bronze are worth a fortune. Robbers have a field day, breaking into houses and armouries. It's no recipe for a peaceful life, which is what we need.

There is another source, however, and when the price of eastern tin rose so high a few years ago, some of the traders began to come in with ingots of good quality, and of a strange shape like a knucklebone. The rumour mill ground away about where these ingots came from. The source, it turned out, was northern. They were coming along the Garonne River and the Consul made it known to me that there was a commission to be had for establishing where they were being found and smelted. It was a valuable commission and set my imagination alight, as a way to fund the journey I had always dreamed of, travelling to the edge of the earth, taking measurements to enable me to calculate its ultimate extent, perhaps even to resolve the arguments about the relationship between earth and heaven, or at least to better understand how land and sea and sky combine to make our world.

Perhaps now you understand one of the gifts that I have given you – the bronze owl. It's my dear Goddess Athena, in all her wisdom. She is waiting for you, waiting for all of us, to listen to her.

*

While I was recovering from my fever, one of Ussa's slaves, a big friendly man called Og, said he would take me to find the source of tin, a heavy, heavy stone, cassiterite.

Og didn't seem to mind his situation. I guess there are many worse slave-owners than Ussa and he had a special role with her, more like a henchman than a slave, really. I sometimes wondered if he loved her. He was almost a body-guard to her at times.

He took care of me with the Keepers, made sure I had everything I needed. When I was finally able to get out and about he walked the long beach with me, and told me what he knew about tin. He had come from a tin mining family and he warned me that it would be hard to persuade a miner to reveal his secrets. The tin is found in stream beds throughout the land, and it washes up on the beaches sometimes, after a storm. I told him I wanted to see it, to watch people digging for it, and also to see them smelt it into the ingots that make their way to Massalia, to prove to myself

21

that I understood the process whereby it is made. He agreed to take me to a place he knew, when I was strong enough. I was eager to go exploring with him.

I recovered quickly from my fever. I now long for the health I had then, the walking I could do, striding out in the morning with no care of where I'd end up. I was in my prime and I was hungry for adventure.

BELERION

ICTIS

I was sitting at dusk on the bench outside my hut, one of the cluster of buildings on the north-west side of the hill. I had been told the Keepers would perform a ceremony on the beach to welcome the rising full moon. This spot had a good view of the shore and caught the last of the setting sun, although unfortunately the landmass behind me obscured the moon. Ussa, as usual wearing her long white fur coat, joined me on the bench to enjoy the sunset painting the sky. I don't remember ever seeing her so calm anywhere else. Perhaps it was the peach and rose-petal clouds.

We watched the Keepers moving on the beach, a line of bending and stretching bodies. They formed into a circle and then a spiral, twisting out from one central dancer. I suppose they must have been singing, but the breeze and the waves hid whatever sound they made. Yet their motion was somehow even more mesmerising in its silent rhythm.

'Don't take this the wrong way...' Ussa glanced sideways at me, with a sly smile. 'I'm rather pleased you got ill. It forced me to spend some time here.'

'You mustn't feel obliged to look after me,' I said.

'No, I know that. But I'm interested in your adventure. I can help you. And something tells me you'll be good for business. Already, just by hanging around for a few days, I've got wind of some opportunities coming this way, which I would have missed if we had moved straight on. And being here is supposed to be good for me, even though I can't stand the place, really.'

The Keepers were back in a long row again facing east. Given their arm movements, I presumed the moon was rising. I wished I was down there on the beach and could get the full effect of their ritual.

'I remember coming here as a child. I used to hate it. I still hate it.' She actually looked pretty relaxed and contented, leaning back, fingers running through her hair. 'It's so dreadfully boring here. The Keepers are so virtuous it makes me sick. All this wisdom and worship and insight and harmony, it's enough to drive a woman to liquor!'

'What brought you here as a child?' I asked.

She crossed her hands in her lap. 'My grandmother,' she said. 'She was a Keeper. One of them. Her father was the Merlin.'

'The Merlin?'

'A great wizard, the chief of the Druids, magical advisor to the King. A powerful man. Some of the Merlins have been renowned bards, but my great-grandfather was just a magician. I say "just". He was an alchemist. There are stories of his metal magic that are hard to believe. I wish I had just a fraction of his knowledge. I could make a fortune. They say he took most of it to the grave, although my cousin Gruach knows a lot of it.'

'It's a shame he didn't write it down.'

'Oh no. That would be dangerous. I'll have no doings with writing!'

'Why ever not?' I have a reverence for the written word that brooks no criticism.

'Anything that can be written shouldn't be.' She got up, and stood with her hands on her waist.

'But why not?'

She waggled her finger at me. 'If it's trade, it will cheat you. If it is magic, it will rebound on you. If it's a message, it will lie to you. What else is there?'

'But think of all the good it does!'

'No good that I saw ever came from it.'

'But knowledge! The wisdom of great thinkers can be shared even after they are gone. Think of Plato! Pythagoras! Herodotus!'

She tossed her head. 'Never heard of them.'

'What about poetry? The great stories. Homer! With books we can learn from the mistakes and the brilliant minds of the past. Without them we merely grope our way blindly into the future.'

She had turned to me, a look of mockery on her face.

'You are a dreamer, sweetheart. I've no knowledge of any of these people, and I don't see how even if I had, they would have brought me more gold than I have gained in ignorance of them.' She shook her head in a kindly way, as if I was a child doing something foolish but harmless. 'Poetry and fine words, whether they're spoken or written, achieve precisely nothing.'

'What about your songs?'

'Oh, a song is all voice and body, the words are irrelevant. They influence nothing. This conversation, it does nothing. It passes the time pleasantly, but it is idle and these idle words, spoken or written down, would be the same. The only words that matter are those of a business deal, or a magic spell or curse, or an instruction or request, and all of these spoken words cause trouble if they are written down and separated from the body of the person who speaks them. Even a messenger who passes on a request or a communication from another knows he risks his soul by acting on another's behalf, speaking their serious words without them being actually present to give them their embodiment.'

'And what about words of love?' I said, thinking of the poems of Sappho.

'Love?' She chuckled. 'All words of love are words of deceit, spoken or written. But at least there you may have a use of the quill, to titillate the senses with a little tickle.' She stroked my nose in imitation of a feather, and I knew it was pointless to argue with her. 'Even you, my dear, must recognise that all that counts in matters of love is conveyed by the body, not by the voice.'

It was hard to dispute the point, although if she had understood Greek I might have tried reciting poetry to her. Perhaps, on reflection, it was as well I desisted.

She turned to go. 'Come down to the beach later. You'll be interested in what is happening.'

ON THE BEACH

Later that evening, when the tide was low, I saw in the moonlight a very large currach, with at least ten hands on oars, sweep onto the beach. The rowers stopped and six got out to haul the boat up into the shallows. A posse of figures emerged from buildings on the slope below me and they included the white, striding form that was unmistakeably Ussa. More people disembarked.

I put on my coat, thinking I had yet to find myself some better clothes for seafaring on these wild waters, and set off, still a little wobbly from the fever, down towards the beach. Whatever the interesting thing was that Ussa had promised, I didn't want to miss it.

The path wended around the hill, past the wattle and daub shacks of the lower level. Even the children who lived there were heading for the beach.

As I reached the sands I came out into the light of the moon, still low in the sky like a huge gleaming coin. I had some little ones like it in my pocket. There had been enough of a glint in

Ussa's eye and I was getting to know her well enough to deduce that 'interesting' could to her only mean profitable.

A wagon was making its way across the causeway towards the island and a second one was not far behind. I guessed they were carrying tin. The boat's crew had unloaded huge bundles, which they were very careful not to get wet. A thin woman hurried about gesticulating and shepherding the carriers up onto the dry sands where a short, fat man stood in conversation with Ussa. They were both watching the progress of the wagons. The causeway was only just visible, and it did not look like a good surface. Wooden wheels jolted as oxen tugged their burdens along.

I made my way over to where Ussa stood.

'Pytheas!' she said, introducing her companion. 'This is Nisien, son of a great chieftain of Silures. Pytheas is a traveller from a southern sea coast.'

We bowed to each other.

'You share an interest in the heavy stone?' I asked.

He shook his head, and my attention was drawn to the bundles that were being untied by the thin woman. The rough leather tarpaulin was pulled back to reveal heaps of thick sheepskins and cow hide.

'You need some of this to make you some decent sea clothes if you're planning to come any further with me. These are excellent quality.'

Ussa bent down and rubbed the fleece inside one of the sheep-skins. It was as thick as any I had seen, it was true. But it was the final, smaller bundle that caught all of our eyes. Silvery fur, the distinctive pelt of wolves. Once my eyes had stroked it, I knew the coat I needed was made of this, and I was soon involved in my first trade mediated by Ussa.

'It's not the winter pelt, is it?' She spoke with a note of scorn, as if the furs were rags. 'It's not going to keep a person warm, really. Not like bear skin.' She stroked her own coat.

27

I couldn't believe this. I reached out to touch it and my fingers sank into the thick hair.

Nisien confirmed what I could feel. 'There's nothing warmer than wolfskin, apart from that, possibly.' He touched Ussa's coat as if it could still bite. 'But that's heavy, where the wolf pelt is light. The wolves are out in the snow and sleet, up in the mountains, hunting in all weathers. Winter is their season, and their fur will withstand anything.' He stroked it beside me. 'Feel that thickness, the long weather-hairs and the shorter layer below, how soft it is. That's what'll keep you warm. And there's nothing more handsome on a man. It is a regal fur.' He turned to me. 'You're a traveller, sir?'

'I am. I have come from the shores of the Great Sea in the south, and I am going north.'

'The wolf is a great traveller. He roams far, his spirit will protect you on your journey.'

Ussa rolled her eyes as if he was talking nonsense and turned one of the furs over to examine the skin. She pointed at some blotches. 'The tanning is shoddy. Look, here. How long will it be before the hair's falling out? Who wants a mangy old pelt like that?'

Nisien pulled a fox fur from a pile and turned it over, lying it beside the wolf skin. 'Look at this. The fox is simply done, and you can see how it is stiff here, especially around the edges. But now, feel this.' He directed my hands to grasp a handful of the wolf skin, so that it crumpled in my palm. 'See how flexible that is, right to the fringe. This is top quality tanning.'

'How many would I need for a coat?' I asked.

'You'll get a short jacket or a long jerkin out of one, but for a full coat, two is better.'

'Oh, you can't do anything useful with a single pelt,' Ussa said. 'And price?'

'I need twelve drams of gold to pay a hunter for three pelts.'

Ussa screeched in outrage and called him a liar. They haggled for a while, Nisien trying unsuccessfully to deal with me directly, but Ussa was determined to drive a bargain. It isn't really in my nature. I always find I'm happy to give people what they want from me if I can. But Ussa had a rapier tongue and guarded my purse from my generosity.

We settled eventually on four drams of gold and a glass bracelet for the two biggest and best pelts, including their cutting and preparation for stitching, plus sinew to sew the pieces together, bone buttons, toggles and some sheepskin mittens thrown in for good measure. Although I felt I'd got the better deal, he chewed on my gold coins with evident satisfaction, complimenting me on my excellent taste. I was surprised by how valuable he seemed to find the glass beads, and I wished I had brought more with me. I thought of them as no more than trinkets to give to people in exchange for hospitality, but clearly they were a valid tender.

By the time I had completed my transaction, Nisien's big boat was settled well up the beach and the wagons had arrived. Three people had disembarked from each. One stayed by the oxen, the other two made their way down onto the beach and stood just above the reach of the frothing waves. The moon gleamed on the wet sand all around them and their shadows reached far up the shore. I wondered why they wanted to be so close to the water and guessed that it must be so they could keep track of the level of the tide and not get caught by the causeway submerging, leaving them stranded on the island.

As soon as the coins had changed hands between me and Nisien, Ussa was off down the beach. She placed herself between the two pairs of men and I saw her beckon them to come closer together.

Even from a distance I could see hostility between them. Of each pair of men, one was carrying the goods and the other seemed to be a kind of defender or bodyguard. When I got closer, I was amazed to discover that both of the men with the items for sale were in fact women. I thought that there had been considerable bargaining for my wolf skins, but once I got within earshot of their trading with Ussa I realised what I had experienced was nothing.

I guessed that Ussa had wanted to get the suppliers together so she could compare their goods, or more likely control the deal, but they clearly wanted to negotiate one by one. Ussa was talking ten to the dozen and one of the traders was having to argue hard with her. She was red-faced and earnest.

'It is pure, pure.' She thrust an ingot towards the side of Ussa's head. 'Listen! Listen!' She stopped, seeing me watching them. 'Who's this?' She pointed at me with the ingot. She was dark-haired and bright-eyed as a weasel. The tin glinted in the moonlight.

I bowed. 'I am Pytheas. I am from Massalia.'

She looked blank.

'Many days sailing to the south.' I thought this might interest her but she turned her back on me and handed the tin to Ussa, who pressed it against her ear to check its quality. The purest tin will crackle if you try to bend it. Buy nothing else.

'Does it talk to you?' I asked, and Ussa grinned, nodding.

'What is it you're after, exactly?' The trader said, swinging around to me. For some reason I was annoying her, but I hadn't come so far to be put off easily.

'May I listen to it too?' I put my hand out to Ussa, seeking to test the ingot but the trader snatched it from her.

'Are you with her, or what?'

'I have come a long way in search of the smelting metal.' I hoped my voice was conciliatory.

But the trader was putting the ingot back in the box and now Ussa was starting to look anxious.

'I came here because you asked me, Ussa, and first they turn up…' The trader pointed at the boat and the other wagon, 'and now this…' She closed her chest lid and gave me a dirty look. She was set to leave and the man beside her was standing too close for comfort.

Then Ussa's hand was in the crook of my arm. 'Pytheas, come and see this.'

She led me off to the other trader who was smiling nervously at me, and I was soon the proud owner of an ingot of tin. She had watched the drama with the first seller and offered us a fair deal straight away. I could see the scales and it was far cheaper than the going rate in Massalia. And it was pure and dense and crackled perfectly.

When I bought only one ingot the trader showed no sign of being put out, and with Ussa's help we negotiated the cost of a larger shipment. With a little persuasion from my charming hostess her prices got better and better. I couldn't believe how little they valued it.

'You Carthaginians always drive a hard bargain.' The trader grinned at me. 'When do you want it?'

It didn't seem worthwhile to disabuse her about my origins, though I had to bite my lip at being taken for a thug from Carthage. 'I can't say.' I had to be honest. 'I have a journey ahead of me, northwards, and I have no idea how long it may take me. But if the gods are kind to me I shall return, and I shall take all the tin my gold will buy. Back home I'll be a hero if I return with tin. They all have enough gold but tin is in short supply.'

'Take it and carry it with you,' Ussa said, hooking her arm into mine. 'There's plenty of room on board my boat.'

I took it that she was as pleased with the deal as I was, so I unburdened myself of a modest weight of gold and acquired a sack of tin ingots that I needed help to carry. The trader and I parted friends and I was a happy man. I wished I could write a letter to tell people back home what I had discovered but I knew no way of getting correspondence to Massalia from so far north. Even now I will have to make a leap of faith to send this epistle to you.

TO PENDEEN

Og took me to see a tin mine the morning after the traders had been to Ictis. I remember it was a delight to stretch my legs, stride out across the land, to get away from the smell of the sea for a while and fill my lungs with woodland scents and the airs of farming, which always remind me of home.

As soon as he was away from Ussa his manner changed and he became enthusiastic. He reminded me of a puppy that is unnaturally cowed around its master, that wags its tail when it sees him and obeys every command but is ever watchful in case it should find him in a bad temper, conscious always of the need to be cautious with every move. Away from his mistress, Og's shoulders went back, his head lifted and he strode across his native land like a wealthy man. I could see why, as beyond the trackways was a wild and majestic country.

It was a marvellous walk. This land of Og's has trackways that are wondrous to behold, hedged on both sides by stone and earth, with all manner of herbs and flowers and bushes on top, especially spiny ones, thickets of thorns that would be impervious to the most determined goat. It is a marvel the lengths these people have gone to, making these divisions across their land, to keep their fields separate from the travelling and herding routes. Og told me these hedged walkways have been there since the beginning of time and when I pressed him he said since the age of the giants, who built both them along with other strange stone formations that he promised to take me to if I was interested. Of course I was!

He led me first to the top of a hill where a stone structure stood, as evidence of giants. He called it a quoit. It looked like a giant mushroom from a distance and closer up it became clear it was an odd construction: a small chamber made from enormous stones. The capstone in particular was almost the size of those raised to make the Parthenon in Athens. But where was the great civilisation that could achieve such a feat? All I met were peasants, and the strange mole-like men of the underworld, and although they were swarthy and strong, and some, like Og, were genuinely big men, they could not lift such stones as far as I could tell, and they had no signs of our technologies. They, too, treated these stone edifices as works of wonder. All around the islands of Albion archipelago there are stone mysteries and I would love one day to return and discover more about their origins. Perhaps these stories of giants are true? Or perhaps there were ancient people whose knowledge has been lost.

Near to the quoit there was a great building work underway, with a huge circular rampart and ditch, almost 100 strides in diameter. The boss of the labourers told Og that the warlord had a plan for a fortress. I hoped to meet such a man. Given the scale of his ambition, he would have had some good tales to tell, but he was away at some gathering of the tribes, the foreman said, along with most of the warrior men. Og was most disappointed.

As we walked away, he said, 'I have friends among them, I'd have liked to introduce you.'

'How did you come to be enslaved to Ussa if you have friends in such powerful circles?' I asked. 'Are you not tempted to run away and seek their protection?'

He shrugged. 'When I was a boy I was given to Sevenheads, Ussa's grandfather, to pay a gambling debt of *my* grandfather's. I was handsome once, and Ussa took a fancy to me.'

'Can your friends not negotiate for your freedom?'

'It doesn't work like that with Sevenheads.'

I never fully understood it, nor still do now. There are favours and systems of repayment in that land that flow down the generations in ways that we would never tolerate here in the civilised world. And yet the people there seem to act as if there is no other way of living.

From this high point we could see the coast for miles and the ocean seething out forever. It truly felt like the end of the world, the last place before the edge of knowability. I know now this is false, but that day I remember feeling I had searched out the margin of the known universe and was in a place where one false step could tumble me over the edge. I don't know what it is about the inhabitants of Belerion, but they have had that effect on me each time I have visited them. Yes, I returned to this place. Why else bother going into so much detail about it if it were not to prove significant?

We continued on our way, Og and I, down from the fortification-in-making towards the coast, with its dramatic cliffs where the ocean rolled in and was brought to an abrupt halt, fuming and spraying white foam. We made our way out to a sacred spot on a clifftop, and Og cast some crumbs from his pocket and water from a skin as a libation to a god he called Belenos, who seems to be akin to Apollo, with the power of protecting seafarers from the danger of the ocean.

I would not want to arrive there by boat in a storm, for the rocks make it a treacherous shoreline. I am sure there are local men who can navigate in and out of the narrow coves that they call zawns, most of which are little more than gullies and no good as harbours. We did go to one good beach, backed by a steep cliff, where at low tide there would be hours of easy access by boat, even from a stormy sea. But what you would do with your vessel there at high tide was a mystery to me – behind the beach was nothing but boulders and sheer cliffs. I was reluctant to make the climb but Og was insistent that I see it, so we scrambled down a stream valley to get there. As I panted back up it to get out again, it was quite clear that a boat couldn't be carried up such a slope.

I asked where people kept their boats. Og merely shrugged. 'There are places.'

The reason he wanted to visit the beach was to seek the heavy stones from which tin comes. We searched the stream bed and swept the beach but found nothing unusual. I soon bored of the endless stone-picking and of Og's scornful shake of his head as I showed him yet another cobble that seemed unusually heavy to me. I gave up the hunt and sat on a boulder watching the sea foam up the beach in that hypnotic pulsing that can be gazed upon for as long as you can spare the time, which always soothes the soul and calms the mind and restores the body to balance. I was tired after our long walk, and I had money to buy tin with. I did not need to grope about in cold water for dubious stones. I already had a sack of ingots of the purified mineral in my luggage at Ictis.

'Yes!' Og ran towards me with a huge grin on his face and dumped a stone into my outstretched hands. I almost dropped it; the weight was extraordinary for what was otherwise a nondescript dark grey stone that I could not have distinguished from a thousand other sleek wet river cobbles.

He snatched it back with glee. 'Come on, let's go to the Bunnies. Just wait till I show Uncle Suil I've not lost my touch.'

He set off up the river, across the boulders and then up the steep slope towards the clifftop. I followed as fast as I could. It was a formidable climb and I was tiring after walking all day. At the top he was waiting for me, cheery as a puppy again.

Still, it was a magnificent place, and I enthused at its grandeur as we strode along the clifftop. Ahead of me I could see him nodding in agreement and not a little pride, I think, at my praise of his native country. Waves smashed and plumed against rocks below us and although part of me shuddered at their ferocity, the like of which we never encounter in our own Great Sea, I have to admit it was exciting.

How enjoyable it is to be with someone who is happy, I thought to myself, as Og stopped to show me a white flower. Everything in the world is wonderful when a slave gets a taste of freedom. I wish I could free them all, although of course life here would be impossible if we were to do such a thing. Perhaps where you are it is different.

A bit further along the cliffs, over some more steep gullies, which were a scramble down and a trek back up again, we reached a cluster of stone huts. At the sight of us, the couple of children who were playing outside disappeared indoors and a moment later a woman came out. Evidently recognising Og, she dashed towards us.

'It's Auntie Suil.' Og gathered her into a hug.

'My heart, what a treat it is to see you.' She peered up into his face. 'My, my. You've not changed a bit. And how long is it?'

'Too many years. Is Uncle here?'

'He's down the Bunnies, where do you think? And who's this?'

I was introduced as a friend, interested in the heavy stones, and the woman smiled at me with suspicion in her face. She was swarthy like the trader I'd bought my tin from, but with wide-spaced eyes, a broad forehead and a big mouth. The wrinkles in her face suggested a life of laughter and tears, a life fully lived. But I could see that strangers with interests in tin were not her favourite visitors, and I was spoiling what would otherwise have been a joyful reunion with Og.

'Shall I leave you two to catch up?' I offered. But the prospect of a stranger with my interests wandering around unaccompanied was clearly even more alarming to her.

'No, no. You come along in, the two of you. Where've you come from? You must be starving.'

Og was always ravenous, and I was thankful for that as I had also worked up an appetite and would have seemed to be wolfing down the bread and butter we were offered by our hostess, were I not beside him. No free man knows how to eat like a hungry slave. He waved away his aunt's apologies for not serving us meat. 'Bread's what I need.'

I nodded agreement, though some cheese or fish would have been welcome after our long day's walking. We ate heartily what she gave us, the children watching us intently. It did not occur to me until Og made a rude remark to me later that his family were too poor to offer us anything else and that we probably ate the children's supper. No wonder the woman's smile seemed unconvincing.

AT THE BUNNIES

After food, we set off down towards the shore and before long reached the clifftop, where Og told me to watch my feet. Sure enough, there were holes and gulleys and the ground was rough. We picked our way down to a place where we could hear the sound of tools, stone on stone, and voices. Around a corner we looked down into the mouth of a cave, and under the rocky overhang three men were at work. One was grey-haired and beside him hunched two young men – one a burly, dark-haired replica of the old man and the second a lanky youth, with a similar visage – presumably both his sons. The dark-haired youngster was bashing away at a pile of rocks and the other was taking up the pieces and rinsing out the heavy ones using a shovel and a bucket of water. The older man seemed about to head off into the cave depths with a sack when he turned and saw us.

With a single hand gesture he silenced the others, their hands literally paused in mid-strike. 'Who's there?'

'Uncle Suil, it's me, Og.'

Dropping his sack, he strode out from under the overhang, barring the way with what I could now see was his formidable body. He was not tall (I imagine that would be a hindrance to a miner) but he was thickset and it was clear from his posture and his bare arms that he had the strength of a bull. He was dressed head to toe in thick leather except for his arms, and he even wore a leather hat, like a round helmet, with a string under his chin. On anyone else it might have looked comical. On this man, all it did was emphasise the thorny blue eyes that poked from under it.

Their glare was directed at me. 'I don't welcome visitors. What's your business?'

I was certain we had made a mistake, but Og seemed strangely relaxed. 'This is Pytheas,' he said. 'He's from far away south where they have no heavy stone, and he is studying it. He has pockets full of gold but he's too mean to part with it. He has come to steal your magic and tell everyone your secrets. I'm his right hand man.'

He was grinning at his uncle, who had braced himself as if about to wrestle me to the ground and beat the life out of me.

'Look, Uncle. I found this on the beach at Pendeen.' He brought it out from his jerkin. He had lugged that stone all this way, wearing it like a mother carries a child.

His uncle reached out a hand but didn't take his eyes off me. He weighed the stone that Og proffered and curled up his upper lid in a snarl.

'It's a good one, eh? Isn't it?' Og said.

'It'll do.' He chucked it behind him without looking at it, and his dark-haired son dodged it as it crashed onto the pile beside him. He picked it up and started to batter it into pieces.

The old man's eyes were still pinning me to my spot.

'Like I said, he has gold,' Og said.

'There are plenty of traders to buy from in Ictis.' His accent was thick and I had to work hard to understand him.

'I will pay you gold just to learn what you do, where you work, how you produce the tin,' I said. Then, noticing the snarl forming on his lips at my use of the word, I rapidly corrected it to the phrase I had been taught, 'The casting metal, I mean.' His face relaxed a little, but he gave no sign of being amenable to my request. At least he was listening to me. I hoped I would make no further blunders of etiquette. 'I need to prove, when I go home, that I have been to the *source* of the metal. If I return with the metal itself, it only shows that I met a trader. But my reason to visit you is to understand the way you take it from the earth, to know its origin. I need a guide to its source and I'm willing to pay him handsomely.'

'How do I know you won't send an army?'

'Traders will come after me, but not soldiers. My land is so far away. When have you ever seen or heard of an army from the Mediterranean coming here? It's not possible.' I thought about Alexander, to whom nowhere is unconquerable, but I wasn't going to mention him. I wondered if the old man, like the trader, had experience of the Carthaginians. If he did, he didn't say so and I had no intention of invoking those warmongers by name.

He was glaring at me, his mouth a thin line. 'Why should I trust you?'

I offered three gold coins. As he bit down on each one in turn, his face impassive, I said, 'I seek only knowledge and only what you'll give willingly. You do not need to show me your deepest secrets, although I am hungry to learn anything you'll tell me. I will pay you for all you show me. I know that to survive whatever is down there,' I gestured to the cave mouth, 'you must have special knowledge. Please share what you can with me. I am sure, though I cannot prove it, that it will increase the value of your metal.'

He fixed me with those piercing eyes, then shook his head and handed me back the coins. He returned to his work, making out he had finished the conversation. I put the coins down on a stone between us and stood, waiting. I noticed him glancing towards me out of the corner of his eye. Og looked at the sky, going nowhere. I took my cue from him, willing Suil to change his mind.

I watched an idea come to him. He looked over at the gold coins and a grin started to form, then he pulled his face back to seriousness. He turned to me, and in a gruff voice said, 'You'll get dirty.'

I had won!

He got to his feet and touched the thin youth on the shoulder. 'Boy, give him your clothes.'

The lanky lad had a face full of amazement but immediately began removing his outer layer.

'The boots'll be too big,' the old man said.

'No matter.' I too began shedding clothes. I must have been smiling like a boy given his first real sword. This was an opportunity of a lifetime. The jerkin and leather trousers of the lad were a bit tight on me but not uncomfortable, and the boots were as big as he suggested they would be. But the leather cap was a snug fit. I beamed at the lad and nodded to my clothes. He seemed awkward about wearing them but I didn't care. I was raring to go.

The old man poured oil into a tallow lamp, a tiny thing of clay, like a cat's paw. He blew the smouldering fire into a flame, then fed a wick into the little spout and lit it from a birch taper. 'Do you know how to ask the earth's permission to enter?'

I shook my head.

A grin of utter mischief crossed his face, then, looking serious again he patted me on the shoulder. 'Come this way.'

He led me away to a quiet corner beyond the overhang. I am not going to tell you what he had me do. It is a secret that I paid well for and have no need to divulge to anyone, even you. Suffice to say I returned with an offering to the earth, in a pot, which I carried down with me into the underworld. I hoped this man was not simply making fun of me, a gullible foreigner.

UNDERWORLD

It was the darkness that made it wonderful. Darkness reveals mysteries that our eyes hide from us.

When we first entered the cave mouth, the great bright sky was replaced by the wobbling light of the little flame. The roar of the sea, pounding the cliffs, faded into the sullen quietness of rock. I felt as if all my senses were numbing as we penetrated into the depths. All my attention was focused on following the bobbing lamp in front of me and not knocking my head on the roof. You must walk in a strange, crouching way. It is uncomfortable and the passage is so narrow you graze your arms and body against the sides.

'Is this a natural tunnel?' I asked.

'No.' The reply came from up ahead.

'Why make it so small?'

'You've never hauled rock, have you?'

That shut me up.

We carried on in silence. The darkness and narrowness began to weigh on me. My back ached from hunching. But we persisted, shuffling along.

Eventually the lamp stopped and I saw the glowing face of Uncle Suil. The flickering lamplight revealed we were in a slightly bigger space, higher if not wider, and there were tools here. We had reached the working edge of the lode. His eyes were gleaming.

I pointed to a glittering strand of rock. 'So this is it?'

'No, that's quartz. This is what we're here for.' He stroked a band of dark, pinkish rock.

It was freshly hewn. I touched it and it felt no different from any other stone but I could see that it formed a distinct band within the granite to either side. I imagined him working his way along the lode. There was barely enough height to throw a hammer.

'The falling rock must be dangerous,' I said.

'There aren't many of us with all our fingers.' He held his right hand up and sure enough, there was a digit missing.

We each said nothing for a while. We were in the depths of the earth. I felt the rock pressing in on me.

'I am here at the frontier,' I said, more to myself than to him. 'This is the source.'

'This is where it comes from. The mother's vein, this is, you can hear her heart beating.'

It was true: there was a deep, throbbing, sound. Perhaps a distant rumble of the waves, or perhaps it was what he said it was.

'You love it in here, don't you?' It sounded trite as soon as it was out of my mouth.

'Where's your pot?' he replied.

I brought it out from where I'd tucked it into his son's jerkin.

'You can empty it there, in that corner, see, far side of the spoil.' He reached over with the lamp over so its light licked a cavity.

I caught my breath. A creature sat there, eyes glowing. Suil put down the lamp and moved away with a chuckle that I can't say sounded benign.

'Feed the mother's little helper. Go on. Feeding time.' His voice was sing-song and strange 'Fee-ee-eeding time.'

I am not a person who is easily frightened but there was something beyond the natural about what I was looking at. I was deep underground with a man who I did not know. He laughed like a demon and his voice echoed; I was not sure if only he was laughing, or also this weird creature sitting in the alcove.

'What is it?' I asked. He only laughed harder.

Then it began to rise from its spot, lifting up off its perch, and into the jumping light of the lamp. My heart lurched as I saw its face fully, eyes glowing with flames and long, slimy hair over its mouth.

'Feed me.' I do not know where the voice came from.

The monster was still rising. 'Fee-ee-eed me,' it insisted. Its paw reached towards me, with strange leathery digits and claws as sharp as nails.

'Empty the pot into its hand,' Suil's voice behind me nearly terrified me out of my wits with its urgency. 'Quickly!'

I poured out my offering. It had come from the deepest part of me and I had produced it, I have to admit, with some difficulty in the old man's presence. I had been glad he turned away but now he was watching every move and would see all I had managed. I fed the beast with the contents of my pot and then it retracted its hand and slumped back into its corner, slurping disgustingly for a while before falling silent. All I could see of it was a slumped shape in the alcove.

I was trembling. And then, behind me, Suil began to make a weird noise, playing a tune on some kind of breathy instrument. It was an odd little melody, just four notes long, and its rhythm was a regular pattern. I remember it clearly: *da-da-da-dee da-da-da-dee*, the long note being alternately the lowest and highest. It was hypnotic, and the echo made harmonies of the most extraordinary sort. It was hard to stay frightened in the presence of such beauty.

And then the light went out.

The tune continued, doubled in intensity. The smell of the underground world sprang fresh into my nose. I felt more alive than I have ever felt before. Between the phrases of the tune, my companion was leaving longer and longer pauses, and in those pauses I reached out into the darkness with all of my senses.

I felt my bodily presence grow as if I was becoming stronger and larger. I tried moving and my hands seemed to have become antennae of huge sensitivity, like those you see a cockroach waving in front of itself. I could feel the rocks before I touched them and their shape was vivid to my fingers, their texture complex and interesting, each crystal with its own smooth or jagged form. Similarly, with two mobile hands that could see behind and above as well as in front, my head seemed to know how far it had to swing more effectively than when it was guided by eyes. My feet had become eyes or noses, too; they reached about, probing like snouts, and the contours beneath me became clear. My firmness upon that patch of earth gave me a sense of security no act of standing had ever done before.

I realised the music had stopped altogether, the last pause reaching deeply into the space around us. It smelled of lichen and mould in there, the air cool and still as a grave.

I remembered that I had sought guidance from Artemis before I set off on my journey. The priestess had taken me into a side-chamber, down some steps, and into a cellar-shrine where the Goddess took the form of the hibernating mother bear. It was winter and the shrine was as cool as this mine, but there the resemblance ended, because it was dry and full of shrouds with painted and embroidered patterns, so our voices had been muffled and softened as we had talked about my journey. I had made an offering of honey, prayed for a successful outcome and asked the bear for courage. And there, the light had never gone out, the candles on the altar had burned calmly all the while.

I felt something against my leg and my whole body stiffened. There was a distinct stroking sensation on my right shin, and sharp claws, pricking. I suddenly needed light. I dared not reach down. I knew somehow it must be the creature from the alcove and now I heard what I can only describe as snuffling.

'Don't worry.' Suil's voice was disembodied. 'The kobold won't hurt you now it has eaten.'

When someone says don't worry in such a circumstance, it is no help at all. The body knows fear in a way that words cannot reach. I was seized by a pounding, rising, breath-sapping sensation. My stomach gripped. My legs shrank from the soft abrasion and the prickling of this thing, rubbing itself against me. My eyes stared out into the black vacancy.

As suddenly as it began, the touch of the creature ended. I could hear it, or I imagined I could, shuffling back into its alcove.

Suil took me by the wrist and said, 'Follow.'

We shuffled deeper into the cave, or perhaps back the way we had come. I had no sense of direction at all. We stopped in a cooler space and I felt a current of air on the back of my neck.

All the time, he was chanting something but I could make nothing of his words. It was all one note, deep and incantatory. He was communicating with some spirit or other, or perhaps with the beast. There was a spicy, soft smell and a sound of scratching. The hairs of my head must have been standing out like a hedgehog's bristles.

A touch on my forehead made me cry out.

'It is just me.' He laid a hand on my arm. Could he see in the dark? I guessed he must have been able to, or this alertness of all the other senses I was experiencing was simply so much more advanced in him that the dark was no hindrance.

There was a long pause, with only the throbbing of the earth. My heart was pounding. I tried to slow my breathing and calm myself down.

When he spoke again, his voice was solemn. 'Southern man, know the earth.'

I think that's what he said, anyway. I was trembling from head to foot, terror and wonder running through me. Every time this man spoke his voice seemed to come from a different place.

'Speak to the earth,' he commanded.

I had no idea what to say. To be utterly honest I have no idea what I did say. I do remember my voice sounded thin and I have no doubt at all that what I managed to produce was feeble as well. The response was a grumbling rumble that seemed to come from the rock itself. It was far too deep for Suil, or indeed for any human to produce.

'Tell her how you are feeling,' Suil whispered in my ear. Once again, I jumped like a frog.

But I do remember what I said then. 'Awe.' That single word echoed on and on and it seemed to modulate into a body-shaking reverberation, as if a throng had picked it up and was passing it back and forth. I felt myself vibrating, pulsing with life. The sound I made came back to me, trebled in intensity. I said the word again and for a third time, and each time it returned enriched. Harmonies seemed to sing it back to me. It was dark through all of this of course, but I swear I could see colours made by the sounds, and they were breath-taking.

'Now tell her what you are looking for.'

The sounds must have somehow given me confidence, for I was not surprised or frightened by Suil any more. I had not been harmed yet, and this was the strangest and most wondrous experience of my life. The adventurer in me knew that this was an opportunity I must seize.

'I seek the origin of tin, of amber and of ivory and I seek new jewels.'

'You seek much,' Suil said, quietly.

There is a passage written by Herodotus, where he says he cannot speak with certainty, *for I do not allow that there is any river, to which the barbarians give the name of Eridanus, emptying into the northern sea where, as the tale goes, amber is produced, nor do I know of any islands called Cassiterides, whence the tin comes which we use... Then he says, nevertheless, tin and amber do certainly come to us from the ends of the earth.*

'Is this the end of the earth?' I asked.

'No. Ho ho ho, no!' The earth guffawed in response. Laughter echoed and boomed. 'I am boundless...' And this boundlessness was tangible in the great musical voice.

I knew Herodotus to be wrong. I knew! Here, this place was the origin of tin. What triumph I felt. This was the Cassiteride Island. I had found it! I had sailed on that northern sea that the great historian did not believe in, and I would sail much more and further. I cannot describe the elation this knowledge filled me with, but let me tell you that it, too, felt boundless. I was sure then that I would also find the river Eridanus and the source of amber.

'You are in the belly of the earth, the place where bears come in winter to merge and die and be reborn in spring. You have made contact. Are you ready to be reborn?'

'No,' I said. 'No, I'm not ready.'

I wanted just to be there for a while, in the belly of the earth with all my senses alive, listening to the drips and the distant murmur of some watercourse – or maybe it was the sea – that made a deeper rumbling from time to time. I followed the sound of one of the drips with my hands and felt where it was making the rock slippery under my fingers. I reached my face in towards it until it wet my cheek and let it drip onto my outstretched tongue – its taste was of life itself, pure, original, untainted, uninterpreted. I breathed in and out knowing my flesh was continuous with the earth. This cool yeasty smell of wet rock was the earth's breath. The mention of bears had made me think of Artemis, and so I offered her a prayer, one of the simple chants we teach all the young children. I am not a great one for the temple most of the time, but I was glad then to be able to speak to the bear goddess in the appropriate way. It is a chant about becoming a bear and there, deep in that damp burrow, it seemed wholly appropriate.

'Goddess of the Bear, protector, make us brave,
make our footsteps sure as pawprints,
make our voices strong and fearless as a roar,
make our spirits shine like the Great Bear of the Sky,
let us know your wisdom,
let us know True North,
Goddess of the Bear, protector, make us brave.'

After my voice had stopped reverberating, the silence seemed profound, as if my words had brought the world to a shocked standstill.

Then the steady drips reasserted themselves and the pulsing throb of the earth returned.

The flute that Suil used to make his music down there began again. Again it was just a simple tune: two pairs of notes, a small interval between them, descending, *di-dee, di-dum, di-dee, di-dum*. There was something restless about it. I felt a hand on my shoulder compelling me back down the tunnel and it felt right to start walking, my feet, *di-dee*, treading, *di-dum*, to the rhythm of the tune. I said, 'thank you' and received a silencing tap on the back of my head. Suil must have been right behind me. So I stayed quiet, and the little tune propelled me back out towards the light.

The light! Oh, by the Gods, what it was like to return to the light! The sea crashing on the cliff foot below, the whistle of wind, the salty-sweetness of it! I had not realised how stale the air in the mine had become until I breathed the outside world.

Having shown me his underground realm, I hoped Suil would show me how the tin is smelted, but he was adamant that that was a secret not even my gold could buy. I managed to get him to tell me a little of the process: after the boys had smashed it and sifted out the heavy ore, it is heated with charcoal to a temperature hot enough to fire pottery, and the resulting prills of metal are hammered together or melted into ingots. It sounded a primitive enough technique. I sorely wished to see his furnace in action, but this is a mystery I was not party to. Still, to have been inside the earth to where tin is born was wonder enough.

Perhaps you're wondering why I have told you about this in such detail? It is not just to express my piety and remembrance of Artemis, nor to prove that I have genuinely been to where tin originates, despite what those people anxious to sully my name would have everyone believe. No, it is to urge you to revel in all of your senses, not only the power of sight, which we depend on so much. If I were to go blind I could no longer do my scientific measurements or read. But I learned that day that life would still be full, enriched by sensory compensation from my ears, nose, tongue and skin. Yes, my dear: do not underestimate the power of touch and of all the other senses. I also tell you so that you understand that I was sometimes frightened on my travels. It was not the last time.

TRADE

In the two days after the full moon the tide was at its maximum, and I was amazed by how many people had arrived on Ictis. The causeway was dry for several hours as the tide was lowest, then at high tide it was completely cut off and this seemed to put everyone into the mood of a festival. Men, women and children had clearly come from far and wide to enjoy the experience of being marooned. They walked on, mostly with something to trade, as if the temporary island could create a special kind of market, add some value to their goods or bring good luck to their transactions.

Another of Ussa's slaves, called Li, took a liking to me and I to him and we escaped from the main throng to a quiet viewpoint where the late morning sun glittered on the water. He had a flask of mead – delicious, sweet, flowery – he said it was made with the honey from heather blossoms. It went straight to my head.

We were sitting on a stone terrace wall at the edge of the path up to the Keepers' temple, looking out across the bay. Rollers swept in onto the sand with a steady, languorous rhythm and I felt myself becoming drunk and enthralled by the delightful accent of the young man beside me. Li kept quizzing me about where I was from and what I was doing there. He was greedy for knowledge of other lands, fascinated by the detail of my journey from Massalia to the Gironde and on up to Armorica. I told him about my Periplus and promised to show it to him. I asked him in turn about his home.

'I'm from Silures, three day's sail north of here, the heart of the world, the very centre. That's my home, or it was, until I was captured. Now I must go everywhere.'

I wanted to know what the journey was like from his home to Ictis.

Li waved his hand to the right. 'Of course, it's wild water here where the ocean is open to the west, but then up the coast there's the huge estuary, where you can find shelter if you need it, and then Eriu gives us calm water mostly.'

'Eriu?'

'The big island off to the west. Surely that is in your – what did you call it?'

'Periplus,' I said. 'It has nothing for this far north in it, I'm afraid. And your people. What do they do to survive in this harsh

49

climate? Are they farmers? Is it possible to grow any decent crops?'

He laughed at me and shook his head. 'Cattle, of course. And not always our own! We love cattle. Fish, all the bounty of the sea. We grow a bit of barley. Bread is a handsome food, for sure, but if we can benefit from others' harvests, all the better.'

'Do your people trade?'

'Of course. Gold, silver, horn, hide; our craftsmen and women make beautiful things. Dogs too. Dogs for hunting, or for in the granary to catch rats, whatever kind of dogs you want. And people, unfortunately for me. There's plenty of demand for slaves. It's not every tribe will deal with them but we're good at it. My dad always said, "we make the best chains in the whole world, we may as well get the benefit." But it backfires. Other tribes don't think twice to do the same to us.'

He was remarkably sanguine about his fate, I thought.

The sunshine overhead prompted me to take a measurement. I fetched the gnomon from my bed. I was very proud of it, with its beautifully engraved symbols of sun and moon and stars, as if it carried the authority and protection of the heavens within it. Each time I measured the sun's declination with it, I felt I was getting a blessing from Apollo or more likely from Athena, who I am sure would appreciate the attempt to understand the world I was journeying in.

I got Li to help me, holding the staff, while I marked the spot on the ground where the tip of its shadow fell. When I laid the gnomon down to measure the shadow's length, he plagued me with questions about what I was doing and took great delight in my answers, as if I were telling jokes.

'You're like the old druids who'll tell you from the distance a frog leaps how old you'll live. What a laugh! I can't wait to tell the others I've met a man who navigates by shadows! You can tell the way, but only on a sunny day, eh? You'll not be able to go anywhere when it's raining then?' He was killing himself laughing at me, tears in his eyes, half doubled-over, the rascal.

I don't think he meant to be unkind and I chuckled along at his mirth, enjoying being a clown to him. I didn't realise how prophetic he was being. Those northern lands have more cloudy weather than I could have imagined possible. I wish I'd known it earlier, I would have taken more readings when I could, rather than hanging back and waiting until noon, when no matter how good the morning it had invariably clouded over. I've learned to take it seriously, but not too seriously, when people laugh at me. There really is nothing funnier than a fool.

The measurement, I was surprised to learn, was only a little lower than that I had taken on Tregor. I had travelled mostly west then on my sea voyage with Ussa, not far north at all.

'And where will you be going next, do you think?' I asked him

Li shrugged. 'Ussa goes where she goes. I heard her talking about Manigan yesterday. That means North, probably.'

'Who's Manigan?'

'He's the Walrus Mutterer.'

'The what?'

He grinned. 'He hunts the tooth-walker.' He saw my evident ignorance. 'A huge animal of the north, walks on the ice with its big bone tusks.' He gestured with his hands, two huge fangs.

I suddenly realised he might be talking about the northern ivory. I quizzed him and that seemed to be the case. I was excited. How smoothly my quest was going! 'So she's going after this man for his ivory?'

'No, not really. He has a stone head she covets.'

'Why?'

He shrugged. 'Don't know. She wants it.'

There was a blast of a high-pitched horn from the beach and Li was up on his feet. 'I've got to go, that's the call for the gathering. Nice talking to you.' He bounded away down the track with the speed of a deer.

I sat for a while watching the melee of people and goods until the smell of food wafting up from one of several braziers became too tempting. I was wondering if I might follow Li to ask him some more questions and whether my journey would take me to his northern home. The brief picture he had given me with its talk of dogs and talented crafts people made me sure I would find it fascinating.

Now that I had found the source of tin, my quest, really, was to go searching for amber and ivory, but I had vowed to explore every interesting lead if it led north, and this qualified as interesting. And in the event, Ussa persuaded me to voyage on with her. She charmed me, I admit, and it was easier to stay with her now I was burdened by my haul of tin, but I travelled with her mostly because she had all the right contacts to get me where I needed to go. Having established the source of tin, she seemed to be quite taken with helping me find ivory and amber. After what Li had told me I questioned her about the northern ivory, and she seemed to think it would be possible to track some down, but only much further north. She also volunteered that amber was bought most cheaply and abundantly from the traders who had crossed the ocean from the east and claimed it washed up on beaches in far northern lands. I already felt I was in a far northern place, but she and the slaves laughed at me for suggesting it.

Why would I not go with her? She had been true to her word and more helpful than I could have expected. She not only knew the trade routes but to some extent, I suppose, she had created them by making deals with people wherever she went. And she was going north.

The evening before she planned to leave, we gathered to eat the meal the Keepers provided for their guests. It was more elaborate than usual, as if she was being given a send-off. Ussa waved me over to her and indicated a man seated at his meal.

'Pytheas, meet Gruach, my cousin.'

He was all dressed in tough leather and the skin of his burly body, where exposed, was tattooed with chevrons and spirals, as if he practiced his decoration on his body before hammering or casting it into metal.

'Pytheas has come all the way from the south of Gaul,' Ussa said.

He smiled genially enough, putting the leg of duck he was chewing down on his plate. 'And you are going where?' He articulated each word as if it mattered, which it did, I came to realise as I got to know him better. He used few of them, spending their coinage with weighty consideration.

'To the edge of the world,' I replied.

He smiled with one side of his mouth. 'And you know where that is?'

I grinned. 'No, but I shall.'

He nodded. 'Don't fall off.' He picked up his drumstick and bit into it, and Ussa clearly understood that this was all the conversation we would get out of him.

'We'll leave at first light,' she said. 'Are you loaded?'

He shook his head as if this was a tiresome question and Ussa rolled her eyes and turned in search of more convivial dinner company. Before I followed, I noticed a waif sitting alongside the smith with similarly tattooed arms, presumably his daughter. She was watching Ussa and me intently and when I caught her eye she gave a little smile then turned away.

The knowledge that the smith was intending to travel north with Ussa clinched it for me. The opportunity to travel with a smith, and perhaps wangle more tin secrets out of him, was unmissable.

I caught up with Ussa and tapped her on the shoulder. 'I'll come too, if that's all right?'

'Good.' She tucked her arm around mine. 'Let's find ourselves some company to share music on our last night in Ictis.'

NORTH ALBION

MEASURING ALBA

I must tell you about my most recent calculations. I have become a little obsessed by them in recent weeks. I am preparing to make a presentation to the Council about the island that its inhabitants call Alba, and we call Albion. It is part of an archipelago. I don't need to tell you that, but it made calculating its circumference a challenge, with all those islands around it. The main island, Albion itself, is a sizeable chunk of ground and I have been work-ing out just how big, based on all the measurements I took and the records I made.

I tried hard when I was there to keep tidy records, but when you're one of Ussa's crewmen, keeping a handle on logic and making records that follow that logic is easier said than done. *Ròn* is an excellent craft, a powerful, seafaring vessel, but life on a boat, any boat, is rough and an open sea boat especially so. And it was difficult living with strangers that I'd been brought up to think of as barbarians.

The journey north from Belerion to the Winged Isle was

straightforward at first: a short southward passage and then west to pass the cape, during which our progress was slow and steady in a light easterly breeze. Then the wind shifted south and then southwest and we made better speed for the next four days and nights, accelerating in fact as the weather deteriorated. It felt like spring when we left Belerion but as we headed north, winter returned to harry us.

It is hard to measure the distance covered. I would estimate that we could travel somewhere between three and four hundred stades in a good day's sailing, and more of course when we continued through the night. But that's no more than an estimate and I tried to adjust my records to take into account our progress, including time when we wallowed about in calm seas (it has to be said that there are considerably fewer of these out on the ocean around Albion than we have in our Great Sea).

We made a short stop on an island in the middle of the strait between Albion and Eriu. The weather there was bright and I managed to get a sun declination measurement. However, Ussa was disappointed because a Silurian trader had passed there recently so the local people had nothing of interest to swap for her goods, so she wanted to move on almost as soon as we had arrived.

A druid of theirs warned us worse weather was coming but Ussa insisted on going anyway, so we set a northwards course and the next day we made good progress up and beyond Eriu, into the complex waters of the Hebrides. There I saw strange sights that made me realise that the tides could hugely influence our speed and therefore my measurements of distance.

The one I remember most vividly was waiting at anchor between two islands while a torrent raged ahead of us. Toma, the skipper, was chanting some incantation to the water. Eventually his pleading calmed it completely, allowing us to sail down the channel. At first it flowed gently the way we were going as if to help us through, but then, as if we were not going fast enough, it accelerated. By the time we reached its mouth Toma was cackling and as animated as I ever saw him, and the water was rushing almost as wildly as it had been when we were anchored at the other end, as if it wanted to spit us out. Only a person in communion with spirits, surely, could navigate such fickle waters.

Over the next week we were in and out of harbours. Ussa could never pass up a chance to trade and I was always keen to be back on land. I love the sea, but you cannot better the drama of a landing and the thrill of a new port. Everyone wanted to know Ussa, so travelling with her I was guaranteed to meet the most interesting people wherever I went. I know she used me like a circus animal, 'her Greek', but it didn't take long for me to learn how to get around that. I'd play dumb for her, but when her back was turned, I had my own games.

Anyway, as I was saying, today I have been totting up all the notes I made of my actual journey times. To calculate the circumference, I've had to cheat a bit. Albion, the big island, is roughly triangular and the long side is on the west where it is a confusion of smaller islands, riddled with rias and promontories. Overall, as the eagle flies, I calculate it as twenty thousand stades. The short side goes opposite Gaul, from Belerion to Kantion in the east, and it is only seven and a half thousand stades. And the eastern shore, I am prepared to hazard as fifteen thousand stades, although my journey took me down only part of that coast and I have had to make calculations based on what sailors told me. By the time I got there after my amber trials I had learned enough to work out whose stories I could trust and whose I could not – or I like to believe I had. I shall never know. Find out if I am right if you can; tell me before I die and I shall go to the Islands of the Blessed a happy man. To be honest, I think I shall be fairly content when I go there, if that is where we really go. I have had a good life. Few have seen what I have seen and lived to tell the tale, although I must admit I also have my share of regret, and the guilty conscience that drives me to write this epistle.

*

Back to my journey. After an extremely long but enjoyable day's sailing with a following wind, we rowed into a perfect harbour on the north side of a large island, where Ussa was well known, but not, from what I could gather, particularly welcome. I hoped we might be there for some time as sailing up the coast, its rock formations had intrigued me. But the people who rather reluctantly took us in for the night talked about the walrus hunter called Manigan, and Ussa became extremely agitated. My interest was piqued. He had been there only a few days before and had told our hosts of his plans to travel north, starting his hunting season early.

This was when I realised quite how obsessive Ussa could be in her chasing after Manigan and his magic stone. She was mad for it. I tried to get her to explain to me why it was so important, and she said to me, 'He's my cousin. It belonged to our grandmother and she was told it should always be in a woman's care. It's rightly mine.' I wonder if she ever got it off him.

On this occasion, ignoring the warnings of rough weather and the offers of hospitality from our hosts, she packed us all off again in the boat at first light. It was blowing hard out of the southwest for the first few hours and the sea was the lumpiest and most uncomfortable I have ever known, worse even than a storm in the Northern Ocean, which, although the sea was huge, had a rhythm about it I could understand. Toma told me the land we were passing was notorious for its unpleasant sea, due to the mixing of water from many different directions.

The morning's sail was nothing, however. Not only were the tidal streams and currents baffling, to me at least, but in the afternoon the sea became wild and a wind got up that seemed to build and build with a ferocity I had never known. I was soon soaked to the skin and glad of my boots and my wolf fur outer layer, which kept me warm even when wet. I swear there is nothing better than good boots and thick wool socks. I can endure a lot with feet that are tolerably warm, virtually nothing once my toes get cold.

The sea that day! I'll never forget those waves. Our boat was lifted and tossed until I thought we were certain to flip over. I clung to the halyard at the mast until Toma told me to come and shelter at the stern where the side of the boat was a little higher and I at least had something solid at my back. I cowered there throughout the rest of the gale, while he and the slaves battled with sails and rope. I couldn't understand how they could even attempt to sail, but it was clear we needed to try, as allowing the boat simply to be buffeted by the wind and waves would have put us on rocks many times. Somehow Toma managed to have enough sail and control of the rudder to keep us off the shore.

There was a period when the wind was at our backs, before it moved to the east and blasted across our beam, building in intensity. Toma ordered the slaves to reef the sail until it was as small as it would go. He was anxious to make for one of the various safe harbours he knew, but these were all on the eastern shore and the wind would not allow us to approach them. For a while, the visibility was so poor I was amazed that he knew where we were, but that was his genius I suppose, and why Ussa had him as her skipper. Then, as the day went on, the cloud lifted.

The safe channel between the island and the mainland was too easterly for us to approach, so we had no choice but to go north into a loch, or west to other islands. Toma gave Ussa a choice of two possible harbours. He favoured one on Rum, he said. She chose the other, due north, Loch Slapin, in the Winged Isle. Her eyes were greedy for the place on account of it being Manigan's land. She was sure she'd find him there.

The loch had daunting crags along its western shore and I was terrified we would be wrecked along them. Behind these cliffs, mountains loomed like the jaws of some great predator. I have never seen a more forbidding place. We hurtled up the narrows and made for a place of relative shelter. Toma ordered the anchor to be thrown overboard when we neared the shore and we came to a halt in the shallows, then he let out rope so we could be washed up onto the rocky beach with some control. The boat yawed and slewed about in the waves and I was sure we would founder there, but Toma's nerves are of stronger stuff than mine and he got us onto dry land without injury.

The boat was battered in the process of landing, and Toma made it clear he wouldn't be able to sail again until it was mended, so we were stranded there for several days.

At first I was simply delighted to be alive, and once I discovered where I was I became fascinated. Ussa, needless to say, could not wait to get back out to sea and on with her journey. Her enmity with Manigan made her an uneasy guest, although I have to say they treated me honourably and made me feel more than welcome, particularly once I learned what a special location it was.

THE WINGED ISLE

On the Winged Isle there is a place I will break a great taboo to tell you about, but because you are who you are, I want to share it with you. Take it to your grave. It will perhaps serve you better there than in this bright world of greed and jealousy and ire. Or go there while you are living. It is a wet and dreary island but it may change you. It did me. I believe it prepared me for my meeting with Rian, even further north.

After our crash-landing, we were spotted by the family who lived closest to the stony shore and they took us into their crag-top house, tall and imposing. The matriarch Seonag stood as we stooped through the narrow entrance and was the first to speak to us, after Ussa and I had made our way in. I was surprised that the old woman of the house had such power.

'Welcome,' she said, 'and bring your slaves in as well. We are all the children of the Great Mother.'

I liked her immediately. She made us all feel welcome and was full of curiosity about our plans. She and her family spoke a dialect of Keltic that was hard to follow when they spoke among themselves, but when she talked to us, she spoke slowly and clearly and it was easy to tune in to what she meant.

The broch was far less impressive inside than out, like an orange with a thick skin; it looks so juicy and inviting on the outside, but once you start peeling it reveals only a few wrinkled, stringy segments on the inside. The people were comfortable enough, I suppose, but the furnishings were all simply made of hazel wattle, cow hide and itchy heather. They don't go for fine cloth, these people, and why would they? For much of the year they need materials that will keep them warm when gales are howling and storms lash in from the ocean.

We were offered seats made of stone along the wall. They were cushioned by hide over something, perhaps heather. They use heather for everything, those people, you can't believe it. Or perhaps you can, perhaps I'm telling you things you are familiar with.

Ussa was given a bench with rather splendid furs to sit on, which no doubt doubled as a comfortable bed at night, and she adopted a queenly pose. There was a good fire going and food was soon put before us, fish mostly, but also cheese and small, delicious, nutty bannocks.

People came and went all the time, and the place was clearly a kind of physician's centre with Seonag, the woman of all cures. There was a pot of something herbal brewing. Grateful-looking people came bearing gifts of food, a few eggs or some roots, shellfish or grains, and their empty cups and bowls were refilled by the ever-smiling matriarch. Those who looked hungry were given a task, like grinding some corn or fetching water, then a bite to eat. It was like watching a mother with dozens of children, only most were adults.

Ussa sat stony and silent much of the time, but after we had been there a couple of hours, men arrived, one older than me, carrying a satchel of tools, and the other, clearly his apprentice, carrying a roll of hide. After a few words, most of us set off with the two of them to mend the boat, while Gruach and Fraoch set up their forge.

I have a great admiration for the way these leather currachs perform in the sea if they have the right people handling them, those with the knowledge of how they can fly. Their lightness and flexibility, far from being a liability, is what gives them the ability to survive those wild waters. They lift on big waves, instead of acting as a barrier, and they can survive a battering by lumps of water that would prise open the planks of many a ship of our waters. More importantly, they are light enough to lift up onto a shore, so in a storm they can be protected, instead of having to hang onto an anchor at risk of being smashed against rocks.

I can give you an example of what impressed me about the boat's design. One day in the northern ocean after being pitched about all day in evil water, our boat sprang a leak where the wooden spar had rubbed against the leather and worn it so thin a rip could open up. Toma calmly took out a roll of cow-hide from his chest, a ball of sinew, a big awl, and a needle made of some kind of bone. With his knife, which he always kept wickedly sharp, he cut two pieces of the material, roughly square, pierced holes along their edges with the awl, then leaned over the side of the boat. With one hand on the outside, he placed one of the patches over the hole, and the leak stopped. He gestured for me to help him, and placed my hand over the patch. He slipped the second piece under the spar on the inside. Despite the boat pitching about on waves, each time we rose up he'd punch the needle through and follow it with twine. With a few deft stitches, he fastened the patches in place. It took less time than the boiling of a kettle and the boat was as good as new again. I tried to imagine the equivalent mend on a wooden boat, the palaver of heating up pitch to try to caulk a leak or the futile attempt to nail a wooden patch over a hole, which would be doomed to seep forever. These boats are watertight and as mendable as a solid pair of riding breeches.

But that day, it was clear that there had been some real structural damage as we had made landfall. Two wooden spars had smashed, and needed replacing. I watched for a while as they cut out the damaged wood and discussed how they would lock in new pieces, but eventually the cold and wet drove me back to the broch.

Seonag was there, chatting with a neighbour, a younger, elegant woman called Cuilc. The interest I showed in Seonag's ministrations to her flock had endeared me to her, and I found myself getting deep into a conversation I shall remember to my grave, and who knows, possibly even beyond there.

'So what's your interest in chasing after Manigan?' she said.

'I've no interest in him at all, except possibly for the ivory I've heard he gathers when he hunts the big horned sea beast.'

'Walrus. Horse of the sea. It has great tusks.' Seonag imitated their curved shape as if coming out of her own face.

'And why does Ussa pursue the Mutterer?' Cuilc asked.

'He has a three-faced head and she covets it.'

'A head?' I said. 'She told me it's a stone.'

'It is. It's known as the Death Stone. She's reckless if you want my view. It's dangerous enough. Riddled with curses.'

'She told me it is magical and can answer any question you ask it.'

Seonag snorted. 'At what cost? Did she tell you that? A life for every question. Manigan gets some hunting prowess from it but I wouldn't want it.'

Cuilc looked impressed. She turned to me.

'What's the most interesting thing you've found on your travels?'

Without really thinking, I told her it was edges. 'I feel myself skirting the margin of the known world and finding treasure everywhere here. It is almost magical.'

'No.' Seonag was sitting on a low stool by her fire, stirring a simmering pot on a flat stone. With her voluminous skirt and long grey hair she seemed to flow out of the floor, as if the rug was an extension of her or she of it. 'It is not magic. Everything valuable, significant and rare is found at the edge of the world. What is the purpose of your journey?'

'I am seeking amber,' I said, 'and tin. I found tin at the edge of the land, further south.'

'And you shall find amber on the coastal fringe as well. It is of the liminal world, as am I.'

'Liminal.' It was my turn to echo her.

'The crossing of boundaries is dangerous enough, but you know this already if you have come this far.'

I tilted my head. 'I enjoy it. There are such interesting things to discover. Between languages, for example.'

'You shift between them easily enough.'

I explained my childhood in the Greek colony, surrounded by Gauls, my nurse a speaker of Keltic, my teacher a Roman who taught me the mathematics I love to this day. He introduced me to Euclid's ideas, which have served me well in understanding the measurements I need to make to clarify the shape and extent of the world.

'Your nurse?' She picked the nugget that related to her. 'What was her name?'

'Danu.'

'A slave?'

I nodded. 'Perhaps that's why I don't see the boundary between freedom and slavery as clearly as some do.' I was thinking of Ussa, who always liked this distinction to be so clear.

'All these borders can be crossed.'

'They must be. I like to remain open.'

'Have you crossed between life and death?' She looked at me hard, waiting for me to answer.

'No, but it is a boundary I know I shall breach one day, probably too soon for my liking.'

'There are places where it is thin enough.'

'I wouldn't want to go too soon, as I may not come back.'

'Of course. But no edge is single-sided. You sail, so you know the ocean might drown you, but more often she returns you to shore. Death is no different, really.'

'You sail on the water of Lethe?'

'Lethe? I do not know it. No, I do not sail. I go down into the underworld.'

'Lethe is the river to the underworld.'

'Ah, then I know it well. The blood of our earth mother is pure and clear. I follow it down, certainly, though not by sail, just by foot, and by strength of will and spirit. And perhaps a little magic. Just enough.'

I was enthralled, but wanted to be sure I did not overstep myself. 'And you return,' I said eventually.

'Of course. I guide, shall we say. There, and back if necessary.'

'Will you guide me?'

'Why do you want to go there?'

'I am Pytheas. I am exploring the edges of the world.'

'Then I am Seonag, your guide to the passage to the underworld.'

Was it arrogant of me to think of myself as Odysseus, embarking on his journey underground, seeking to appease the gods of the ocean and acquire advice on how to get home safely?

BRIGID'S LAND

As if it was completely matter-of-fact, Seonag began to make a plan to show me the sacred portal to the underworld. I could not really believe what I was hearing.

'We shall go later. It is half-moon, which is a good time of balance, a safe-enough time when most of the restless spirits are sleeping. You must prepare yourself. I will find you something to wear and gather firewood. It is a fair ride from here.'

'Where do we go to?'

'A gateway. You'll see soon enough.'

She handed me a bundle of soft woollen fabric dyed the colour of a summer sky, deep blue flecked with white. It was a shapeless robe like a long shirt. Then she gave me a soft, plaited rope, coloured pale green. I had no idea what to expect, but her swift purposefulness intrigued me. Now she had decided I must see this place, she was clearly following a familiar set of preparations. She had a big leather bag into which she placed my clothes and a bewildering array of vessels and powders. I was pleased to see fresh bannocks going in along with nuts and dried berries and a decidedly unappetising dried fish. Twice she went outside and yelled, 'Ishbel!' and eventually a dark-haired girl with shy eyes appeared with a boy, no more than a toddler. He ran up to the neighbour, Cuilc, clearly his mother, who gathered him to her in a hug. He was a beautiful child, dark-eyed and round-faced. I was introduced to him as Eadha, which I was told is the name of the round-leaved poplar, the aspen, which always quivers in the wind. I tried to engage him but he was at the age where almost everything except his mother is too strange and more than a bit frightening.

Ishbel seemed at a loss without the child but she brightened up when Seonag told her we were going to Brigid's Land and set about her own gathering of objects. I saw a flute go into a pocket, and a lamp. We were introduced to each other, but at first she seemed too shy to talk to me, although I caught her eyeing me curiously at one point and she returned my encouraging smile. She was perhaps eighteen years old.

'Ishbel will follow me as priestess,' said Seonag. 'I had no daughter. Perhaps Brigid was angry with us for something. But fortunately I have Ishbel to pass on what I know. She'll lead the ceremonies there soon enough.'

Behind her calm voice there was a tension. I sensed that some deeper conflict had gone on that she was not willing to talk to me about, and that she was making light of something grave. But she was keen to be off, and led us out to where two white ponies were grazing.

There was a shout from behind us and a man appeared on a knoll towards the shore.

'We're off to Brigid's Land,' Seonag called. 'Cuilc says she'll cook for the guests.'

He nodded and went back into the barn.

'She's a good friend and always keen to talk to people from other parts,' she said to me.

We rode the two ponies, Seonag and Ishbel on one and me on the other. I'm no horseman but these were biddable and remarkably strong and sure-footed, so it was easy going. There were thickets of contorted birches and hazels with drooping catkins on the low slopes. A leafless bush made russet patches on the bog among green moss hummocks. The cores of the blond rush tussocks were greening too, but between them the peaty ground lay black and menacing. The hill was a pattern of a pale grass and heather, two shades of dull brown, and an amber scatter of bracken completed the atmosphere of brittle decay.

Seonag pointed out the odd landmark along the way, but mostly we plodded quietly. I looked out for spring flowers, but they were sparse. The weather was disgusting, as it is so often in that part of the world. I was tired and wet when we reached a long valley where our paths divided. Ishbel and I were sent with a bag down to a beach to gather stones, while Seonag went ahead.

The beach was a clutter of gneiss and sandstone pebbles of all possible sizes and shapes. Ishbel had an air about her that belied her age and she instructed me with gravity through the ritual gathering, step by step. We walked down to the sea. She made me take off my boots and put them in the bag, then stand in the freezing water. The stones were slippery underfoot and the waves unsteadied me. Ishbel chanted something and I thought about what Seonag had said to me about liminal places. This was one. This was the same shoreline I was following all the way up north. Although I had made libations to Apollo for each sea voyage I made, I had not thought to honour directly the boundary of sea and land. My feet ached with cold when I came out, but stepping on dry land was hardly a relief as it was almost as wet out of the sea as in it.

'Is there a god or a goddess for the shore?' I asked Ishbel.

She looked at me blankly.

'Who were you chanting to?'

'The sea.' She pointed to the stones. 'You have to gather three dozen bigger than your fist.'

I started to get my boots out but she shook her head. 'You have to go barefoot.'

Once filled with stones, the bag was heavy. I hoisted it on my back and we set off uphill. It was a steep stumble following a stream. My feet were soft after weeks in boots. I have spent more pleasant afternoons. I wondered if Ishbel was secretly laughing at me, going along with all her demands, and I was reminded of the Bunnies in Belerion, where I had had similar doubts about Og's uncle until he took me underground.

The horse was not allowed to take my burden, Ishbel said. She led it while I toiled up the slope. The stream petered out into a bog where I slithered about in my bare feet. The hills all around were covered with the scrubby birches that are all they can muster for woods in this part of the world. They were still leafless and a strange, if rather marvellous, wine-colour.

Springs trickled together into another stream which flowed out of the mire. We followed it down. It was a bright chuckle and I noticed that the stone in its bed was different from the rock I had just walked through, and from the stones I was carrying. It was a grey limestone, smooth-surfaced, unlike the gritty gneiss and red sandstone.

We smelled the smoke first, then suddenly we were on a soft green sward, despite the early season. It was a threshold to a new world: a gentle pasture, with two huge, hairy, black cows grazing on it.

Seonag walked towards us and bowed to me as if we were meeting for the first time. Her face was painted, her hair tied back and wrapped in a blue cloth, and she was wearing a splendid, voluminous black robe with a huge sunburst embroidered on it. She led me to a crescent-shaped mound and indicated I should put down the bag of stones beside a strange dome. I felt light and childlike once relieved of my burden.

Then she gave me a wooden bucket and led me back towards a pool where the stream gathered before literally disappearing into the ground. Beside it was a splendid clump of primroses.

'Fill your bucket,' she said, so I bent down in the channel and angled the pail so water flowed into it. It was the clearest looking water I have ever seen, so clear you can't see it.

'May I drink it?' I asked.

'Of course,' she said.

It was delicious, like drinking pure crystal. I said so, and she laughed in appreciation.

'You'll need three buckets full.' She beckoned me to follow her.

I splashed water on my legs from the bucket as I walked but my feet were so numb I barely felt anything. She led me to the dome. It was a hide tent. She lifted a flap and bowed in through the low doorway. A fire was burning inside. There was a stone tank sunk in the floor and she told me to pour the water into it, then go for more.

*

When I had filled and emptied the bucket three times, Seonag said, 'Now fetch your stones. They go here beside the fire.'

68

Ishbel was nowhere to be seen.

I did as instructed.

'Remove your cloak and come in. You can put it there.' There was a peg to the left of the doorway. She told me to sit and bustled around me, sealing the flap, bringing the fire to a blaze, showing me how to arrange the stones to heat up, laying out bowls of dried petals and leaves. I felt myself settle into the dim space, enjoying the warmth. The dancing firelight and rain pattering on the hide roof were mesmerising.

Seonag sprinkled something onto the fire and the tent filled with a sweet, pungent smoke. She lowered herself onto a rug beside me and reached for a small drum. Then she paused and closed her eyes. The ceremony had begun.

As she chanted, she made a running patter on the skin that sounded like the raindrops on the roof. Weaving through the smoke, Seonag's song told of the birth of the first people out of the earth. She had a sweet voice but I felt as if I was an imposter in a private ritual, or that I was being led into something deeper than I had bargained for. I had a tickle in my throat but managed to stop myself from coughing until she had finished. I don't know if it was because of my cough or not, but she offered me a drink of herbs and something alcoholic. I really have no idea what she gave me, but as I supped, it burned deep in my belly. Had it not been for my need to suppress the cough I should have been more tentative with it.

After several gulps, she took it gently from me with a raised eyebrow. 'That's probably enough, if you're not used to it.'

I'll never forget the wry look on her face, the way an indulgent parent watches a child. 'It'll take you over the border, that's for sure.' She winked, and took a healthy slug of it herself.

From that point on I don't think you can rely on me to tell you what happened. I do not rightly understand it. She left me to wash, after piling the hot stones into the water tank. I began to feel queasy and worried, but as I splashed I suddenly found myself marvelling at the feeling of wetness on my exposed skin. My body became oversensitive and my legs and arms felt long and gangly. I dried myself beside the fire and dressed in the blue robe and green belt. It felt delicious to be clean and I felt young again, capable of anything, although when Ishbel returned I wasn't completely certain that I knew what was happening.

She led me into a cave. I took amber with me and I distinctly remember giving it to the spirit who dwelled in the cave. Everything else – well, it was beyond words. It was the place of the goddess. Brigid's land. I scribbled some notes afterwards. This is what they say. Paraphrase is beyond me. Make any sense of it you can.

Darkness, starlight, glittering.

A jewelled cavern.

Golden drips.

Black chert boulders, white marble stripes, spiky limestone. A wet rock tapestry.

A smooth waterworn channel and a trickle underfoot.

A pool of pure clarity. Blood of the goddess. All the wisdom of the ages.

Rippling light on the passage walls. Drops of gold, a pool of gold, golden gleams and glitter everywhere.

I looked deep into a channel that delved into the depths of the universe, a pillared chamber of silver and ivory.

I drank blood. Fangs hung ready to drink my own.

Among breasts like the teats of a sow, dripping with milk, I wept for the lack of my mother.

Ears of goblins and elves listening to the murmur of water.

The lyre! Strings echoing the trickling stream, the stream leading the song.

Pure joy. Pure love.

Spirits of the dead howling from deep within. Roaring.

Terrifying struggles, thunder, agony.

The other side. Darkness. Coldness.
Only a whirling stillness and the trickle of water.
Clammy horror. Mud. Slime.
Emptiness.
Shaking. Uncontrollable shaking.
A trickle of sound through the darkness, a stream of light.
Fingers, stroking a ripple of song, most beautiful music.
Rippling glimmers.
A glow.
A hand.

ABOVE GROUND

I do not know when I emerged. I had passed beyond the edge and I returned to my senses back in the tent beside the fire, wrapped in a blanket, warm again. I was given a fresh, minty hot drink, sweetened with honey, and my nausea was tempered by it. Seonag was not there but Ishbel was attentive and gentle, encouraging me to stay where I was, lying down, asking me how I felt, what I had encountered. She had lovely pale skin. I wanted to touch her. It was impossible to answer her questions.

'Where's Seonag?' I said.

'Talking with the spirits.'

'But where?'

'In the cave.'

'Have I been there?'

She nodded.

'Why am I not there still?' I really did not understand how I could be here by this fire.

Ishbel just smiled.

I became infuriated by her. I was confused, not really rational. I think I might have shouted at her.

She seemed fearful and begged me to be quiet, promised me

we would go to find Seonag.

I was scared too, to be honest. I felt unhinged, as if I was losing my wits. I wanted Seonag like a child wants its mother. I let Ishbel soothe me and, still wrapped in the blanket, we emerged into the night and saw the moon seeming to chase the clouds. It was no longer raining. We trod the wet ground back to the cave mouth.

I didn't dare to re-enter. Proximity to it set my mind wheeling again and I had to crouch, huddled against the entrance at the top of the steps down into the world below. The lyre was playing and fragments of its melody flowed up towards me. Bathing in them I felt myself settle again. I sat on the top step, my feet tucked into the blanket, and listened to Seonag and the spirits singing to each other.

An owl hooted in the woods nearby, but this was not Athena; I had moved beyond her realm, and had to grapple for a different kind of wisdom. The bronze owl that you have is my symbol for this moment and all that came before it on my voyage. It embodies my discovery of tin's origins, the knowledge I found in the strange underworlds of the Bunnies and of Brigid's land, and the preconceived ideas about the supposed 'barbarians' that I abandoned along the way. I discovered that, far from being ignorant savages, they could be elegant and make beautiful music, and that they had wisdom and expertise in astronomy and navigation that was truly impressive.

After a while, Ishbel placed another hot mug of sweetness into my hands. I supped it, drinking in the sounds from below, bathed in moonlight and steam. I allowed a honey glow to smile from my belly to my face. I knew then that I was the luckiest man alive, to share in such a mystery, to be granted this place I inhabit upon the edge of our society, exploring the margins of the world, granted the chance to go over and back. I did not want to cross too soon again. It left me with a healthy respect for the infinite darkness that lies beyond the small pool of light we dwell within. I know I shall go there permanently one day, and I also realised that night that part of me is there already, perhaps that is where we go in sleep, to re-join the subterranean part of ourselves, our under-minds, where all our urges and anxieties hide. For that hour, or however long it was I sat there, it was all exposed. All my desires spoke. All my fears stood, disarmed. I knew myself.

Later, the waves of the soul closed over everything again. I've never experienced that absolute clarity of spirit since, but I gained something lasting that day. I knew myself. It was the greatest gift I have ever been given. Until that day I was making my journey in order to take back to Massalia the secrets of the north and thereby become rich and gain the status of councillor. I was going out in order to get in – into the elite that is. But that night in Brigid's Land I realised there was really no need to take anything home, and that no amount of formal status would satisfy me if I was not already satisfied by my own discoveries. To return was still there as an aim, of course – it was my intention, shall we say. And to return with gifts and revelations – that was something I had in mind to do as well. But these were no longer the centre of my purpose. The journey had become its own end.

Looking back on it, I think this was the start of a process in which I came to realise that all people and perhaps even all objects have an intrinsic value, and we do wrong when we treat them as merely means to an end. But that realisation, as you will soon learn, had yet to take shape in my mind.

I was there, in Brigid's Land, listening to the music of the underworld given voice by the strings of a lyre and by a kind and undemanding woman who had offered me this gift for nothing, for no reason I fully understood, simply recognising in me my need for passage over an edge within myself. I was there, sitting on a chilly step, back in this world after an indescribable and essential journey into a world beyond normal reach. By being given the chance to gain that place it was as if I had been forced to let go of a support I had been clinging to without realising it – my ambition, if you will – and I found myself walking hands free, upright and strong. I was rid of the burden of ultimate purpose. I was here. I was free.

It left me in a state of unrefracted joy for quite some time that night. I was still in that state, now I look back on it, when I first encountered Rian. You might say, if you were fanciful, and I do not know if you are or not, that I was being purified by the gods, or by the spirits of that wild and beautiful place, to meet her. Or you might say it was all just a long string of coincidences. I cannot tell. From inside my own story it has always seemed to make perfect sense, while being, when I think hard about it, completely incomprehensible.

I conceive it as a moment when a tide turned inside me. There's a long chapter in my book, *On the Ocean*, about tides. It includes all my measurements and the work I did over the course of my journey to verify my theory. I already had a good idea of how they worked before I got to Brigid's Land but I had one of several conversations there that made me understand their rhythms more deeply.

It was after Seonag came up out of the cave. She was radiant in that robe of sun, her eyes huge and dark, carrying the wooden lyre cradled in her arms like a baby.

'How are you?' she asked.

'Happy,' I said. 'Happier than I have ever been. My soul is clean.'

She smiled at me and bowed deeply at the cloud-furled moon. 'Thanks to the moon. She will set soon enough. Another day. Moon rhythm, sun rhythm. All of life, coming and going. It is all tidal: bleeding, birthing, sleeping, ageing.'

I asked what she meant. She saw rhythms everywhere, linked to phases of the moon, the dances of the white goddess as she described it… What she said has transformed how I think about tides. How sad it is that when I attempt to discuss this with my fellow countrymen I am met only with scoffs and jeers.

'Each day and night, we begin asleep, we wake, we live out our bodily functions of eating and moving, and then we sleep again. Meanwhile the tide goes out and in, twice. Many of us sleep in the middle of the day as well, allowing the tide of our thoughts to go out twice, as the watery tide does. Each month the moon waxes and wanes and so does a woman's womb, but just as there are two tidal fluxes for each full day-night cycle, so there are two tidal fluxes with each moon. At both full and new moon, the high tide is high, the low tide is low, its range is maximum. Between them, on the half moons, the range is modest enough. We have words for this. We call the big tides 'springs' and the small tides 'neaps'.' That's what she said.

She also told me something I have been unable to verify, which is that the northern ivory, which comes from the tusks of the great sea-creature called walrus, is also linked to the moon and tides. The animal has two tusks, one of which represents the waning moon, while the other is in the waxing mode. An amulet made with one will increase the influence of the thing it represents, but if made with the other it will reduce its power. So if you want to be kept safe from the danger of a bear, you should make an amulet in its form from the waning tusk, whereas if you want a boat to sail well, you should make a little ivory ship from a waxing tusk. She pulled a necklace out from inside her clothes – it was made of polished ivory beads. 'This is pure waxing moon,' she said. 'I wear it next to my skin so her influence is always strong in me. But with or without such a thing, we all ebb and flow with her.'

People here mock me for the assertion that the moon influences the tides. I am sorely challenged to produce an adequate proof and I am the first to admit that there is much about tides that I cannot explain. There are places I have been to around the coast of Albion where the tidal range is as much as 30 podes. I have seen it with my own eyes: huge areas of flat land dry out and are inundated twice each day. In narrow channels, the force of the tidal water runs in and out like river rapids, as fast as a trireme with full crew. Narrow passages between islands can be filled with swirling water and even out at sea a tidal flow can stop a boat dead with the wind behind it. No doubt the gods play with these forces, but there is also a regularity about them that has its own power. Surely their mystery is open to analysis.

I am entranced by the fundamental tidal rhythm, the swelling to a cusp, then the slide out to a minimum. I told Seonag so, and she smiled.

I was sleepy, and she let me rest. When I came round I was aware of someone playing a flute somewhere outside and a robin answering from a tree, or was it the other way around? It was innocent and beautiful. All of it.

I have never told anyone about my underworld experiences. I feel I am becoming confessional and that is not my intention. It is as if my guilt is tidal, ebbing and surging, and when it rises I have an urge to go off at a tangent, to divert from the tale I really should relate.

I shall press on. North!

AMBER

NORTHERN LANDS

GNOMON

My gnomon measurements have often caused amusement. People think I am simple-minded to measure shadows, and they laugh because they lack my knowledge of what the measurement means, what I can do with it. The laughers think they know where they are, but I can calculate exactly where that is, how far north, how far from home.

I always need a helper, and I've learned a lot from the people who have assisted me, through their responses. Rian helped me the day after we arrived in Assynt. It was the first time, indeed one of very few times, that we were ever alone together.

She was gathering wood and at first I think I frightened her. She was a slip of a thing, a skinny little creature, but those bright green eyes like emeralds, coupled with her amber-coloured hair, were unique. I had never seen such a combination on a person. That alone wouldn't have been enough to persuade me to buy her. Rather, it was her intelligence that clinched it, and this day was the first time I noticed it. We seemed to have no language in common so I thought it would be a challenge to work with her, but she turned out to be easy to communicate with. We used signs and gestures and she was so smart, she never needed to be told or shown anything twice.

It was a beautiful day: crisp and blue. The landscape there is extraordinary, I have never seen anywhere so unintelligible. Mountains and bogs butt up against woods and rocky crags and everywhere you go your way is blocked by water: streams, rivers, ponds, lakes, swamps or the sea-shore, so you must meander and swerve and constantly lose your way. It is impossible to keep your bearings. Yet everywhere I found myself marvelling, either being caught unawares by a sudden vista of sea or mountains, offset or reflected in water, or by being forced to watch my feet and noticing some of the wonders of the season unfolding. Although it froze at night and the trees had no leaves, there were signs of spring everywhere. The woodland was dotted with little flowers, pale yellow primroses, and a three leaved plant with delicately pink-veined white petals. A bright green beetle charged ahead of me on the path and a golden bird hopped along, patiently, as if showing me the way. There were birds in the treetops and a light breeze that stroked my skin like a lover. I suppose spring was touching everything equally like that, and maybe this is why the birds sang and the flowers and mosses glowed.

But I am a scientist and I was trying to find out how far north I had come and for that I required an unobstructed exposure to the sun, where the shadows of the trees would not obscure my measurement. I gestured to Rian to follow me, trying to explain what I was seeking. It sounds strange, but what I required was flat ground, and that place seemed to have none at all. I should have just taken the measurement out on the fields behind the broch, but I wanted to gain some height and get a vista. She obliged me by going up to the brow of the slope we were on, but that landscape is perpetually confusing. I saw that there were successions of other knolls, rippling out, obscuring and occluding the landscape in all directions. There were small bodies of water, lochans, they call them, in every hollow, glittering in the sunshine, their surfaces wrinkled by the breeze, catching every glint of light and doubling it. It was a jewelled land. From here too I could see the sea reaching out and islands, hazy in the west. A headland obscured the beach and the lagoon where the broch stood to our north.

Below us was the perfect spot, a grassy patch above the shore. I gestured to it as the destination and she showed me the easy way down through the birch trees and willows. I saw she was watchful as we broke out from among the trees. There were four black shaggy cows grazing the sward. This was clearly someone else's place and I could see she was readying herself in case we encountered them. It is strange how at times I seemed to be able to see her thoughts and at other times she was as calm as the windless ocean, as featureless and unreadable. I heard many people call her cold and unfeeling, whereas I think of her as deep and capable of a serenity that mystics only dream of.

She looked at me expectantly once we were on level ground, but a cloud had covered the sun. They were fast-moving and seemed to billow out of the northeast where I later saw there were mountains. While the sun was out and they were rising they looked white and fluffy as lamb's wool, but once they reached overhead they were grey-bottomed and menacing. Yet as they shifted out over the ocean, they seemed to dissipate as if the sea's reflection up into the sky was too blue and pure to tolerate them. The edge thinned, like strands of a fleece pulled apart by a spinner, and then disappeared into the blue: fluff, then flecks, then gone.

We stood watching the cloud disintegrate over the languorous sea. She pointed out a seal lolling on a seaweedy rock in the bay. It rolled onto its side and lifted its tail, as if in greeting, curving its back, fluttering its flippers, then collapsing back into a slump of apparent bliss. We shared, Rian and I, a smile of admiration for the good example it was setting us.

The cloud split open, the sun broke through, the water blazed into a million shards of dazzle and my gnomon cast its line. I pointed to the tip of its shadow and gestured for Rian to stand there, precisely, and she positioned her left toes with perfect care exactly where it fell. I measured the distance between the staff and her, laying the staff out horizontally. The pole/shadow ratio was 5/8. A golden ratio: the ratio of 5 to 8 being the same as 8 to their sum, 13. Many of our greatest thinkers, not least Plato, see this ratio as the essence of life's generative force. I like to think everything that followed between myself and Rian was destined from that moment.

I knew from the height of the sun that it must be about noon and I was worried that I might have missed the moment. I waited just a minute and then took another measurement. She seemed to find this amusing. It was exactly the same. I paused again. The next reading of the shadow was marginally longer. I waited to be sure then took a fourth reading. It had lengthened further, so I knew my first reading must have been at noon, if I hadn't missed it. The second reading was comforting, its implication was that I had caught the sun, by chance, at its cusp.

I do not know how much of what I was doing made sense to her, but she paid close, perhaps I can go so far as to say rapt, attention to it all. I've said it before, but it bears repeating, that being in the presence of Rian often made me feel that a moment was happening where life was brimming, a tide reaching its zenith. She seemed to inhabit the perfect calm that occurs between storms. Did joining her mean inevitably passing from one phase of life to another? Was that her mysterious magic?

I know she changed me utterly, and I look back at myself as the person I was before I encountered her, and the person I have since become. Perhaps it was because she was on the knife-edge of transformation from maiden to mother. But I think it is deeper than that. She exemplifies a universal tideline between the people of nature and the people of things, or rather between the people controlled by nature and those who put nature under their control.

It is hard to express this, but one image stays with me from those days I spent in Assynt. There are many herders in the fields behind Massalia and I was accustomed to their way of herding: they drive the cattle where they want them to go with a stick and often a dog or two. I saw the same in Belerion, up those marvellous trackways I told you about. In other places I have seen the cattle lead, and I watched it often in the north. The herders follow their herd, allowing the animals to choose where they will forage.

This is the distinction I mean. The former controls nature, the latter is under nature's control.

In Assynt I watched Rian with her cow and I could not tell who was leading whom. I can only describe their movements as of two individuals together who knew where they were going. The cow grazed, lifted its head, moved on, paused to munch again, and at any moment you would have sworn the girl was simply drifting along at the mercy of the cow's urges. She had no stick, nor did I see her slap the cow or push it along or steer it in any way. I'm not sure I heard her issue any commands, though I can't guarantee she wasn't humming to it below earshot. No whistling or calling, anyway, none of the characteristic hullaballoo of the herders in our place bringing the cows in for milking. Just a stroll, punctuated by frequent mouthfuls of grass; but over the course of a sunset the cow was down from the hill beyond the woods, across the field without damaging the young crop, and back to the house. Did the cow want to come home and did she just allow it to follow its whim? That is what it looked like. But somehow it also looked as if, had she not gone to encourage it home, it might have stayed out in the wilds.

And something similar was involved in the nature of our relationship. Whereas I was her master and she my slave in theory, in reality I felt possessed by her. If she coughed I would look up. If I heard her singing, I would try to watch her without her noticing. If love can enslave a man, I was her slave, although I didn't recognise it at the time.

I am telling you this because you need to understand me. It is hard to explain oneself to another, to tell one's story truthfully. I think there are only ever a few moments in our lives that really define us. Fleeting instants when we know ourselves for who we really are, when we feel the pure mineral lodes that run within us, the bones of our soul. The rest of our lives we hide from ourselves, attend to our flesh, fuss about with pretence and tricks to try to convince others as well as ourselves that we are moral, upstanding, disciplined, good-natured people. In my vanity, I have wanted to appear benevolent, a giver of gifts. But I know myself in my heart to be greedy.

Do you know the story of Patroclus and Briseis? It is one of my favourite sections of Homer. She was a princess, beautiful and clever, and when all of her family were killed in the Trojan War, Achilles claimed her as his war booty. Patroclus tried to comfort her, explaining that Achilles was a gentle man, and would treat her with honour. By belonging to him she would escape the indignity of being a mere chattel, which would have been her fate if any of the other princes had taken her as their prize. I like to believe it was in this spirit that I bought Rian.

Life is a long curtain of self-deceits, and there are only very few moments when a chink of the true light of our nature breaks through. It is those chinks I therefore dwell upon, so you may be familiar with the unadorned truth of me, even if it is not pretty. The strongest desire I have ever felt has been the urge to possess a person. I have tried to pretend it was simply a wish to take care of them, but that is disingenuous. The compulsion to own another human reduces them to something like a commodity: it is a denial of their sacred reality. I know that now.

PURCHASE

I bought Rian from Ussa with a piece of amber in the shape of a tear-drop. Yes. I'm sure if I told her, my old nurse Danu would shake her head and mutter about omens.

There were some wild nights of drinking on the journey north, and the broch in Assynt where Rian lived led to one of the most memorable. Og was on fine form on his whistle and Ussa danced and sang her way into the headman's bed, making him think she was doing him a favour while stripping him of his valuables through trade and gambling. She noticed far sooner than anyone else the most precious thing he possessed. She had a way of seeing everything in terms of what she could sell it on for, and persuaded people to give it to her for a fraction of its value. She would pay so well for all the mundane goods, like skins, pottery, metalwork and even hospitality, (although that was normally given for free), so people thought she was generous. They wouldn't question when she offered a pittance for a priceless gem, persuading by her that it was just a shiny, pretty stone.

I don't think Ussa even bought Rian from her foster father. He gambled her away in hope of winning a bronze blade, which was handsome enough, but nothing special. Unlike Rian.

Looking back I wonder if Ussa saw my attraction to her and calculated the profit she could make by facilitating my acquisition of her as my slave. I'd put nothing past that woman. I'm sure I wouldn't have offered to buy her from her family, and I'm even surer that those people wouldn't have sold her to me. The grandmother protested as it was. I would surely have acquiesced.

But to Ussa such scruples were meaningless. I don't think she understood the concept of love. Lust, for sure, which is just a form of greed. She wielded lust as a deadly weapon. But to her, family devotion signified little other than a kind of bondage best broken, ties to be severed. Although she travelled with her cousin, the smith, she seemed able to abandon him without qualms. Her enemy, Manigan, was also her kin of course. What unhappiness lay behind that family rift I never did discover. I'm not sure I wanted to. Perhaps you know?

Anyway, Ussa dragged Rian awake in the middle of the night and won her at craps from that thug who was supposed to be her guardian. She was branded next morning, while I was out getting the lie of the land. I returned to a furious hush, the smell of burned flesh and Ussa, smug as a cat with a songbird in its mouth.

She put on a show of leading a hunt, which was a farce. I don't think she ever caught anything hunting, she was far too noisy for wild animals, and I think she did it deliberately, playing a game with the man she was toying with at that moment. During the long trudge that her expedition involved, I observed Rian closely. She limped, but bit back tears when the new brands pained her. I felt quite sorry for her, she was such a pretty little thing. When Ussa made Rian bend down in a muddy hollow, then put her feet on Rian's back to refasten the thongs around her boots, I hatched the idea of buying the girl.

I slept on the thought, but it would not dislodge itself from my mind. At breakfast she waited on Ussa and I was envious. I wanted her to hand me a bowl of food. I wanted her to brush my hair. So I offered Ussa the amber teardrop, and Rian was mine.

ON BROCHS AND SLAVERY

My experiences in the northern lands made me question almost everything about myself, about what I knew and about the order of the world. Take this relationship between a master and a slave. You would think it is a fairly simple thing to understand: one has the power and the other, powerless, obeys. I was once told that power is like pregnancy: you either have it or you don't and it can't be shared. But I met people in the north, and Rian in particular, who defy that simple picture.

Some slaves, like Og, are pliant and adaptable, and these are the ones who survive, or even thrive, sometimes, given the right owner, someone who can appreciate their merits. They are obedient and do not suffer from their role. Og and Ussa were a team really. He had moulded her life almost as much as she had shaped him to her will, creating a niche for himself, doing mostly what he does well, like cooking. He helped to control the other slaves, making everyone's lives together as comfortable as they could be. I got the impression he smoothed the way for them. You would see Li and Faradh grumbling but they would not rebel, they would fall in with him.

I saw him trying to give Rian the kind of tasks she could perform easily. There was of course lighting the fire, which she seemed to have a magic for; she could make flames anywhere, with anything, effortlessly, it was a part of her being. But apart from fire-raising, everything she did for Ussa appeared to pain her. She chafed visibly.

I don't think broch people make good slaves, in general. I met a few in my journey. They are hard, like the stone of their buildings. They resist or they are blank and discontented, like Rian.

*

The brochs are impressive buildings: some are as tall as eight men, as tall as Athena's statue in the Parthenon, and made of stones so massive you wonder who built them. They're skilled architects, but they use this skill to make brutal buildings. They stand for strength and they stand strong. These are the houses of hard people who can withstand the wildness of the northern ocean, who even thrive on it.

I have been wondering about those towers of double-walled magnificence. All around the coast the people dwell in these majestic structures, surrounded by various huts, barns and hovels. It is perplexing. The inordinate lengths they go to in order to craft these extraordinary buildings makes me sure their architects must have some kind of blessed status with the gods. It is impossible for us in the civilised world otherwise to understand them. They adore their boats and they adore these circular towers and they adore the promontory structures and the old circles and underground chambers of the ancients, and all these are indeed wondrous. Yet they are barbarian people. They do not understand the order of the universe: the gods in their hierarchies, the motions of the spheres, the geometry of the world. All of this, when I talked of it with them, met with utter incomprehension or mockery. They make music of a harmonic depth and with melodic beauty and complexity, and they build structures of such cleverness, even brilliance, I will go so far to call them mystical structures, yet their spiritual lives are completely lacking in what is needed to explain such gifts. How can the Gods on the one hand bless them with these skills yet on the other hand tolerate not being honoured?

Of course the broch people have gods, yes, but they comprehend them in peculiar ways, full of what I took to be misconceptions at the time, in my arrogance. Should I consider you one of them? You are descended from them, so perhaps I should. In which case I should say, 'you broch people'. Now, looking back, I wonder if they were, (and if you are one of them, if you are) so misguided after all. I have asked for favours from Apollo, especially safety at sea, of course, and assumed that when this was granted it was him I should be thankful to. But how, really, should I know it was him? What if it was Artemis who actually favoured me, or perhaps even the cow goddess of those people, Brigid, who was looking on and taking care to fulfil my wishes. Or what if, (I shall be condemned as a blasphemer but I am beyond caring), what if Zeus, Apollo, Artemis and all the rest of the Gods are a figment of our collective imaginations and we are all actually at the mercy of the whims of some wild sea spirits from the ice lands?

Did you know Rian lived in one of these brochs when I met her? Her foster father, Drost, I think he was called, was the headman, and had been there along with his mother, since they built it. She was one of those matriarchs, like Seonag, who made me wish the world was run by women, not by men. This was one of the things I learned on my voyage, that the world is not ruled by men everywhere, and I admit I found it ridiculous at first. It's odd, when you are in a house where it is obvious that the most sensible person there is a woman, and that the things organised by her are the best part of their lives and the matters presided over by the men are a shambles. I suppose that's why Ussa went there. She did not always get an easy welcome. There are some headmen who cannot think of trading with a woman, although in my experience of the north, some of the best dealers were of that sex. People laugh at me here in Massalia when I tell them this, but I'm sure I wasn't just imagining it.

On the sea, though, it is mostly men. Ussa is rare, although not unique. Few women own a boat and ply the ocean but the barbarian women have skills and roles that have surprised me often. Her helmsman, of course, was a man. Ussa never directed the affairs of the ship, really. It was a tool for her I suppose, and Toma was the brains of the boat. He never left it, as far as I could tell. He slept on it or as close to it as he could. He would wait on it whenever we came to harbour, only ever going on land to get something the boat needed – hide or rope or tar or wood or tools. He was as devoted as a mother to that boat. He was a part of it, or it was a part of him. He's not unusual I know. Harbours are full of these men married to a vessel, but his marriage was somehow more intense than most. I never did understand why. I think Ussa acquired him when she got the boat, but I don't think he was a slave. I presume he built the vessel and he certainly knew how to sail it better than I've ever known anyone sail, apart from the Walrus Mutterer of course, but his boat is a slip of a thing compared to Ussa's. It's like an arctic tern, too fleet and light ever to be caught but capable of long, long journeys. Ussa's boat, *Ròn*, is a skua, fierce, strong and proud, a raptor, and with Ussa on board that's not a bad analogy. But she never seemed able to hunt down Manigan, although I have watched her catch gulls, both real and metaphorical, and I've been horrified at the cruelty she is capable of.

*

There was a day I realised my feelings for Rian went beyond the care of a responsible slave-owner. We anchored in a steep-sided geo and Ussa hurtled off, sniffing for trade, while Gruach unloaded in his normal, unhurried manner. From Ussa's excitement I got the sense that this was going to be an interesting location, so I packed up all of my belongings on the assumption that we would be there a good while. I gave my bundle to Rian to carry.

I was cross with her because of a kerfuffle on the shore involving a sailor from another vessel that had anchored beside us. She and Gruach's daughter were flirting with him and I considered their behaviour rather too fresh. I don't think I was consciously punishing her, nor was I really aware that it was a flash of jealousy that made me lose my usual gentleness with her. Not until I had cause to reflect later, after the ardour of my rage had cooled, did I understand its source: the sailor, who was my rival. I didn't know then who she was frolicking with on the wave-lapped rocks, although I learned later that it was Manigan, but his identity was irrelevant.

I thrust my baggage-roll at her and strode on, leaving her to lug it up the near-vertical gully wall. When Li helped her with it, I made her go back and carry it herself. It was a matter of principle: she had to do my bidding. But it was also more than that. I wanted to show everyone watching, including that upstart sailor, that she was mine. I stood at the cliff top watching her struggling, but pushing on, like a poor little kitten trying to clamber out of a bucket, and when she reached the top I wanted to fold her in my arms. But before I could she collapsed into a dead faint. The other slaves carried her to the nearest habitation, a big roundhouse, and I asked the lady of the house to do anything she could for the girl. She took her in and brought her back to herself. I was embarrassed by the force of my feelings, the remorse I felt at my cruelty, and it made me realise I was unnaturally attached. The fear that she might die – it was brief, but long enough to recognise that I loved her, and that my annoyance at the sailor was in fact jealousy.

I was enamoured of my slave! I have to tell you, this took me aback. Yet on the other hand, it also took me onwards.

*

I found Rian endlessly fascinating. Enchanting, even. Yes. I came to believe a kind of spell had been cast on me. Looking back I think I lost all sense of myself in the weeks that followed. I play-acted a man, Ussa's pet Greek, a charming traveller, but if I am honest I felt completely out of my depth in that strange land where women were strong as rocks and men as baffling as the tides.

We chased Manigan, never catching him, and the pursuit took us so far north we reached the veritable end of the world, Thule, where sea and air and land congeal and make no sense at all. A strange spirit of the sea, a monster, rose from the ocean and Rian and Toma sang a song to it that completely unhinged me. I struggled to keep a grip on myself through calm and storm and near starvation. The skipper's boy died and was tossed overboard, as if he was no more than a dog. One of Ussa's slaves, Faradh, followed.

Among it all, I don't know why, I tried and failed to be a master to Rian. That is all I seem able to say about this now.

THULE

After writing yesterday, I walked for hours and reached the conclusion that I have to be more candid with you than I have been so far. I cannot simply skip over what is difficult for me to write.

The northernmost part of my journey has developed, in memory, a dreamlike quality. I spent many happy hours musing, glorying in my momentous achievement. I was further north than any of my compatriots had ever been, I was sure of this, further even than most would believe possible. I didn't appreciate then what I know only too well now, that they would mock me, that people like to feel safe and contained within boundaries. Even powerful people, those I used to admire and those whose respect I hoped to gain through my discoveries, hate change. I have learned that we are few who thrive by pushing on into the unknown, revealing what lies beyond.

The sky above me swathed in cloud, I exulted in what I had seen. For all that day we had sailed among ice, plates of it, like a temple mosaic. We crept our way between the floes, slush parting before the bow, shouldering and shoving aside, where necessary, big slabs of ice. The pack ice is well named: the blocks of ice swarm like wolves, menacing from all directions at once. The barbarian slaves were nervous but the skipper had my faith. He couldn't have got to the age he was without knowing all he needed to know to survive in those waters; he would have perished long since otherwise. He followed a sea creature with a horn for a while – a genuine unicorn – which seemed to understand a song he sang to it. It guided us to where the ice thinned, which it did suddenly, and we were out in open water.

Beyond the ice we sailed on, and it was then I took the helm to let Toma rest. Contemplating the ice and its sharp boundary with sea, I made up my mind that it was time to take my slave across a similar threshold. Rian was a virgin, I was sure of that, and as I steered the boat, keeping it in the groove where the breeze could be most help to us, water trickling under the keel, I reflected how like ice Rian could be, and yet how much I desired to set her on fire.

We had, as the poets say, been playing with smoke and sparks, or so it felt to me, and it was time to build a blaze. This metaphor was not random, for the place we found ourselves in beyond the ice was a marvel of volcanic mystery rising right out of the ocean. A mountain belched smoke and its steep side glowed, as night fell, with lava. There was a pungent smell and a hiss as brimstone flowed into brine. It was extraordinary.

Toma took the helm from me. Then the wind died. We were carried in by a current, closer and closer towards the fuming shore. Eventually, we had to get the slaves to row and my Rian pulled her oar alongside the men, like the tough little creature she is. I was full of admiration and watched her, imagining my hands on the muscles of her back, my body against hers in a rhythm similar to the heave and thrust of rowing. Ussa was impatient and wanted to use her holly whip on them, to lash them into greater speed, but Toma and I pleaded lenience and, for once, prevailed.

So when Toma let them stop, deeming us to be once again at a safe distance from the shore with the tidal stream easing, I led Rian under the shelter at the prow. She was exhausted and shivering, drenched with sweat, so I helped her out of her wet clothes, wrapped her in my wolfskin coat and took her to my bunk, where I warmed her against my body, bringing myself to a perfect height of readiness. She writhed like a kitten trying to escape and I had to hold her firmly to overcome her resistance.

It is only natural, I suppose, to fear being taken across a threshold. I felt sure that once she was over the other side she would share the flames I felt inside, and relish the heat of a mutual fire. And so I pushed her bodily across the boundary that held her as a girl, puncturing it, thrusting her through it into womanhood.

But afterwards, far from being joined to me, she seemed more distant and withdrawn than ever. It was unbearable, her ashen sullenness. I felt as if I had bought something sparkling bright and now it was doused and dull, mere dust. She would not speak. She would not even look at me.

In my disgust I sold her back to Ussa.

It is only looking back that I can see how much that disgust was displaced from me onto her, how inside my petty hatred and scorn a deeper shame was hiding. The real boundary violated that night, I see so clearly now, was within me.

ON SONGS

Songs contain a strange magic. I can't sing a note myself, have never been able to hold a tune. I don't know why. Perhaps it has something to do with having lost my mother so young, so all the songs I heard as a child were sung by slaves and servants, almost never in my mother tongue. Perhaps that is what makes their power all the more intriguing.

One of the things I noticed about the slaves aboard Ussa's boat was that they were in a continual state of lethargy unless a song was being sung. It was part of Toma's genius as a skipper that he used tunes to work the crew.

I remember when I became conscious of this. It was somewhere close to Rian's home. The wind was favourable, and there was that delicious sound of the sea slapping under the keel. As always, Toma was singing along with it, some shanty that seemed to make all the crew's work easier, the ropes coil more evenly, the sail hide more pliant and the sea and the wind and the boat join together in a kind of unity. 'The chicken rock is a dead man's sock, a head on a block, a funeral frock, oh give it a wide berth, let's give it all you're worth, stay off and away to the inner bay, off and away to the cosy bay'. There were lots like that. I guess they were really useful in some places, but they seemed to sing them at all kinds of odd times.

Wherever I have been in the world since that voyage, if I overheard a sailor or a person in some drunken gathering or a beggar or a slave at a task, whoever it might be, singing one of Toma's songs, I always recognised them immediately as his and seemed to hear him in the distance, in the background, singing along. He sailed that boat by his voice, I swear it. I never heard him sing when the boat was not in motion, and never on land. And I never heard Ussa sing on the boat at all. They each had their domain. They still have, I assume. Perhaps in some strange way their very different styles of singing united them, bonded them, and defined their relative strengths and the loci of their power. When the sea played under the keel, Toma was master, and he sang the tunes. All the rest of the time, Ussa was in charge.

Most of the time, Ussa was in charge.

Toma's songs were primarily utilitarian, with a definite nautical purpose: to make light of a hard task, like hauling up a sail. They would allow work that needed to be done repetitively, like bailing, seem to symbolise something else, sometimes joyful, sometimes violent, sometimes moving from despair to the ineffable, so that as sails filled with air or an anchor rose from the deep, those making it happen would feel their spirits lift. Sometimes his songs were pure mischief and I don't know if Ussa realised how many of the mermaids were mocking her, or how many of the inclement winds in the songs were intended as metaphors of her moods. Often the songs were pure innocent fun, ridiculous stories regaled for the sheer mirth they invariably created, or so lewd you'd blush if I told you them.

Occasionally he sang strange, mystical wonders, and these could unmake a person, but most often his songs were navigational, verse after verse pointing out the landmarks needed to steer a safe passage from one place to another, an oral version of the periplus. Some of these were downright strange. I remember one: *The flat face of the salty fisher winks across to the shaggy rock. Roll among the seals, cock a dog leg and throw yourself down upon the block.'* It meant something to him, no doubt.

*

After Thule, on the approach to the Cat Isles, I remember Toma muttering to himself in a sing-song way: '...stack with a hat, under if flat, wind against tide, half a mile wide...'

I was curious. I asked what he was singing.

'It's the inshore lore for here, that's all.'

I listened to him, chuntering on. As he was singing he looked intently at all of the stacks and geos. He nodded and sang to each rocky outcrop we passed with a kind of chanting voice. Birds passing led him to another kind of recitation. More than half I could not catch, as he was murmuring to no-one in particular. Throughout the western coastal journey there had been a boy, Callum, with him, but he had died in the northern ocean, and I realised now that in his seemingly endless chat to the boy, what he had probably been doing was reciting all this lore, teaching the youngster, as we travelled. What I had taken as the endless idle chatter of an old man with a captive audience I now saw as the passing on of ancient wisdoms. He was a walking almanac, this man. Inside his head was an intimate knowledge of the coastline, expressed in verse or song, gathered and passed on by generations of seafarers.

What a loss it must have been, therefore, to lose his boy. I don't know if Callum was his grandson, or even related to him. I never asked. But he wasn't just a companion for the old fellow. He was, or he would have been, the repository of all that knowledge, journey by journey. I didn't understand then, but now I do, how he must have mourned his passing, and grieved for his loss. I wonder if he ever found another boy to take his place?

NORTHERN ISLES

You know, I wasn't the only one fascinated by Rian. In the Seal Isles, where I spent much of the short summer after she had been sold to the Black Chieftain, I encountered a druid who believed she was the stuff of legend.

We were in the Seal Isles because Ussa had run out of bronze goods to trade and wanted to track down Gruach, the bronze smith, and his daughter, who we had left there on our way north. They were exactly where we'd left them, in a friendly community centred on a big roundhouse which had an endless traffic of people in and out, cooking and sharing, bantering and bartering, presided over by a hugely jolly, buxom, loud-laughing hostess.

While I was there I heard about a huge ring of stones, at Brodgar. Perhaps you know it? An extraordinary edifice, an astronomical device of stone on a massive scale, built by the ancients, and still in use, like a calendar in the landscape. It allows them to map the moon and stars' journeys in the sky. As there is nothing like it where I am from, I wasted no time in getting a guide to take me.

I arrived in the late morning. It was damp and still and the biting midgies were wicked. A group of longhaired, bearded mystics were gathered around a smoking fire. One of them got up to meet me. He was a wispy grey-cloaked man who introduced himself as the master of the stones. He gave brief evasive answers to my questions and, although he allowed me to take a gnomon reading, when I attempted to measure the dimensions of the circle, he told me politely, but firmly, that I must leave.

I wanted to protest, but one of the druids by the fire separated from them and offered to walk with me back to the roundhouse and explain some of what I had seen. He was an ugly man, pock-marked, with an arm missing, and a straggle of dark hair and beard. He spoke Keltic with the southern twang that Ussa and Og had, and sure enough, he too was from Belerion.

'I'm a wanderer,' he said. 'Uill Tabar's my name and happiness is my business. How are you? Where are you from? Far away, I can see. Tell me all about your travels.' He was loquacious and funny and he said he could drive out bad spirits, intervene in difficult times and foretell the future. 'Mostly, I collect prophecies.' He grinned at me. 'What can I do for you?'

I asked him about the ring of stones, and he was rather secretive about it and changed the subject back to my journey. Eventually we got talking about tides. I described my amazement at some of the strange currents I had observed around the islands. This was clearly something he was interested in as well. He told me that the channels between the islands have flows of incredible power and what I had seen was nothing exceptional. The local fisher people think nothing of the sea between islands flowing west in the morning and east in the afternoon, reaching speeds as fast as a rapid river in each direction. He talked about eddies and whirlpools. He explained the dangers of standing waves and overfalls if the wind is in the opposite direction to the tidal stream, and the violent seas caused by strong cross winds.

Most importantly, he showed a keen understanding of the tidal rhythms and their relationship to the moon. He confirmed that they ebb and flow each night and again each day, a little later each day than the last, in a cycle that follows the moon, reaching their maximum strength when the moon is full and when it is new, then weakening again when it is waning and waxing. This knowledge confirmed my belief that there is great knowledge among these barbarian people, and I wished their astronomical lore was less closely guarded.

At the roundhouse he was clearly well-known as 'The Prophet' and welcomed for his humorous stories. After dinner, he and Ussa were joking with each other.

'You're going to have to stop the slaving my dear. It'll bring you bad luck, I've told you before. The only fortune it's going to make you is bad fortune.'

'Pshh, what do you know?' She elbowed him. 'I'll have you know I've done rather well this year. I've a boatload of fine whale-bone tools, a piece of amber you'd be amazed by and a handsome new crewman, all thanks to a ginger girl I won at craps in Assynt.'

He turned round to her. 'A ginger girl, did you say?'

'She was his for a while, wasn't she? Your wee pet, Rian.' She pointed a long fingernail towards me and I nodded an acknowledgement.

'Rian.' He turned his head back slowly but his eyes were wide. 'And where is she now?'

'You're interested, are you?' Ussa chucked him under the chin like a child. 'Come on Mr Prophet, spit it out. What do you know of her?'

'Ach I'm just feeling sorry for a lassie ripped from her home. And are you still chasing that damned stone?'

His diversion worked and the conversation fell to the Stone of Telling and the prophecies associated with it. One was that it would make a good king kill his son, which had come true, and that incident earned it the moniker of the Death Stone. A second said that anyone who held it would be infected with a kind of bloodlust. The third was that it would be neutralised by a child whose mother, grandfather and great grandmother were slaves, but whose father, grandmother and great-grandfather were free.

'These three generations uniting slavery and freedom will end the Death Stone's tyranny,' he said.

We were all rapt listening to him. The fire had died down as we talked and we were sitting in a dim glow, his eyes glinting as lamplight caught them with each movement of his head.

'You mean it would destroy its power of Telling. And that will never happen. It's a curse that can never come true,' Ussa retorted.

They argued on and I lost interest in the debate.

The next morning, Ussa and Og appeared with Uill Tabar in tow. He looked much the worse for wear and I didn't like to ask what might have ensued. I suspected that Ussa had resorted to force to get what she wanted to hear out of the poor man. Whatever it was, Ussa now wanted to leave straightaway. I was used to her sudden whims by now and I was optimistic that we might be heading east across the North Sea, but in fact she wanted to go back north to the Cat Isles. She claimed 'unfinished business' with the Black Chieftain and I surmised she had got wind that Manigan might be there with the stone.

'After a quick visit, we'll find you some amber, I promise,' she said to me.

Of course, I agreed to go with her. My tin was still in the hold of her boat.

Gruach and his daughter Fraoch came along with us, plus a local seaman who led Toma right through the centre of the islands, along a succession of fascinating tidal channels. We dropped him at the north end and sailed on, overnight, to the Cat Isles.

Early in the morning, as we approached an island, Toma called to me. He was pointing out to starboard. At first I couldn't make out what he was seeing, then a big round head, like a whiskery barrel, broke the surface. It had two impressive fangs.

'Tooth-walker,' Toma said. 'Sea horse.' He raised his voice and called to the beast. 'Greetings, Old Gentleman.'

The creature lifted itself up, like a seal does, to get a better view of where the voice was coming from. It was just like a seal, after all. A big seal. Just an animal, like any other. After all that I had heard, all the mystery and moon magic of its ivory, that was all there was to a walrus. It bobbed, then dived, its rear flippers like a pair of gloved hands. They seemed to wave, and then it was gone.

MOUSA

It was fair this morning so I ate my breakfast out in the court-yard, basking in the low-angled sun. At this time of year it feels so health-giving, as if it can burn away the misery of winter. As I got up to go indoors, to return here to my desk, I passed the entrance to the kitchen and the servants' quarters, where one of the female slaves was sitting in the doorway, stitching a fine cloth, catching the light. I deduced that she probably belongs to my sister-in-law. She is pregnant, very much so, which I suppose is why she hasn't gone to Greece with her mistress, nor out to the vineyard.

The woman's pale face had a kind of translucence, as if the child makes itself visible as a glow from within, signalling that it is more than a mere lump in the belly. Seeing her reminded me of when I first learned that Rian was pregnant.

We had been to an island off the mainland of the Cat Isles, which had on it a most impressively built broch. I was in a good mood, I seem to remember, having been enjoying our passage, particularly the tidal streams which are so strong. I had been sketching the layout of the islands in my notes, and fitting together an understanding of how the rips and races follow a fixed schedule, running, pausing, then running back, twice each day, in synchrony with the tides. We had on board a crewman pilot who knew these waters since childhood and had the patience to explain their flows to me, and although he kept referring to an undersea serpent as their energy source, which frankly I believed to be nonsense, he was otherwise lucid about the flows and ebbs. So I was greatly stimulated when we made landfall and looked forward to the good hospitality I had come to expect at a broch.

I was sadly disappointed. The building itself was large and belonged to the Chieftain's wife's family. Maadu was a dour, stout woman with an equine face and a gaudy clutter of bronze and silver jewellery on her neck and arms. She welcomed Ussa like an old friend and was delighted that Gruach was with us. She urged him to set up his forge as soon as he could. She was making preparations for the wedding of her son later in the summer, so she wanted gifts of bronze as well as the usual repairs to kitchenware. She told us this as we walked up towards the broch from the shore. She remembered me from when we had first made landfall after our great northern ocean voyage, and flattered me that I was looking much less drawn and hungry now. I replied to the effect that everyone benefits from summer's largesse.

Although the broch was substantial, there were very few people there. Maadu explained that she used it as a summer residence and had taken just enough slaves there to manage the summer crops and tend the cattle.

Among them was Rian. She ducked in through the doorway, backwards, pulling a pail of milk in after her and as she turned, I recognised her. To say I was shocked would be a grave understatement. She was filthy. It disgusted me that I'd ever touched her, to be frank. Dressed in nothing better than rags, feet bare and crusted with cow dung, that amber-coloured hair matted and dull, her face so bony her eyes seemed to bulge from it.

I am a clean person, fastidious in my ablutions whenever I can be, and such a state of ill-kempt slatternliness revolted me. She smelled of the midden. She did not make eye-contact and I did not want to look at her.

The broch was untidy altogether and there was nothing and no-one to amuse me in it, so I took myself off to explore the island, and was pleased to leave. I believed that this sight of Rian had cured me of my fascination for her. My admiration curdled to contempt, or so I told myself.

It was only later, on the boat returning to the mainland, that Ussa told me what she had learned there. I wished I had found out sooner, so I could have looked more closely at the girl.

We were seated on a bench on the boat. Ussa's hand latched onto my knee. 'So, have you left a string of bastards all along your trail? You're a sly one. I had a hunch you and she were up to it. No doubt the child is yours, eh? Given the timing. Or it could be Maadu's husband's of course, though she swears not.'

'What are you talking about?'

I looked at Ussa. She was fuming. 'And now Maadu won't sell her because she's pregnant. Her excuse is that as it was the Chieftain that bought her, she'll have to consult him. He might want to breed from her. I told her I think it's your brat.' Ussa curled up her lip as if I was a flea-ridden dog.

'So?' I could not understand why she was so angry with me.

'You heard the prophecy. Now I'll have to wait for the Chieftain. Damn it all. Men. Can't keep your hands off…'

It dawned on me eventually that she was trying to buy Rian back because she believed she would fulfil the prophecy Uill Tabar had told. I wanted to say, 'It's only a story,' but I didn't, of course.

Ussa looked smug. 'It turns out she belongs to the Winged Isle. One of those round houses near where we stayed, when you were off meeting the spirits of the underworld. I wish I'd found that out earlier. But anyway, I can make full use of it now I know.'

'Did that druid tell you that?'

'I got it out of him.'

Something about the way she said this made me leave off questioning her. There was steel in her eye, and fear, something trapped, like a caged hawk, and I had learned to leave her alone when she looked like that.

My mind raced. Father of a child of that bag of filth and bones I had just witnessed? I was horrified. But I said nothing to Ussa, shrugging it off with a laugh, making some dismissive, enigmatic remark. And Ussa took me to mean that I had no interest in any bastard offspring I might leave behind me. Nothing could have been further from the truth. That woman had no insight into me on such a matter at all.

It was a busy landing and I was taken to a house belonging to a widely-travelled sailor who kept me entertained until late that night. So it wasn't until I lay down in my bed that I could think through what Ussa had suggested. It was so hard to match the maiden I had taken to my bunk with the slut I had seen that morning. I tried to imagine a child growing in her belly, but I hadn't looked closely at her at all. My impression was only of dirt and skinniness, and because of this, for a while at least, I dismissed any thought of her as the possible mother of a child of mine. I lived, for the rest of that brief summer, in a state of denial.

ON AMBER AND IVORY

Amber was what I was searching for, really. The tin and ivory were part of my quest, but what motivated me most was the mystery of amber. Devotion to Artemis and the memory of my dead mother were perhaps part of that, but also sheer curiosity about the origins of such a peculiar material.

It was amber that drew me to Rian and why I have never really been able to let her go, even though of course I have abandoned her. In person, but not in my soul. In my heart she still stands there with that glowing hair, those quiet features, those bright eyes, that calm. She is the human embodiment of the gem, which although stone-like, is not exactly a stone. It is the living stuff of a tree, magical and supernaturally alive.

I have met others who believe it is a bird secretion, but I prefer the traditional story, that it's the tears of the sun god's daughters, the Heliades, who have been turned into poplars. It smells of tree sap and it has a kind of pliability, a plasticity, which makes it like resin, but in reality it is stronger and denser than anything a normal tree can exude. Perhaps in ages past trees were different, or perhaps it is the ageing that it has undergone since Helios' daughters' days of weeping that has given it its texture. Whatever, it arouses my passion. It is the most magical of all materials and it pushes my scientific understanding more than anything else I know.

It was Manigan who first told me where I would find it. I talked to him in the court of the Black Chieftain of the Cat Isles. Well-named, he was black-haired and black-hearted. I was invited to go sea-hunting with him and I turned him down, and ever afterwards he treated me as only half a man, not even half. Ussa went with him, of course. I've never known a woman more thirsty for blood and killing, and no matter how often she hunts she always seems momentarily victorious at the moment she walks through the door, and then disappointed not to have killed more. The day they returned was like every other. She paraded in with her slaves carrying the gutted carcase of a seal and within minutes was making withering remarks about their failure to catch even one of a pod of pilot whales they had glimpsed. 'I would like to be eating whale meat now', I heard her say, the juice of the seal steak literally dribbling down her chin. I was always amazed she dared to be so rude. It was a slight on the Chieftain's hospitality. I could see it drove his wife nearly to distraction but the Chieftain and his son were in thrall to Ussa. They treated her like some kind of queen.

Anyway, while they hunted I did not go. I wanted some time on land to take a gnomon measurement and do some careful observations of the sun. I took a slave and marched him up to the highest point of land, where our position on an island in a sheltered sea loch, which they call a voe, was clear. I had been keeping track of time and it was by my calculations only about ten days before the summer solstice. I measured the ratio of the noon shadow to the length of the gnomon, and from the length of it was able to calculate that the height of the sun was only three cubits. I had some hour-candles with me, and although people thought I was completely crazy, I burnt one continuously from one sunrise to the next. By measuring the length of the candle at sunset and again the next sunrise I calculated that the day length was almost exactly four times the length of the night, which lasted barely five hours. It never really got dark. I was now sure that no Greek had ever been so far north. I was hungry to find out more about the land where the sun does not set at all in summer from some of the sailors of those islands who frequent the northern ocean.

After we came down from the hill I sought out some of the elders with knowledge and experience of the seas. There were some great wayfarers among those men. They have a special affinity with the sea and no doubt many old customs that they kept secret from me. Taboos are strong among the seamen, many won't let a woman on their boat, for example, some have a phobia of the colour green, and they don't trust easily. Quite rightly, in my view.

There was a lively discussion among three grey-haired sailors. They exchanged a few words with me in a friendly enough way and took my questions, one with a nod of his head, one a scratch of his bulbous nose, the last with the tap of a calloused finger on his knee, checking with each other for confirmation before giving me back an answer. Most of the time the conversation flowed between them in their own dialect like a flow of jabbling water between boats in a harbour, full of chuckling and back-slapping and moments of thoughtful, gloomy contemplation. I wanted to ask what they were saying but I also did not wish to be rude or make myself a burden to them. Then we were joined by Manigan, who seemed to know two of them, and he began to act as an interpreter for me, passing what was said back and forth between us. I was surprised that he was willing to be here, given Ussa's presence, but when I asked him why he wasn't worried about her he just laughed.

'She's hunting. What she doesn't know can't hurt her. I'm not going to let her ruin the fun of the wedding feast,' he said.

Then he started quizzing me, and he must have made me sound interesting enough to the old fellows because they seemed to become curious about my journey and wanted to be helpful to me in my search for amber, although like I said, it was Manigan who actually told me where to go.

'The lynx stone, they call it. It washes up on beaches on the far side of the North Sea.' He gestured eastwards. 'If you're lucky you can find it.'

'Why do they all it lynx stone?' I asked.

'Because it's the colour of cat's piss.' He laughed.

'And where, exactly, is it found on beaches?'

'On the eastern shore of the North Sea. There's a long beautiful beach to the north of a promontory where there are polite but very dull people who may show you exactly where to go, or they might not, depending on how boring they are being.' This was typical of Manigan; if there was a joke possible, he would make it. He said something rapidly in their dialect and the old men laughed. Then he proceeded to give me good directions of how many days' sailing south and east the coastline in question lay, a few key landmarks and the name of a village.

I committed all he told me to memory, thanked him and asked how I could repay him for the information. He looked somewhat offended. 'I have given you nothing at all. If you expect to pay for nothing you must get taken for a lot of gold.'

'Knowledge is valuable,' I said.

He sat back and crossed his arms. 'Most valuable things are not worth paying for, and the most valuable of all cannot be bought.'

I could not accept this philosophy. Everything has its price, and I didn't want to be in debt to anyone, especially not to an enemy of Ussa.

He exchanged words with the old men again. Then he said, 'I know. Tell me a story! That's what I want in payment: a story from your country.'

So I told him this. 'Phaethon was the son of the god Helios, and like all sons he believed what his father did was simple, that it was nothing much at all and that he, his father's son, could do it easily. But Helios' job was to drive the chariot of solar fire across the sky from east to west each day. No-one else had the strength of will and body to control the fiery steeds on their great daily climb across the firmament, across the high noon plains and down to their evening resting place. But Phaethon was young and like all youths he thought himself bigger than he was in reality.'

Manigan smiled at this, his eyes on mine.

I was encouraged by his attention. 'One day, he got up early, took the chariot and drove it up into the morning sky. As the horses got into their stride, he had to use all of his strength to keep them running straight and of course the animals realised that the boy didn't have full control of them so they started to gallop. Once they were out of rhythm the chariot began veering and slewing about. The horses panicked.' I was probably gesturing with my arms by this stage. 'One of the steeds broke out of its harness and the chariot tumbled. Its fire spilled across the firmament. In minutes, there was smoking, flaming chaos and all the gods were calling on Zeus to do something before the whole world was destroyed by fire.'

'Zeus?' Manigan furrowed his eyebrows.

'The chief god.'

He nodded.

I continued. 'With a thunderbolt, Zeus struck Phaethon down to earth. He sent water sprites to dowse the flames. Phaethon fell into the Eridanus River and drowned, and we were all saved from being tinder. His sisters, the Heliades, rushed to the river and stood there, wailing and grieving until eventually Zeus turned them into poplar trees. Their weeping, with the clarity of tear-drops and the colour and intensity of sunbeams, is electrum, the shining one, amber.'

Through it all, Manigan listened intently. 'What was the river?'

'Eridanus,' I said.

'Eridanus,' he repeated.

I corrected his pronunciation, which he didn't seem to mind at all.

Once satisfied he could say it right, he said, 'Thank you for this story. I like it, and I shall tell it, but when I do, I am going to make them the tears of the girl who loved him, not his sisters.'

'But that isn't what the story says. It was the Heliades.'

'Let me tell our friends.' He turned to the old men and gave a little preamble, then told them the story. I could tell he had begun because it was as though he was suddenly a different person. His voice changed, its tones were richer and had a sing-song lilt. There was a rhythmic patterning as he repeated phrases and his body was alive with gestures. I wondered if the same transformation had come over me when I told it, but I doubted it.

After he had spoken there was some debate among the old men.

'We're discussing the sisters,' Manigan told me.

There was a bit more banter.

'They agree with you.' He pointed to the oldest two men. 'But me and Tor think the story is better if there's a broken heart, not just sisterly grief. It's a good story, though. The arrogance of youth and the wild horses of the sky, amber has all of that fire within it, we agree. But what we're debating is what kind of tears are needed for it. We like that there are women, so that the amber contains both masculine and feminine, and that they are tears of grief, of loss. I think there must be an erotic charge to it as well, hence wanting it to be a girl who lusted after Phaethon, who loved his courage, his headstrong bravado, maybe even egged him on to test himself, so sure was she that he could make the sun shine for everyone, the way he made it shine for her. Aye. The old boys say the amber is pure and so it is better if it is sisterly love, with no eroticism. But I want that charge. I feel it in the stone.'

'Do you know that when you rub it, it attracts things?'

He nodded and spoke to the men. One of them shook his head.

'I have some.' I got out my pouch, opened it and took one of the larger amber pieces out. I held it on my open palm.

Manigan, without missing a beat, took it, rubbed it vigorously on the sleeve of his shirt, then wafted it close to the silvery head of the eldest man. Hairs lifted, and he made them dance and wriggle, clinging to the amber. Everyone laughed and Manigan said something lewd no doubt, echoed and augmented by comments from the others. They giggled like schoolboys and Manigan winked at me.

'I think my version of the story is the winner!'

'But it's not the true story.'

He lifted both hands. 'Truth? What matters is whether people like what they hear.'

I wanted to argue, but he had my piece of amber.

'What do you want to swap for this?' He let it drop from one hand into the other in turn.

I seized my chance. 'A piece of your walrus ivory and the knowledge of where it comes from.'

He was taken aback.

'My livelihood and my secrets too.' He put his hand into his pocket, together with my amber. 'You don't ask for much, do you? I'll give you one or the other, which is it?'

'I'll take the ivory,' I said. 'I always trust hard evidence before a story.'

He sniffed with indignant scorn. 'You turn down a sacred mystery.'

'I have more amber, I have no ivory. That's all. I've learned that the ivory comes from a tusked sea horse. I got a glimpse of one on the way here. I gather you hunt them.'

'The Old Gentlemen are my compatriots. I am the Mutterer. It is my duty.'

'So, you'll give me a piece of ivory, and I'll shake the hand of the man who hunts the animal it comes from.'

He took a shard of ivory from an inside pocket, and laid it on his palm. 'This is a tusk tip. It contains all the mystery of the northern ocean. Treat it with the reverence the Old Gentleman who gave it to me deserves.'

I took it off his palm. 'It's a fair swap.'

'Swear that you will revere it.'

'I can't swear that. It's just a piece of ivory.'

'No, no. It's not just anything. If you treat it like that, if you don't recognise it as sacred, then one piece is the same as any other, and any piece can be swapped for a coin or a gem. Then everything is reduced to exchange and nothing has any sacred value. Believe me, that way lies greed that can never be satisfied.'

'It's just bone. It's beautiful, I give it that. But to me it's no more sacred than meat. If everything was sacred then trade would not be possible.'

'Not so. I just traded you this sacred thing for a beautiful gemstone with a memorable story behind it.'

'But surely any bit of amber would have sufficed. Or gold of the requisite value to allow you to buy some amber, if that's what you desire.'

'Not at all. I have no interest in gold. I've seen what it does to people. Look at Ussa, for goodness sake.'

'What's wrong with her?'

He shook his head at me as if I was an idiot. 'She sells people as if they're trinkets.' He took the amber out of his pocket and held it up to the light. 'I wanted this because of the story that introduced it, which is now contained within it. This is the object that lifted my friends' hair with its strange attraction, that gave us all this good time together. I wouldn't want another piece. And in exchange you have this tusk tip. It is unique, true, but you turned down the chance to hear a story, which would, I can promise you, have been more memorable.'

I told him I was satisfied with just the ivory, but if he thought I should hear the story I'd be delighted to listen to his yarn.

He shook his head. 'You have a strange idea of value. I don't want to trade with you after all. I'll have that back.' He switched the amber for the ivory on my hand, and slipped the tusk tip back in his pocket.

From that point on he made no secret that he didn't like me. Or maybe he just wanted a chance to show off by telling a better story than I had. More likely. He beats me at story-telling, I'll give him that, though I think my loose ends are becoming as bad as his. He always seemed to have a tendency to leave a thread of a tale hanging. I think he did it deliberately, to leave the listener wondering, to give them that feeling of teetering on a cliff, so they want you to carry on. No doubt he often used this trick to get a drink or a bed, by leaving his audience feeling that if they treated him well, he'd cough up something more. I don't think I did that with the Phaethon legend, yet here it is the opposite extreme: I'm leaving so many hanging threads my entire garment of a memoir is fraying. I am getting old, my dear, forgive me.

Anyway, I had missed my chance to get a sample of walrus ivory from its hunter, and it took me a long time to get the piece from which the dolphin amulet was carved. You'll have to be patient with me. I am trying to weave the threads of this story together, even if it is threadbare in places.

THE CHASE

My feelings about Rian erupted again at the wedding feast. I wasn't really looking forward to the event, as I have a dread of the dancing that inevitably follows such things and I had vowed to myself to leave early. I delayed my arrival, fussing about with my notes on the tides, so that when I reached the wedding feast the celebrations were already well underway. It was a big crowd. People must have come from all of the islands and they had set the party up outside the broch. I was shown to a bench next to

Ussa and treated as an honoured guest. And who should come to fill my cup, but Rian?

What a transformation had come over her! Dressed in a simple frock and apron, her amber hair tied back in a plait, she looked radiant, with clear skin and those sea-green eyes. I feasted my gaze on her. She was exactly as beautiful as I had remembered and although she didn't meet my glances, her modesty only made me keener to watch her.

As she carried a jug of ale to the guests I was reminded of the gilded statue of Athena at her temple in Massalia. Such poise, such elegance, and the haughty superiority of a goddess, untouched by the filth and lewdness of men. The squalor of the summer was an aberration I soon forgot. The farmyard muck had blinded me to her grace, but now it was all washed off I knew with absolute certainty that I had not been wrong to take her as my own, and I wanted her again.

Yet I held back, observing her. Several times, Ussa had to tap me on the arm to attract my attention back to the conversation with the Chieftain's family. Yet as soon as I could, I returned to watching. I had a good vantage of the broch doorway. Whenever she ducked away inside with an empty jug or dirty dishes, it was as if the sun went behind a cloud, and each time she tripped back out, balancing a tray or with another pitcher for the thirsty throng, I felt myself latch back onto her like a dog. So when Ussa started hussling the Chieftain to buy her back, I joined in on Ussa's side, hoping, really, to get her for myself. I was drunk enough for it to feel like a game. I would have paid anything to touch that tender, bronze skin again.

Ussa haggled with the Chieftain until he had agreed that she could buy her back from him. She offered him bronze, but what he said he really wanted was ivory, and she gave him a beautiful creamy slab of it.

I was furious. If I'd known she had it I would have bought it off her like a shot, but when I challenged her on it, she simply laughed, and told me to ask the Chieftain's steward, who could procure anything I wanted.

So, the morning after the feast, I was asking the steward whether there were any walrus hunters other than Manigan who might be willing to trade a tusk for gold, when Ussa dashed in, her hair in a frazzle as if she'd been dragged out of bed.

'That little bitch slave has run off with my thieving cousin.'

'She seems to think herself no more yours than she was ever mine. Perhaps you're better off without her.'

Ussa tossed her head in that scornful way she has, as if I am a child who understands nothing.

My pride was dented. I had thought Rian might prefer to travel with us than to be with that bunch of barbarians, particularly as she was so filthy and emaciated when I had seen her on the island farm. Surely being with us on our adventure would be preferable? Yet given the opportunity, she had instead chosen to flee with a man who can at best be described as a ruffian. Yes, I was jealous. Of course I was.

Ussa was determined to track the runaway down. She was intent on chasing Manigan anyway, because of the stone. 'I'm leaving as soon as the tide is falling and we can get safe passage out of the channel.'

'When is that?' I asked.

She looked at me as if I was an idiot. 'Immediately. Are you coming?'

'Are you still planning to head east to the amber shores?'

'Eventually yes, of course.'

It wasn't difficult to weigh up my options. There might be other traders heading straight to the Amber Coast who would be willing to allow me to travel with them, but then again there might not. And my tin was on board her boat, of course, so it was easiest just to go with her.

'I'll come,' I said.

'Well, hurry up. I'm not prepared to wait for you if you slow me down.' She stomped off to gather her crew.

I packed all my belongings together and donned my furs, and with my writing box under my arm and gnomon in my hand I was ready to travel.

As it turned out, I was down at the harbour before Ussa and her slaves. Toma was ready to go. I wondered how many hours he had spent ashore in the time we had been there. Not many, I guessed. Perhaps he was perpetually in a state of readiness to sail, just waiting for the opportunity to be off.

I stowed my gear on board, then wandered off to find some food. In my haste I had not eaten, and my previous experience of travel with Ussa pushed me to take some precautions by way of a few extra personal supplies for when her estimates of how much provision the crew needed failed to provide us all with adequate vittles. I don't think she meant to deprive her crew and passengers, but she seemed to treat food as a mere convenience rather than an essential aspect of life. Perhaps this habit of not eating regularly was what made her so bad-tempered. I think because she relied on Og to cook, she had little real sense of quantities required for preparation of meals, or maybe she simply didn't entrust him with enough goods for bartering when they were in places where supplies could be obtained. Anyway, there were plenty of people around the harbour who were willing to give me food in exchange for coins and I settled with a fat woman who chuckled and stroked my fur coat as if I was a pet dog, furnishing me with a big bundle of dry food, plus bread and cakes, all wrapped up in a handy piece of hide, waxed and waterproof with eye-holes in the corners strengthened with sinew. I have it to this day. It is one of my few souvenirs of the trip. I have been kept dry, or my goods have, thanks to it, more times than I can remember. A fair exchange for a piece of silver, there's no doubt about that.

By the time I returned to the boat, Og had arrived, and soon Li and the new slave, Samhain, were stashing supplies on board, running up and down the hill as if Ussa were whipping them along, which was, I suppose, precisely what they were trying to avoid. Li's back showed the signs of a thorough lashing, so I deduced he had taken the blame and a taste of Ussa's fury.

When Ussa swept down the hill to the harbour, predatory in her long white coat, I received a nod of acknowledgement from her, before she launched into a barrage of questions to Li and Og, checking that everything she had wanted them to do had been done. It had. The tide was right. I poured a little wine into the sea and asked Apollo to favour our journey, and then we were on our way, warps hauled in, the sail up.

Toma sailed with a mad glee. I think he wanted to push his boat to its extremes, to let it do what it was capable of, yet I do not believe he really wanted to catch the prey. Ussa ranted at him about Manigan's stone, which had, she said, been stolen from the boat. Apparently Li had managed to acquire it from Manigan, presumably by some theft of which I wasn't aware, but although he swore that he had stashed it on Ròn, no amount of questioning by Ussa resulted in an explanation of why it was no longer on the boat.

The wind was light and so Toma let the sail out to its maximum size and stood at the tiller to keep the twitching breeze in it. He sang a high-pitched wailing song with his chin lifted, his throat stretched up like a howling dog: 'Sky flowing, going, going, fly flee-ing, sea-wing, sea-wing.' It was something like that. I don't think he believed it was possible to overtake the sleek boat Manigan sailed, but he was excited by the chase and seemed delighted by attempting to gain on them using whatever advantage he could find from his own vessel. What sailor doesn't love to race?

His fervour was infectious. Li and the new slave Samhain, Og and I were all enthused by it and we rowed when the breeze fell away, as if our lives depended on it. The Black Chieftain's kitchen, and those of the other places we had stayed over the summer, had done us all good; we had all regained weight after our long trial at sea. I was happy to work the oars beside them, much to Ussa's mocking amusement. I rowed beside Og and I took pleasure in the rhythm. I thought of our magnificent triremes, how one of them would have closed on Manigan in minutes.

We didn't catch them. We were like a child trying to catch a pigeon, always thinking, when the breeze settled and its flight stopped, that we could creep up on it and take it by surprise. But Manigan was ever watchful and we could find no advantage. The wind was tricky that day. The gods toyed with us, not revealing who they favoured. They are fickle. Even more fickle than we are. I had poured a libation on the water, but they favoured Manigan.

We nearly took his boat, but he defended himself with fire, and there's no more powerful weapon on the water. Rian made that possible, I suppose, or some Goddess I do not claim to understand. It was a day I will always feel ambivalent about; did I want us to capture her or did I prefer to relish her freedom, her ability to escape? Of course I admired her pluck, but like one who flies a hunting bird, I wanted to see her return to the hand. I wanted the impossible. I know that now and I think I probably knew it then. I found it hard, that day, to control my temper. The only way I did was by watching Ussa failing to control hers. After they had torched our sail, she threw the mother of all tantrums, like a child in a playpen whose toy has been taken by another child. She railed at the escape of Manigan, the departure of the dreaded stone, the loss of Rian, perhaps most of all the shame of being out-sailed. I have to admit there was general panic on board. Fire on a ship is enough to make the calmest of sailors fear for his life.

After the flames were put out, Ussa stood at the mast, clinging on with one hand, gesturing between the ineffectual sail and Toma at the helm, who had been heroic in pursuit, in my opinion. Every now and again she would sweep her long arm forward to point at Manigan's boat, as it made its way out of reach of us, chewing up every morsel of breeze. She moaned at her loss. Eventually, thankfully, she retreated to the bow. Toma and the slaves found some unscorched rope and used the bow-shelter covering to rig a temporary sail and we limped back northwards, the tide, fortunately in our favour.

I would like to say it pleased me to let Rian go, to imagine her free on the ocean, even with Manigan. I would like not to be jealous. Sometimes I do not know whether I am or not. I must have been then, looking back, mustn't I? But I threw the feeling aside and focused on my new target, which was my original quest. I made what felt like a heroic and true re-establishment of the purpose of my journeying. It glowed, it sparked, it was warm and it was healing: it was amber.

Toma grinned conspiratorially at me when I asked him, 'How would you sail to the coast where amber is found?'

I could tell by his face that he was ready to set his course eastwards as soon as Ussa gave the word.

'I would make my way south through the Seal Isles to Alba, and skirt her eastern coastline,' he said. 'I'd wait for the weather to look settled with a gentle westerly and I'd set a course south east across the North Sea. I've done it a few times and if the weather is with you it's a beautiful journey but if the wind gets up, especially if it gets a bit of northerly to it, it can be hell. So I'd pick my moment. And then, on the far side, I'd be looking to take a pilot on board. I don't know those waters enough to sail safely there, but there are always folk who'll help you out if you have the right inducements, which you do, of course, and Ussa's never lacking in interest.' He took his hat off and rubbed his head.

'Right now I'm most interested in that.' He gestured ahead. We had land in sight again. 'I'd like a rest after that sail. And these boys deserve a drink.'

I had never known him so talkative.

We came around a headland and crossed the mouth of a huge inlet. I remembered this place from the summer. We had found a warm welcome here, and I guessed Toma was heading back to the place we had stayed then.

I was right. It was another of these broch communities, a friendly headman who was clearly fond of Toma and amused by Ussa, although not susceptible to her charms. His wife, on the other hand, was entranced by Ussa's wares, and once we had settled in, she demanded to see what new jewels Ussa had gained since we had last visited. She was anxious to ensure possession of one of the pieces of silverwork, a brooch with a symbol of an eagle engraved on it. I've no idea how she paid Ussa for it, other than in lavish hospitality. We dined like kings. Perhaps the deal was knowledge, or perhaps there was a favour owed. It was often obvious how Ussa's trade worked, but this was not the only time when I wondered what benefit she won for her riches.

It was a foul, very windy night and I was glad we had made it safely to land. The next morning I went for a stroll. It was a pleasure to be in such a well-ordered farm after the chaotic drama of the sail. Toma and one of the chief's sons had returned to the boat. I passed them talking about the damage that the fire had caused. Perhaps boat repairs would be the price of Ussa's gift of jewellery. The fire had been swiftly put out, but we certainly needed a new sail and rigging.

I strolled on, happy that they showed no sign of wanting to involve me in the work. A small boy was trailing me at a distance, curious, or sent to spy on me, I do not know.

A little inland, near some scrubby willow, a black cow was munching grass. I gave it a wide berth as I passed it on my way up to the brow of a little hill where I hoped to get the lie of the land, but when I turned to look out across the bay, the broch standing proud below me, I saw that the cow was following me. I carried on up to the summit, but there I saw the cow still dogged in pursuit.

The cloud was almost thin enough to be able to cast a shadow, and I wished I had brought my gnomon, so I could determine exactly how far north we were. The cow slowed as it approached me and stopped a few feet away. Perhaps it wanted to be friendly but it was on the brink, hesitant, as if it had suddenly realised

I was a stranger. Black and hairy, not large for a cow, it stood barely up to my chest in height but was bulky and strong-looking with short horns that could do damage if necessary, or serve as a delicate drinking cup. I was nervous. I'm never very confident near cattle, but I thought I should be friendly to it. I smiled and said something foolish, as you do to an animal you want to like you, and put my hand out.

The cow stepped forward and stretched its neck out to sniff my fingers. It snuffled my hand and I apologised for having nothing to give it to eat. As I said, I'm not much used to cattle, but I felt at peace with this animal. Its big shining brown eyes seemed to look at me kindly and, inevitably, it made me think of Rian. She loved cows. I remember seeing her through the barn door saying goodbye to one before we took her away from her home. I longed to see her again.

Cows are sacred to these northern people, not surprisingly given all the goodness they provide: meat and milk of course, but also warm coats, hide for sails and bone that they use where we would use wood. They make tools from things we would feed to a dog, and in late winter, I was told, if the spring is late and food runs out, they will bleed them alive and make a meal of their blood. These creatures really are the lynchpin of the people's survival. Their goddess Brigid takes the form of a cow sometimes, or cows are sacred in her honour. I'm sure you know all this. That evening on the hill, I have to say I felt blessed by hot, sweet cow-breath.

When I turned to go back to the settlement the boy approached and, with a little stick, poked the cow along in front of us. We didn't talk, but I could see he was showing off to me, demonstrating his prowess at herding the big animal home.

The cow set me reflecting on Rian, and the amazing idea that I might have made her pregnant. I took great gulps of the hill air and felt my chest bursting with this huge, life-changing concept.

A child. A baby. A son, perhaps. My son. I might become a father to a boy like the one beside me. I don't know if you realise what that means for me, a Greek man. Until fatherhood, we are merely boys, no matter how old we may be in years. Some men choose to remain in that state throughout their life, and although they cannot hold office or take a formal position as a leader, this means they are free of responsibility. I had always enjoyed that freedom, and thought it unlikely I would ever want to relinquish it, but that day I had the first inkling of the pleasure that might come from feeling myself a man, a father, capable of heading a household and standing shoulder to shoulder in council with other men. If Rian were with child, my life on my return to Massalia could be completely transformed.

Yet she was a slave. That my son would be born into slavery was unthinkable. And now, anyway, she had escaped with that man, and was heading who knows where. Would she really do what Ussa said, and get rid of the child? I couldn't believe it of her. I didn't want to believe it, now the thought of fatherhood had hatched in my mind. You know the answer, of course, and that I was right. But can you imagine the state of uncertainty I was in?

When I am faced with something I cannot know, which is often in my investigations of geography, astronomy and mathematics, I have learned to push such questions aside and focus on what I can discover, what calculations and measurements will reveal. I have little interest in ethical dilemmas or religious mysteries, other than for what they can tell us about the people who believe in them. So, as the state of Rian's womb was unknowable, I buried my curiosity, or attempted to, and turned my mind back to my quest. I still had to find the origin of amber.

THE GREATMOTHER

A NEW LAND

Ussa was reluctant to give up her pursuit of Manigan and Rian, but I suppose she had to acknowledge that she had been out-sailed and they could be anywhere. Toma insisted that the wind was perfect for a crossing of the North Sea, and argued that there were excellent prospects for exchanging tin for amber on the eastern seaboard. Her greed for trade prevailed and we set off for the amber lands.

We had a brisk westerly wind and the boat flew across the North Sea to the amber coast where we followed other boats into a trading port. Here, Ussa was unknown but a few enquiries and some of my gold soon gained us a pilot, and I found myself back in the ascendancy with her, an equal partner on a new frontier. I was surprised she did not know this place, but I suppose everyone's sphere of influence must have an edge. It was a novelty to discover there were places where her reputation did not precede her, and she must approach people, as I did everywhere, as a stranger, with a foreign face and voice and no friends to recommend her.

The pilot's name was a long mouthful that none of us could pronounce properly, but he answered to Miki. He was small and very intense with light hair and dark eyes. Always speaking quickly, with clipped, sharp phrases, he gave a sense of urgency to every utterance. Next to the thoughtful ease of Toma he was manic, and clearly baffled by his inability to rouse our boat crew to the kind of frenzy he took as normal.

His face lit up when I showed him the big piece of amber I carried with me. He took it in both hands and breathed on it, then rolled it around in his clutches so lovingly that I thought I might never get it back. His delight at our quest for amber was clear and he assured us that one of the best places for finding it was his home territory.

As we got close he became more and more excited, telling us repeatedly how near we were. He must not have been home for some time. I didn't see what there was to be so excited about. There were no grand vistas like in the Northern Isles or on the Albion coast I'd travelled, no snowy peaks in the distance, nor volcano plumes like Thule, just a green, lumpy land with atrocious weather: dull, grey and wet, and plenty of wind to keep us moving. In retrospect, I wonder if his zeal was due to the expectation of a reward for delivering us up to the people there.

*

We arrived towards the end of the day at a long beach. The tide was high and we anchored the boat then let the waves take us ashore, hoping for decent shelter from the rain. Miki ran off inland after telling us to start scouring the sands where apparently amber was often washed up or unearthed from among pebbles thrown up by storms. I looked idly and found nothing, but Og found a lump the size of his thumbnail and was well pleased until Ussa forced him to hand it over to her in exchange for some promise that sounded weak even to me. I wanted to get a look at it but she shook her head, teasing me, 'It's mine. My slave, my amber.'

Og sat in a huff looking out to sea and refused to hunt for any more. Ussa paced about and I don't think she even looked at her feet. Her body language seemed to say that she bought gems; she didn't stoop to gather them, even if they were strewn around her.

Eventually, I saw her stiffen and followed her eyes. Our pilot was returning with a delegation. At the front strode a long-haired old woman, wearing a full-length coat. When she reached us I saw it was made out of a patchwork of furs. Every animal of the north was there: bear, wolf, fox, badger, wildcat, otter, marten, no doubt others. Her eyes were shining stones within a crag-face.

I bowed deeply. I could not help myself. I knew I was in the presence of power. Real power, not the steely control that people make by ruling over other people, enslaving them, and making grand buildings and structures of rules and rituals to prop themselves up. No, this woman embodied the raw power of nature.

When she spoke her voice was deep and smooth as a river. The pilot translated. 'The Greatmother welcomes you to this amber shore.'

I wondered whether the Greatmother was the name of the woman or whether she in turn had referred to a deity. Perhaps both. It did not matter. We were blessed by the presence and welcome of a goddess.

She spoke again. 'The bears will expect gifts. Do you bring gifts for them? Are you ready for their judgement?'

I looked at Ussa. To my surprise, she was trembling, her face a rictus. The old woman looked calmly at her, before turning her glimmering gaze on me. Ussa's terror set me on edge, and yet I felt drawn to this majestic crone.

'I have gold and silver,' I said.

'Are you ready for judgement?' she repeated.

I did not know what this meant. Glancing behind me I saw Toma and the slaves bunched together defensively between Ussa and me and the boat, as if ready to take flight.

The old woman was waiting for an answer.

'We are ready,' I said.

Ussa breathed out and took a small shuffle back, then stopped, as if pinned by the crone's stare.

'Give me the gem.'

I turned my head and watched as Ussa reached inside her big white coat and produced the pebble of amber. She held it out to the crone, who plucked it from her palm and lifted it to the light, scrutinising it.

'Who found this?' The pilot's voice followed hers like a coracle drawn on a current.

Ussa gestured behind her and Og took a step forwards.

'It has something within it. Come, look.' She waved him towards her.

He walked up the beach warily.

'You are a slave.' It was barely a question.

He nodded.

'Here is your freedom.' She handed the pebble to him.

He examined it closely, then quizzically looked up at the Greatmother.

'Come.' She turned on her heel and led us away.

There were a dozen or so other people with her and they surrounded us. I realised they were carrying spears. They marched the three of us away, myself following the old woman, Og at my back and Ussa behind him. We were flanked on all sides by the armed retinue of the Greatmother. The pilot stayed on the beach with Toma, Li and Faradh, and when I looked back they were following us at a distance.

*

We were taken to a place of what I took at first to be natural mounds with flowers growing on them, but when I realised smoke was coming out of their tops I realised they were buildings entirely coated with turf. We were led into the largest of these. Inside, huge timbers arched over a big oval space. The smell inside was almost overpowering. I could not make out what it was.

Then, as my eyes adjusted to the gloom, I saw that at one end there were three brown bears chained to massive wooden posts that held up the roof. I took them to be emblems of Artemis, proof that my quest for her sacred material was soon to be fulfilled. Two of the bears were adult, the third a cub. The biggest of the adults lay sleeping. The other, mangy and thin, paced backwards and forwards. The cub was sitting up with a branch of some sort held in all four paws, gnawing on it.

Still, the smell could not be the musk of these bears alone. In one corner, two women were sifting a huge pile of flowers and leaves on a wicker framework, presumably a drying platform. I was reminded of the way my mother dried rose petals and lavender from her garden to put among her clothes during the winter. But this was flower-drying on a scale I had never imagined. From the mound a rich pungent aroma wafted.

'The bears.' The Greatmother was gesturing to them as if introducing us. She walked confidently forward and the pacing animal allowed her to approach it and stroke it between the ears. She touched a bald patch where it must have been rubbing against its post and it tossed its head away in discomfort.

The sleeping bear woke, lifted its snout and turned its head towards us. The cub dropped its stick and trotted towards the Greatmother until stopped by its chain. It stood, straining at its limit until she approached it and fed it something from inside the folds of her coat. It gulped it down and clearly wanted more.

Ussa had wandered over to the flower sifters and idly stirred her hand among the petals, lifting a few to her nose and smiling at the women there, who stared blandly back at all of us. One of them began to drag a bench out from beside the wall, then stopped at a word from the Greatmother, pushed it back and instead took some skins from a pile net to the bench and laid them out on the floor just beyond the reach of the bears. Three deer hides, like puddles, several paces apart in a line. Then the Greatmother gestured to the three of us to sit, one on each skin.

Og tugged me on the sleeve. He was proffering his piece of amber. 'Look!' He pointed at one end of it. 'Put it to the light.'

I took it from him and held it towards the doorway and examined it as I had been taught. It was a lovely shade of orange, flame-coloured, and slightly crazed. It was the shape of a small pear, and as I rotated the bulbous end I saw a fleck of something. I squinted, turned it a bit more and then I saw what it was: a little moth, tiny, perfect, trapped inside the stone. How long had it been there? How had it got in there? How was that possible? Had this solid once been liquid? Had it flowed and caught up this little insect and solidified around it, sealing it away? And if so, how long ago?

I looked up. Og was beaming at me. The Greatmother watched us with a benign expression, as if approving of attention being paid to the amber. Ussa was frowning at the bears.

I passed Og his amber and the Greatmother made it clear that I should sit on the leftmost hide. Og was placed in the middle, Ussa on the right. She seemed resistant to the idea of sitting, but the old woman was implacable and eventually she did as was required. I wonder now if she suspected what was coming.

The crone said something to the two women and they brought handfuls of the plants they were drying. They strewed a sweet, green herb in a circle around Og. Then the younger woman scattered a ring of little pink clover flowers, like fluffy balls, around my mat. Finally, Ussa was surrounded by white petals – daisies perhaps.

I asked Miki what was going on but the Greatmother said something to him. He put his finger to his lips to indicate I must not speak any more. 'The bears will judge you.' I handed over my gift of three silver coins and he passed them silently to the old woman, who tucked them away without reaction.

JUDGEMENT

The Greatmother ushered the two women away out of the hall, and closed the door behind them. She stepped across the room towards the bears and proceeded to loosen them from their chains, first the cub, then the sleeping adult and finally the pacing animal. The cub immediately ran to the sleeping bear and as the Greatmother undid its chain, it seemed to wake from its stupor. It cuffed the cub away, but so gently that the youngster simply rolled and ran back in to snuggle. Was this its mother, I wondered? But it was not motherly, and shoved the cub aside, so I concluded not. The cub ran to the other bear, gambolling and happy to play. The thin, pacing bear continued to march its habitual steps as if oblivious to the lack of chain, and it ignored the cub as it would a fly.

The Greatmother had taken up a perch on a big wooden chair in the corner and was watching intently, holding an ivory wand in one hand. Miki stood behind her, ready to translate. But all my attention was focused on the bears: the creatures of Artemis!

The cub returned to the snoozing bear and rammed its snout into its side with a grunting squeak. The big bear stirred again and the cub had to get out of the way to avoid being rolled on. Faced with the impassive back of the animal, the cub tried to make it rock, pushing with both front paws, but it was like trying to push a boulder and there was no response.

The cub then trotted over to the Greatmother, who patted it on the head, but when it tried to climb up onto her legs she pushed it down and gently kicked it away. So then it decided to come and investigate us.

I was closest. It stepped warily towards my mat, sniffing. I sat stock still as it familiarised itself with my legs. Curious, it investigated my face with its snout. As damp nostrils touched my nose I breathed out, a tiny snort. The cub jumped back as if I had hit it, and eyed me, scratching at the deer hide. Then it turned aside and approached Og.

He must have smelled good, because the cub stepped more confidently towards him, making a beeline for his pocket, where it turned out there was a stash of nuts. Og's hand and the bear's snout struggled for control of the pocket and soon the creature was literally eating out of one of Og's hands, while with the other he scratched it between the ears. It was an instant friendship. It takes a slave to trust a slave, I thought.

The gift of nuts exhausted, the cub bored of Og and decided to explore what Ussa had to offer. The sound of nuts between teeth had caught the attention of both the other bears. The pacing animal had stopped and was staring towards Og, trembling at the extremity of its non-existent chain, nose twitching. The bigger bear tilted its ears back and forth, lifted its head and shifted its paws. Then it sat up like a dog, head raised, scenting the air. In one smooth move it was on its feet, its full bulk awesome and huge. It took a few steps until it was breathing over Og, who put his hands in his pocket and opened it out.

'It's empty, I'm sorry.' His voice seemed very small.

The bear huffed and Og flinched, but the big animal simply turned its back on him, licked up some of the herbs and padded away.

At that moment the pacing bear broke free of its non-chain and was suddenly on top of Og, nosing in his pocket, rummaging him for non-existent food. He was pushed to the ground as the bear tore at his coat, its long claws scratching him greedily.

'I've nothing for you. The cub got them.' Og shoved the bear off. It gave way, surprisingly, as if disliking being touched and stood just out of arm's reach with a look of shock in its eyes, staring at Og as if trying to make a difficult calculation. Then it lowered its head and took a mouthful of the scattered herbs, its long tongue rasping the floor as it scooped them up. Spotting the clover flowers surrounding me, it turned its attention to them.

I sat frozen to my mat as the bear approached.

Then Ussa said, 'Get off,' and we all, including the big bear, looked towards her. 'Get off, get off, get off!' The cub was clawing at her, standing with its hind legs firmly grasping her fur coat, its front legs pawing at her head, snout chewing her hair. She batted at the little creature with her arm, but it clung on. The biggest bear approached, sniffed the ring of flowers around her and its tongue swooped up a strip of them. Then it too was snuffling at Ussa. The poor woman screamed in panic, flailing, but her punches did not seem to remotely interest the huge animal, which remained placid, systematically smelling her, as if making up its mind where to take the first bite.

I felt the hairs go up on the back of my neck and then something touched my cheek. Hot breath in my ear. My eyes swivelled and met those of the scrawny bear, too close. Far too close.

Its tongue rasped across my face. Huge teeth. The smell almost made me swoon. I knew every level of fear. I could not breathe. I wet myself like a child. I do not think I cried out. I had no breath to call with.

You know, because you are reading this, that I must have survived. But I had no such knowledge and I was certain of my doom. Those fangs were sure to take hold of my flesh. They were my destiny. I waited for the puncture, for the pain.

I remember breathing out, then breathing in again and thinking, as the air flowed in to me, that this was my last breath. And then I breathed it out and felt strangely at peace.

The bear licked me again and snorted onto my face. I inhaled the breath of the bear, savouring it, tasting the impossibility of this moment of life. I was light-headed, crazed with fear. The bear rubbed the underside of its snout across my head, side to side, pressing down on me with the weight of its head.

I bent my neck and the pressure eased. A shout from Ussa jerked my attention sideways and seemed also to disturb the bear, which jumped aside.

Ussa screamed again, a series of short shrieks, and then a long, high wailing. She was hunched in a ball. She had taken off her coat, and the cub was playing with it, trying to work out how to make this big, white inert bear respond.

The big bear was batting at Ussa with its paw, like a cat playing with a mouse. Ussa's hand was over one eye and I could see blood pouring down that side of her face. She was trying to mop it and her hands were bloody too. The bear huffed, and cuffed her again.

'The bear knows you are guilty. What do you say?' It was the Greatmother's voice.

'I'm sorry, I'm sorry, I'm sorry, I'm sorry.' Ussa was sobbing, hunched. The bear stood over her.

The animal beside me licked up more clover flowers, then seemed to lose interest in me. It began munching on the greenery surrounding Og. He sat with his knees up to his chest, trying to take as little space as possible. The bear, ignoring Og completely, worked its way systematically around him, then joined the bigger animal beside Ussa.

The cub was still playing with the coat but everyone else's attention was riveted on the terrified woman, whose sobbing gradually abated. When she fell quiet, the big bear batted her again, as if shaking her awake, or prompting her to continue. It had blood on its paw, and as it stepped aside it left red claw prints among the white petals strewn around her, tinting the flower pool as though it were the white of a bloodshot eye.

The Greatmother sat watching, impassive. 'Confess.' Her voice was a bark, the pilot's an echo.

Ussa began jabbering. 'I know I shouldn't have done it, but I did it, I did it, I admit it, I killed him, I couldn't stand it, I just couldn't do it, so I killed him, but it's all over now. It was a long time ago and nobody knew and it was best, no, no, I know it wasn't best, I know it was a wicked thing to do but I was young and I've been punishing myself, I have, I know it doesn't look like it but I have, I have, the guilt's been there all along. I am sorry. I am.' She broke down into sobbing again. I'll never forget it. She was weeping tears of blood.

The thin bear seemed interested in the blood on her hand and was sniffing at her. She must have felt its breath because she half-turned and beat at the bear's head with her arm, flapping, screaming and swearing at it. The bear, frightened, opened its mouth wide and made a high growling sound backing off a little, but Ussa didn't seem to notice and kept howling until the big bear cuffed her again.

Ussa rolled over into a tight ball, arms covering her head, and no amount of shoving from the bear could gain any response. Whether she was unconscious or just playing dead, I couldn't tell.

Og and I exchanged horrified glances.

The big bear nudged at Ussa a few times more but, getting no reaction, seemed to lose interest. It started licking up the white petals, then turned and looked at me, as if registering my presence for the first time.

The hairs rose on the back of my neck as its little eyes focused in. Swinging its head, it paced towards me. With one bloody paw it knocked me down into a sprawl on my mat. I shrank into a defensive ball, my hands on the back of my head, elbows trying to shield my face. I felt the weight on the bear on me, its paws on my back, stroking my coat.

The Greatmother spoke and the pilot said, 'So, you are guilty too. The bear has judged you. Now confess.'

As if the bear understood the words, it bounced me, shoving at me, trying to shake words out of me. But I had pride inside me as well as fear and I uttered only denial. 'I'm not guilty. What is this? Guilty of what? I'm not guilty of anything.'

With a blast of fury I threw it off and it stepped aside and licked up some clover flowers as if it had done nothing.

'You have soiled yourself,' the Greatmother said.

I could smell that it was true and my anger was fuelled by shame. I shouted at her. I don't know what I said but I remember

132

the old woman just shook her head and said, 'Anger will not help you. Consider your words.'

The big bear was staring at me again. Some part of myself realised that I needed to calm down, that my anger was a danger to me.

'Enough.' The Greatmother got off her throne, took a few paces and drew the bolt on a big wooden door beyond the roof pillars at the end where the bears had been chained. At the sound, the big bear began pacing towards the doorway, soon followed by the cub, at first dragging the white coat, then abandoning it as the smell of fresh air overcame everything else. The scrawny bear stood, as if trying to make up its mind, staring at the opening, then made a bolt for it and was the first through, followed by the scampering cub and finally by the big bear who padded out slowly, wearily, it seemed, as if the humiliation it had witnessed, or brought about, was just the latest in a long series of tiring and unpleasant ordeals it had had to endure.

After the bears had left, the Greatmother closed the door behind them and faced us, sizing each of us up in turn. I sensed that the trial, if that is what it was that we were undergoing, was not over yet.

INTERROGATION

I find the next part of the experience difficult to write about it. I could leave you wondering but that would be cruel, wouldn't it? Perhaps the time has come to be honest. It's my only hope of redemption.

Once the bears had gone, Ussa took her revenge. The Great-mother, via Miki, began an inquisition. I think I was at a disadvantage. I was bewildered by what is considered acceptable and what is sinful by these various barbarian tribes.

Ussa looked ghastly. Her eye was streaming blood and she kept her hand over it as she ranted, which she did incessantly for what felt an age, hurling accusations at me and at people I had never heard of, casting blame around like a farmer scattering seed in every furrow hoping some of it will grow.

She also confessed to her own sins, and some of these were truly awful. The neglect of her sick mother, causing her death. The murder of a baby. Enslavement of people through tricks and deviousness. I knew of some of this. I had seen it: Rian was one like this. But she blamed the people like me, who bought such slaves from her, as the real villains, as if she was just an instrument, as if Rian's enslavement had been premeditated by me.

She turned to me. 'Do you remember when we met Uill Tabar?'

'The druid?' I said. 'The prophet.'

'Yes. And do you remember the third prophecy of the stone?'

'No.' At that moment old superstitious stories were the last things I had in my mind.

'Rian, the slave girl, fits the prophecy, and she's carrying your bastard child, which means if it's born and gets its hands on the stone...'

'What are you talking about?' the Greatmother interjected. 'What stone?'

Ussa took her hand from her eye, looked at the blood, and put it back. She spoke in a dull voice, not looking at the Greatmother. 'The Head of Telling, a magic stone with three faces. It answers any question. It's my birthright and it's been stolen.' Then she sobbed out her story about why she needed it.

Apparently she had gambled it away, pretending she possessed it when she only wished she did. She believed it was rightly hers, but the real reason she wanted it so badly was not for its own sake but because she owed it to her father, Sevenheads, the last in a lineage of warlords with gory reputations. She said he would kill her if she didn't get it and give it to him. Then she turned to me again.

'But what Uill Tabar told me is that little slut of yours...'

I wanted to point out that she was no longer mine, sadly, but Ussa was in full flight.

'Her grandmother was a queen-slave, a shaman, and concubine of one of the Kings of Eriu. Her bastard son became the secret lover of a chieftain's daughter on the Winged Isle, and when she got pregnant she had the child in hiding and guess who it was? Yes, Rian. And what have you gone and done but give her a third generation – King, noble woman, stranger, all breeding into the line of slaves.' She pointed her finger at me as if I was a devil.

'So what?' said the Greatmother.

Ussa turned to her. 'Their spawn will nullify the stone's power.'

The Greatmother shrugged. It didn't interest her. Why should it? 'What else?'

Ussa's rant got worse. She confessed to procuring little children for old perverted men to have their evil way with. She alluded to my behaviour with Rian on that account as well, as if Rian was a little child and not a young woman. She painted me in the most unpleasant light. The way she explained it all, weeping and fearful and contrite, she painted herself as a tool in the hands of the conniving men like me who would travel to the ends of the earth to satisfy their ugly cravings.

It was my turn to be humiliated. I'm not proud of what happened. At first, I got angry and I shouted at Ussa and called her a liar, called her worse things than that. And then the Greatmother turned her attention to me and extracted my confession, if that is what it was.

I have wondered ever since how to understand what she drew from me. It was a portrayal of myself that was new to me. Any life story is partial, constructed from events like a necklace of beads strung on a thread. So is this chain of writing I am creating for you, but it was different from this one, different in every respect. I am not sure whether up until that day I had ever told the story of who I am, but I am certain that if I had, it was nothing like the version of myself the Greatmother pulled from me. I have re-told my tale over and over since that time, to myself mostly, trying to make sense of it, trying to rediscover myself. I have concluded that any life story, this tale I tell you and the one the Greatmother got, reflect more about the person told to than about the teller. A knapped flint is just a slice of the original stone and mostly reflects the skill of the knapper. That woman knapped stories sharper and more deadly than anyone I have ever met. I wonder why. What was it about her? I'd like to say it was her eyes, which were uniquely penetrating and blue. But that is no doubt oversimplified. It was what was behind her eyes, something powerful, something dangerous. All this is by way of an excuse, I suppose. I must give you some sense of what I told her, even though it shames me.

She began by asking me where I was born and who my parents were and what happened to me in my early childhood before my memories began. This is what I told her.

CONFESSION

I was born in Massalia. My father was a councillor and wealthy enough to be able to control a large vineyard, or perhaps it was the vineyard that enabled him to be wealthy enough to have a house in town where traders would come, so he was asked to be on the city council, the Boule. First land and then power, as always, follows. Our wine was prized and traded far and wide. My father sent amphorae away by the cartload every autumn, by the boatload every spring.

My mother was a daughter of a priestess of the temple of Artemis in Massalia. I told the Greatmother that the symbol of Artemis is a bear, and she was interested in this and asked me to speak about my mother. But she died when I was young and I was brought up by my nurse, the old Keltic woman, Danu, who gave me her language, so I have no real memories of my mother to draw on. I sketched to the Greatmother what I could about

136

the Artemis temple, but that was precious little.

I began to relate the story of Callista, who was turned into a bear by Artemis after becoming pregnant by Zeus. But Ussa, who had been moaning and whimpering ever since she had finished her outburst, flew into a temper about her wounded face, the need to tend the bloody mess around her eye. She was thirsty, she said, and hungry. We all were. It was true. And she needed to clean herself. She got to her feet.

'And I'm bleeding. I'm bleeding.' She was crying again, sobbing and tearing at her face. There were red splashes on the floor all around her and as she took her hand away she revealed a gash from her eyebrow to her cheek that had surely punctured her eye.

'Do you want to hear what this man has to say?' the old woman asked her.

'I don't want to listen to another word. I don't care about anyone else.'

I had never seen her so completely shameless. She was like a spoilt little girl. Not a shred of her trademark poise, her stylish composure, remained. She was a shambles, a mess, a wreck. Yes, like a wrecked boat, she seemed simply to be smashing herself onto rocks, unable to resist each wave of emotion as the storm shook her.

Og seemed safely moored on his hide raft in the centre of the floor and I too felt I still had an anchor somewhere beneath me, though I was being tossed about on the Greatmother's sea of questions.

'You forfeit your slave,' the Greatmother said.

'Take him. I don't want him.' Ussa was apparently willing to agree to anything, without protest.

So Og was a free man.

'Look at your amber stone,' the old woman said to him. 'Melt it and let the moth be relinquished into the air, or keep it as a reminder of what you used to be. Do you want to stay to listen, free man?'

Og nodded that he did.

Then the Greatmother said something to Miki, who took Ussa roughly by the upper arm to the door, where he called for someone to take her away.

Then only Og and I remained and the questions continued. I told her irrelevant things about my early childhood, stories from my father about things that did not concern me, his wine trade, a trip we made to Narbo, two days sail east of Massalia, which was perhaps what got me hooked on travelling and boats. The very mention of boats made the Greatmother visibly bored. She interrupted me.

'What frightens you?'

'Bears,' I said.

'You are lying.' She was right. 'Don't.'

'I am afraid of dying.'

She nodded. 'What else?'

'Drowning. Being knocked overboard in the wide ocean. Storms at sea.'

Boats again. She changed the subject. 'What makes you sad?'

'Making mistakes. Being stupid. Not being able to remember my mother.' She lost her bored look when I said this. It reminded me of being a child, sitting there on that mat on the floor, like being with my tutor, Angelus, who had taught me everything worthwhile: the stars, the fundamentals of mathematics, the geography of the world. He taught me from the great works of Thales and Anaximander and Herodotus. He even introduced me to Aristotle, the genius of our time. He used to sit, as the Greatmother did, on a high backed chair, his sandaled feet planted firmly on the floor, reading from a codex of leather-bound parchment spread across his thighs while I sat on a woollen mat in front of him, cross-legged.

But the Greatmother had no book, and if she was trying to teach me something it was not benign. She was leaning slightly forward, one hand on a thigh. The other was holding a piece of ivory, which she was rubbing with her thumb.

'Tell me more about your mother,' she said.

'I don't remember her.' I clenched my hands. 'My father rarely spoke of her. She was a wonderful singer.'

'What makes you ashamed?'

I had to think how to answer this. Her questions did not seem to follow any logic I could understand.

'Do not think, just answer.'

'When I see someone being beaten I feel ashamed for the person who is beating.'

'But what about yourself? What aspect of yourself makes you feel shame?'

'I think my feet are ugly.'

She looked at me with contempt, then lifted her eyes in irritation, making clear how stupid she found me. 'Not your appearance. Deeds.'

'I am ashamed of what I did to Rian.'

Og swung round to look at me, and I caught his glance by accident and we both looked away again.

I was embarrassed. 'I am ashamed of that.'

'This is the slave? What did you do to her?'

'I treated her badly.'

'Why?'

'I was frustrated. She is beautiful.'

'So?'

I wanted to say, 'She was only a slave. It was only once,' but I could not bring myself to make excuses, nor to speak the feeling of her under me, slight and cool, her tightness as I pushed myself inside her, the little cry she made, her strange stillness afterwards. I didn't want to remember that the only words she had spoken had been, 'No.' And again, 'No.' But I couldn't forget it.

'I treated her as my possession, and then I sold her. I did not buy her with that intention. I bought her to save her from harm, but in the end I inflicted it on her anyway. So then I sold her.'

'Why?' The Greatmother's voice was high and sharp, with Miki's voice a whisper in pursuit. He had moved from behind her chair and stood beside and a little in front of her, as if that enabled him to pass her words on more easily.

I thought of various replies: 'so I would do nothing worse'; 'so she was no longer available to me to repeat what I had done.' What I finally said was, 'Because I had ruined what she was, and that disgusted me.'

'What was she?'

'As free and pure and bright as the moon.'

'And you raped her.'

I breathed in sharply. It was a dagger of a word. I wanted to deny it. I had not used force, not really. But accused here, beside Og, beneath the gaze of this old spirit woman, I could not utter a denial. I could not say anything.

'Speak.'

I could not.

'Did you rape her?'

I did not want to speak, but silence was, eventually, worse than assent. What manner of torture was this? No pain except in my mind.

'No.'

She laughed. 'Speak the truth.'

'No.'

'So you lie.'

'No, no, no.'

'Your denial makes it obvious you did. You wanted to possess her.' She paused. 'And afterwards, you sold her.'

'Yes.' I realised as I said this word, that I had implicated myself.

'Because once you possessed her, she no longer interested you.'

'No.'

'Why then?'

I had never thought about it until this moment, really. I had simply done it. I started to babble. 'Because she was ashamed and

140

I was ashamed to have reduced her to shame. I wanted her to be free... of me at least. But of course selling her didn't, couldn't, achieve that. I saw that afterwards, after it was too late. I had not been thinking straight.' If I wasn't careful I would start to make excuses. I stopped myself.

'I am mostly ashamed that I sold her.' But I saw this was not true.

The Greatmother was waiting for me to say more. 'You are weighing your shames. Good.'

'The biggest shame is that of selling her.' I said. 'It has so many implications. There are so many ways of thinking of what might have been if I had not and what might have happened since I did. I wondered if I could make amends by buying her back. But the shame of...' I would not use the word, '...what I did to her before, is heavier. More dense. More painful.'

I could still hear her voice, tiny and cracked. 'No.' High-pitched, like the yelp of an animal in a snare. I had done that to her. I had taken the little creature to pet, and instead I had broken her. And then I saw her as she had been on that island in the Cat Isles, filthy from the midden, and inside her my son was growing. I felt sick.

I thought of copper and tin. Tin, heaviest of metals, lead-like in its density, that was the feeling inside me when I acknowledged my despoliation of the girl. I had taken copper, unburnished, which had not yielded to the flames of the world, and I had tarnished it with a baser metal. I thought of her copper hair, and of the pliancy of a copper bracelet, its healing power. And I knew that she was, as a result of me, alloyed, hardened, and it was irreversible.

'There are many who view sex with slaves as nothing to be ashamed of at all,' the Greatmother spoke lightly. I looked up. Her face betrayed no light. She was the shadow of an eagle.

'There are people who make swords and sleep at night,' I said. She nodded.

'I could ask you to whom you have caused pain, whom you envy, who you want to see again before you die.'

I could think only of Rian.

'I see there is no point in asking these things.'

I asked myself anyway, and I knew I would ask myself these things many times, looking back across the desert of my jovial life. I considered the many characters whose lives had intersected, however briefly, with my own, on my journeys from Tanais to Gadir, from the ruins of Delphi to the wonders of Thule. I knew I would find there only detritus, glittering perhaps, but ultimately dust.

I had allowed everything else to fall, to hold lust in one hand and greed in the other, and now both my hands were burning.

AMBER

After a long, uncomfortable silence, the Greatmother, sitting upright, held the ivory wand up in front of her with both hands, like a lighted torch. 'What are you looking for?'

I stared at it. It was just a bone. 'Amber.'

'Why?'

I thought of many possible answers. I could tell her about the ceremonies performed in the temples, the magic it catalysed. I could tell her about the people who had made fortunes controlling its trade, stockpiling it when supplies were plentiful and creating artificial shortages to make it more valuable. I could tell her of the healing miracles it brought about. I could tell her the story of Electrum, the tale of Phaethon. I could tell how every bride in our land must have a piece to wear on her wedding night to bring her fertility and protect her from violence by her husband, to keep him mild and gentle with her. I could tell her about the old woman I knew as a child who cured sick cattle by treating their drinking water with an amber heart she carried on a chain around her neck. I could tell her of the hunters who burned it, ceremoniously, to propitiate the weather gods before embarking on a dangerous hunting expedition. I could tell her that Rian had hair its colour.

But I told her none of those things. I said only, 'I am curious. I am seeking its origin. I live in a land where there is no amber, but we revere it, and from time to time it comes into our lives and it is full of power. My quest is for its origin, to discover how and where it is made and by whom, and if it is not made, to see it growing naturally, to watch it wash up on the shore where the gods of the sea discard it, or to find it hidden within rock, as some say it can be found. If possible, I want to understand more of what manner of thing it is and if, as we believe, its origin is the sap of a tree, to see the special trees that can produce such gum, or to learn what treatment the resin undergoes to harden it into a gem.'

I don't remember exactly what I said, to be honest, but it was along these lines. I presented myself as a scientist.

The Greatmother lowered the ivory wand and nodded slowly.

'Where will you go with this knowledge once you have found it?'

'Home.'

'And what will you do with it there?'

'Share it,' I said. 'That is what knowledge is for, isn't it? That's what I believe. I can't abide secrets, and people lording over other people because they know something someone else doesn't know.'

She was staring at me as if baffled. 'But what will you *do* with it?' It was as if she had not understood my answer at all. Perhaps Miki the pilot was not translating effectively.

I tried to explain about the Akademie in Athens and our respect for knowledge in its own right, but she clearly grew impatient with me, shaking her head as if I was an imbecile.

'Will they come here, these scientists?'

'Why would they come here?'

'To find more amber. To take our amber. We will defend ourselves.'

I saw that I needed to avoid the impression that I would trigger some kind of invasion of amber-greedy warriors, and I was also intrigued that the implication of her concern was that she had at least some of the knowledge I was looking for.

'Do you know how amber is made?' I said

'It is not made.'

I waited.

'Where exactly are these people you will take the amber to?'

I explained where our Great Sea is relative to her but she seemed not to comprehend. She was shaking her head. Perhaps she did not believe the distances involved.

Then Og murmured something. The Greatmother snapped at Miki, who said, 'Please repeat what you said.' Miki stepped respectfully aside from where had stood between me and the old woman, partly blocking her view of Og. Now the Greatmother could see us both clearly. Her eyes were on Og.

'He is a rich man.'

She frowned, clearly nonplussed by this unsought-for judgement.

'He is generous with his gold,' Og went on, 'if you tell him what he needs to know.'

The Greatmother seemed to contemplate what Og had said. Silence billowed into the hall as we all waited for her to speak. But she said nothing, just sat watching us, her eyes switching between the two of us. I would indeed have been generous with my gold to know her thoughts. Og's last words seemed to linger, smudged by the murmur of the translator, who eventually broke the pause with a question to the crone, who shook her head. Breaking out of her contemplation, she waved the wand around in the air and, finally, staring at me hard, spoke. 'Your punishment will be the amber knowledge you seek.'

She rose to her feet, in that creaking way an old person does after sitting a long time. She said a short phrase to Miki, then shuffled to a little lamp burning behind us, which I had not noticed before. She lit something smoky from it, and began creeping about the hall, wafting the fumes. It was resinous and pungent, and reminded me of the Artemis temple. I suddenly wanted to tell her all I could about the ceremonies they held there, but I dared not speak. She was in the midst of some ritual, murmuring to herself. She made a point of smoking me thoroughly, waving the smouldering pot in front of my face, then blowing on me as if to be sure that I was clean. She treated Og similarly, then bowed to all four cardinal points, before stubbing out the fire, putting the pot down on her chair and leaving the hall without a further word to either of us.

TRAPPED

IN THE VILLAGE

Miki turned, smiled, and said, 'Food! Follow me.'

We traipsed out and over to a round building where smoke and food smells welcomed us. We were presented with bowls of porridge by the same two women who had been at the flowers earlier. I realised I was indeed ravenous and tired, almost trembling with fatigue. We ate, then one of the women, seeing my yawn, showed me a pallet at the far side of the fire close to the wall, and gave me a blanket. I curled up and slept. My last memory was Og's voice telling Miki about his beloved homeland.

When I woke the fire was out, everything was quiet. I was the only person in the building.

I was thirsty and needed to urinate. I got up and went looking for water. Outside it was raining. I relieved myself by the side of the building, and was spotted by one of the women, who took me to a smaller hut. I mimed drinking, and she gave me a beaker of a disgusting, sweet milky substance. I did not know how to ask for mere water. I tried to indicate it by pointing to the rain, but she failed to understand me. I sipped the foul paste and then sat the beaker where the drip from the eaves could rinse it and gather what I needed. She seemed amused and left me alone. I hoped she would return with bread. I was ravenous again. The whole time I was in that place, on the amber shore, I was hungry. Those people seemed to live on air, or expect me to. I was thin as a reed by the time I left there.

I sat in the doorway of the miserable little hovel I'd been taken to, looking out into the rain. Pigs rootled about, making the mud worse. Pork is tasty, but it is not worth the mess pigs make, I don't think. Cows can be nearly as bad of course, although they're more useful, and they have a good smell. One of the pigs was friendly and it came to me to be scratched. It looked at me with its almost-human eyes as if to tell me it knew something I did not yet know, but would soon find out.

Og was wandering about, aimlessly, it seemed, and he came over and talked to me about his freedom and what he might do now. He asked my advice, seemed at a loss, unsure, after so many years of following another's whims, of how to go forwards under his own command. I asked him what he wanted and he said, 'A home.' Where would he make it? Would he go to the tin-mining village he had taken me to? 'Maybe.' He seemed so unsure. 'I could go anywhere.'

'Start there,' I advised him. He seemed pleased to be told what to do, and nodded and went away. I saw him talking with Toma, but the other slaves appeared to shun him. I foresaw that he would be lonely.

Suddenly, into the quiet morning, screams erupted from one of the other small huts. Blood-clotting howls that froze me where I crouched and made me want to hide further back in the shadows, or simply to run away. In retrospect I should have done the latter, but instead I watched with a horrified fascination.

Women came and went from the hut. I saw Og try to investigate and be turned away. I went over to talk to him but I was also led away, asked politely with gestures to return to the place I had been assigned. It was like being sent back to a sty. I was brought a fleece to cover the wooden bench which was the only furniture in my hut. A thin, silent lad stood watching me for a while, before giving me some bread. Then Li came with my sleeping roll, writing box and gnomon from the boat. I asked him what was happening but he wouldn't stay to talk. I ate the bread, washed down with rainwater I had gathered in the beaker from the roof, and continued watching from the doorway. I saw the Greatmother leave the hut of screams, and then she sent the bread-boy and Miki over to me.

'Follow the boy, Arald. He will take you to see what you want to see,' Miki said.

Arald was a shy, lanky youth. He made an attempt at conversation but soon realised I did not speak his language. This seemed to suit him. We set out in the drizzle, through the village fence, down to the long beach and along the shore southwards. When we crossed a stream that ran across the sand, I drank my fill. We clambered up onto the dunes, then onto a stronger trail across a headland to another bay where a river poured out into the sea. Was this the Eridanus River of the fables? On this side of it was another long sandy beach where we began to look for amber. Arald spotted a piece almost immediately and offered it to me. It took us a while to find another, and once again it was the boy's sharp eyes that spotted it. Before long we had three pieces, one quite substantial. I wanted to know if it came down the river or out of the sea, but Arald nodded and smiled at everything I asked him, understanding nothing.

By the afternoon, he was getting restless and we returned to the village. As we came over the brow of the headland into view of the beach close to the village, I saw that *Ròn* had gone. I looked out to sea. There she was, sail up, heading away. They had left me behind, and taken my tin! My chest tightened with fury. I started shouting, swearing, I don't know what I was saying. I stamped my feet. I ran into the sea and back out again. I thought I would lose my mind. The boy ran away, scared.

Eventually, as the boat vanished over the horizon, I calmed down. There was nothing I could do. I was, once again, entirely on my own. I would have to use my wit to complete my voyage.

The screams, I can tell you now, were from Ussa, as the Greatmother cut her eye out. I spent a lot of time with the Greatmother and I got to know her rather well, and I want to assume she took out Ussa's eye because it was so damaged it could not be healed. But I can't be sure. She is capable of terrifying strength when she is judging people, as I know to my cost. She has a ruthless thread like iron that runs through the fabric of her soul. Perhaps it was a punishment. I'll never know.

WALKING ON THE SPOT

After I was abandoned, my journey changed. At first I hoped each day a boat would pull up on the shore, but as luck would have it, when one eventually did, I missed it. I was on an amber-gathering expedition to the south, and when I got back to the beach I saw a ship at the far end and started running, but by the time I got close the vessel was already heading back out to sea, a strong crew of twelve men at the oars. How I cursed and fumed.

Several weeks passed before the next seaworthy boat came. There were boats plying in and out from the shore, of course, and some fishing, but only light craft that were not capable of weathering a storm. The people from the village never seemed to go anywhere else. Why should they? They had everything they needed right where they were, but people came to them for amber and to trade from time to time, and I pinned my hopes of getting away with them.

The next boat came late one evening, and the crew hauled it ashore on the high tide and stayed in the village overnight. I do not know whether they were judged like us. Possibly. I tried to ask for passage with them when I eventually got close to them as they were eating, but they refused any offer. No gold, no amber was enough to persuade them to take me. I guessed the Greatmother told them things about me that put them off. I was effectively her prisoner, her slave, although it took me a while to see it that way.

I've already said I became thin while on the amber coast. I never adjusted to their food and during that winter I was always cold and damp and got sick frequently. They do something disgusting to fish that makes it almost inedible to my taste and their bread is hard, dark and heavy on the stomach. I did not eat meat for the whole time I was there except for a handful of occasions, when everyone feasted: the winter solstice, a celebration of spring, a harvest festival. They have fat cattle and pigs, but I swear their dogs got more meat than I did. I don't count the strange grisly sausages they made, smoked until they stank. If it were not for the cheese I swear I would have starved to death. Those big cows yielded plenty of milk and although much of what they made with it was a rough, bitter curd, there was a woman called Uine who made delicious cheese. She and her husband Don, a mild fisherman, tolerated me. They were the closest I had to friends there, apart from the boy Arald. He was an odd, obsessive little creature, not quite normal, somehow, too clever and single-minded to play with other youths. The pair of us lived in our huts on the fringe of the village, shunned by most of the community, not quite ostracised but never treated like real people.

Meanwhile, I learned their language and gathered amber on the river outfalls and along the beaches. I became skilled in spotting it and Arald seemed to like my company. We invariably returned with a few pieces. At first I tried to keep them to myself but I swear the Greatmother can smell amber if you have it on you. She sniffs it out of any hiding place and uses the threat of the bears to ensure it is handed over. I learned to show her everything I found and she said that once I had paid my due, whatever that meant, she would let me keep some of it. I reconciled myself to this. They had given me the use of the little hut, they fed me and I had few useful skills to offer. I could have paid them gold but a share of the amber seemed a fair exchange. The rest would make me rich on my return home. I hoped, always, to learn more about its original source and more of its mysteries, but although I gathered hundreds of pieces, I made no new discoveries.

I learned their language largely so that the old woman might let me into some of her many secrets. Rather than her prisoner, I wished to be her student, but she was a reluctant teacher; even when I had reasonable mastery of their tongue and knew the shape of their land, from many expeditions across the bogs behind the coast, along the shore and up the meandering river inland, she never let her knowledge come my way.

I tried to interest her in my scientific work. I took a gnomon measurement on a sunny day soon after I arrived. It was sixty-four days after the summer solstice and when I adjusted for this, I calculated that the sun height was around six cubits. I deduced that we were a similar distance north to the island of Monopia, on the west coast of Albion, where I had taken a shadow-reading on my journey north from Belerion.

I asked the Greatmother for an audience and intended to tell her about my method for calculating our relative position. She saw me in the Bear Hall. She was sitting on her big chair and indicated that I should sit on the floor in front of her. I said I wouldn't be able to show her how I did my measurements if I wasn't standing. She pursed her lips and narrowed her eyes. 'Why would you want to do that?'

I showed her my staff. 'This is my gnomon. I use it to measure the height of the sun in the sky.'

She reached out with both hands and snatched it from me, then scrutinised the engravings from top to bottom. 'What is this?'

It was one of the dolphins. 'A symbol of the god who looks after sailors, Apollo.'

'There is no such god. This?'

It was an owl. 'Another symbol. This is of the goddess Athena, the wise one.'

'There is no owl goddess. If you were not so stupid I would think you dangerous.' She showed no sign of wanting to give me back my gnomon.

I stepped forward and took it from her. She sat back in her chair as if I had hit her. I started to talk about my method for measuring shadows but she simply turned her head away from me and said, 'Go.'

'But this is useful. It would be useful for you. You could measure distances more accurately. For example, when you need to take amber to trade at Abalus.'

'What do you know of Abalus?'

'Very little. Just what I have heard people here saying, that amber from this coast is taken there to exchange for bronze.'

She seemed completely uninterested in the possibilities of improved knowledge of the world, simply flicking her fingers at me in dismissal.

I went to find Arald. But he simply laughed at the very idea of measuring shadows. The rest of the villagers treated me as if I had a stupid, if harmless, obsession.

I am always surprised by how few people have interest in understanding the world beyond their immediate horizons, but at that time, with no-one to talk with about navigation or cosmology or geography, I began to wonder if I was on my way to madness. I became desperate to return to the sea, to continue my survey of this northern land, to work out how far exactly this place was from a port reachable by future traders from my homeland. I had reached the location where amber came from, even if I was still no clearer on how it came to exist, so to that extent my quest was almost complete. All that remained was to find out where this place was in relation to the rest of the known world, to chart its distance from Albion, for example. I also wanted to learn more about its geography. What was the extent of this amber coast? Where was the island of Abalus, which Uine had let slip was the market place? Were there navigable rivers going south that may act as trade routes? I could only find out by going there. And meanwhile, I longed to know more about the origins of the electrum I gathered almost daily.

In spring a ship made of planks arrived, rowed by a gang of rough-looking men, so I told Arald I would not join him that day. My hopes lifted that I might be able to travel away with them. One of their party came ashore with his hands tied behind his back, and he and three others were taken to the Bear Hall. He was carried out dead a little while later. The men took him to the beach, built a bonfire of driftwood, got out several flagons of some kind of liquid from their boat and proceeded to get blind drunk while they burnt the body. They sang and danced in a frenzy, while the Greatmother and several other villagers kept watch over them. They also kept me away.

Although I asked what was happening no-one would give me any kind of explanation. I tried to get close enough to address the men directly but the villagers repeatedly dragged me away. This was the day I realised I was no longer free to leave. If I had been stronger I might have acted differently, but I still hungered after knowledge of amber's mysteries. I found it impossible to give up hope that the Greatmother's promises would come to something, and I tried to live within the bounds of the situation I found myself in.

I began to feel like the bears. Mostly they were imprisoned, but sometimes the Greatmother paraded them around the village on leashes. At the harvest festival, in a ceremony that I watched from the margins, the dark, pacing bear was killed, whether by accident or not, I never quite understood. It had always been demented, I thought. Perhaps death was a release. If the bears felt anything like I did about life there, I pitied them.

Every day, after hours spent scouring the beaches for little orange stones, I would go down to the shore and stare out into the distance, trying to will a ship into existence that could take me away. I thought longingly of my stash of tin in Ussa's hold. I became very miserable and struggled to retain a sense of who I was. Although I tried to treat it as an opportunity to become familiar with the northern sky, tracking the stars over the months as they rotated around the celestial sphere, this intellectual activity could not fully satisfy me. I made ink from oak galls when my supply ran low and wrote in increasingly tiny letters to try to keep myself company. I was a misfit. Perhaps I always was, still am, always will be. It is enough to say I learned the art of loneliness in the amber land. If it weren't for Arald I would have been utterly alone.

Arald might have been my friend, but one day I discovered he was a thief. He stole my gnomon. I had been doing some work for Uine and Don and when I came back I noticed it was missing. I had a habit of strolling out early in the morning to the high point on the headland to see if I could see any boats, and to gauge the weather as best I could. I always took the pole as a walking stick. I like the feel of its engravings under my fingers. Over time, I have worn them almost away where I hold it. Anyway, it was missing. I knew I'd had it with me during the daytime the day before, and I knew Arald admired it.

When I challenged him, he admitted right away that he'd taken it. He had the awkward, newly deep voice of puberty even though he was quite a big young man. 'I need it for my wedding.'

'You're getting married?' I was amazed. 'Who to?'

'The Greatmother.'

I didn't believe him.

'She told me I must collect some special things for my wedding.'

Light dawned. 'If I'm still here for your wedding, I'll give you something special, Arald, I promise, but for now, can I have my gnomon back please? It was a gift from my teacher and I promised him I would take great care of it.'

He fetched it and gave it back reluctantly, and I carried it with me everywhere after that. What I had not realised at the time was that this was not a boy's wistful hope for the future, but that the Greatmother did in fact have a plan for him.

I settled into a rhythm of life as an appendage to Uine and Don's household, eating with them, helping in their fields in spring and autumn, and gathering amber with Arald in all seasons. I found myself considered useful for my woodwork skills, which are nothing special, but I like to make joints, fit wood together neatly, and once I had acquired the necessary tools from an itinerant smith (who nearly agreed to take me with him when he left, but did not dare, in the end) I made various useful bits of furniture in my hut, and paid for my food in kind that way, which gained me a reputation as a competent, if not particularly talented, joiner. But Don always treated me with suspicion and Uine something closer to fear.

The moons waxed and waned and the seasons passed. It is strange how time slides by like that, once there is a rhythm to life. It is dangerous, I think, to fall into habits and routine. You think each day you are moving forwards, but in fact you can be walking on the spot.

My advice is, when you find yourself like that, stand still. Think hard. Look around and choose which direction to run away. Then take a deep breath one morning and sprint off at a tangent. Then your life will start again.

That's what happened to me.

THE WEDDING

Arald's 'wedding', it turned out, was a winter ceremony, equivalent to the one you probably know as Imbolc, after the winter solstice but before there is any sign of spring, when the dark cold has seeped into everyone's bones and the barrels are getting low.

Arald informed me excitedly the day before that the Great-mother had told him he had gathered his body weight in amber so now he could be married. I was intrigued who the woman would be that would get this skinny, gauche youth for her husband. As I had promised him, I gave him a gold coin and my leather belt with its fine bronze buckle, which he was most taken by.

The morning began with a feast. Everyone had been baking, it seemed, and there were cakes and pastries decorated with seeds, preserves of summer fruits, all kinds of delicacies that I wished we got to eat more often. Arald was given gifts of food by everyone in the village and was plied with mead, which normally he was not allowed, so he was soon incapable and stupid drunk. There was no sign of a girl, and I became increasingly perplexed, until Uine explained that he was to 'marry' Nerthus, the spring god-dess, and so I began to understand that this was all just symbolic. Still, in my limited experience of such 'marriages', there is usually a pretty girl to play the part of the deity and keep the rest of us entertained. So far she had not appeared.

After feasting, Arald was led away by the Greatmother to the Bear Hall. He reappeared after a while looking tear-stained and with a rip on his jerkin. Still, he looked relieved that his ordeal was over. I had wondered whether the Greatmother would bring her pet animals into play. She usually had a role for one or other in her ceremonies. The big bear still dominated every occasion it appeared in. It was fatter than ever now and the cub had grown into a big strong adult with no apparent fear of anything. They were a terrifying pair.

It was the younger bear that was brought forth to join the ceremony. It had a neck ring and the Greatmother pulled it by a chain. It followed the old woman obediently, trusting her. I think this trust was the source of much of the awe the crone managed to conjure from her people.

*

We all processed out along the track running east from the village up onto the heath. There were drums and whistles, and everyone was drunk enough to be in a lively mood, but not so much, except for Arald, to be stumbling. He had sobered up after his session in the Bear Hall, but was soon plied with mead again to reduce him to slurring, and now that the bear was on a chain he goaded her with a stick, trying to get her to dance, which she did, in a shambling way.

Out on the moor there were three pools. Into each, as she passed, the Greatmother threw a piece of jewellery as an offering to the Earth Mother. A silver earring went into the first, a string of amber beads into the second, and into the third she tossed a bronze neck ring with chevron markings, which glinted in the low-angled sun. I wondered at the wealth this woman could offer to the deities, then reflected on the value of Arald's body weight in amber, all of which I surmised had ended up in the Greatmother's hand. The occasional visits by traders must have enabled her to prepare for such ceremonies.

She showed Arald to a place where peat had been dug and piled up into a kind of altar. She made him kneel by it and then she used a stake to chain the bear nearby. She gathered the drummers and silenced those with whistles. A girl with a wooden flute began a heart-piercing melody over a slow drum beat. While they played, the Greatmother arranged various pots and bowls and lit a fire beside the peat stack, which I could see was acting as a windbreak as well as an altar. She spent a long time chanting and burning something. At first I couldn't see exactly what, but I shifted to get a better view. It was amber! The hard-won stone I slaved to gather was simply going up in smoke in her ceremony! I wondered how much of it she got through in this way. What god or goddess could possibly be pleased by such a waste?

She fed something to both the bear and Arald. It clearly made the bear docile and soon the boy seemed to be swaying in a kind of dream state.

Then the Greatmother said something to the flute-player and they brought the slow tune to an end, switching straight into a crowd-pleaser with a regular foot-stomping beat. Three men and three women stepped out of the crowd singing a song, not all the words of which I could make out but it was about a marriage of a man to a bear, and gradually it seemed to suggest that the bear was not satisfied by the man. I don't really know what nonsense was in it all, but the three men singing took hold of the bear, and the three women took hold of Arald and they pulled the two pliant creatures around into some very strange, lewd positions as they sang. Both the bear and the boy were floppy as dolls.

The song picked up its pace, with a regular 'yah'. Gradually everyone joined in a dance that involved side-to-side steps. On the 'yah', people turned to their side and slapped hands with the person next to them. I found myself alternately clapping with Uine and an old man, both of whom were a head shorter than me. I felt as if I was dancing with children and this and the mead made me feel altogether more joyful than I had for a long time. The sleepy bear and the drunken youth rolling about in mock sex perfected the sense of being at the craziest wedding ever. I laughed away at the silliness of it all.

Arald was now astride the bear and the three women dancers had tied rope around his upper arms and neck, controlling his movements like a puppet. The men had ropes too, around the legs and torsos of the bear and the boy. The dance they were doing was intricate, and the result was a plaiting together of the ropes, and as the tension rose and the song's 'yah's rang out, the ropes tugged and tugged until I saw Arald writhe up into an ecstatic climax. His eyes bulged. And then a final 'yah, yah, yah!' and a huge flourish on the drum and the men and women let go of their ropes and Arald fell back. I saw his face in a rictus, his tongue lolling and blue. He was strangled. He was dead.

*

The laughter froze on my face. I was suddenly in a nightmare. The drumming resumed and all around me the singing continued, faster now, a mad stomping dance that was more frenzy than fun. Arald was lifted away from the sleeping bear and I saw that the peat-pile was no altar at all, but simply the discards from the grave that had been dug and into which his body was now lowered, on those same ropes, his arms and legs dancing like a child's puppet.

I watched, horrified, as the Greatmother, beaming with satisfaction, leaned over the hole in the ground, sprinkling dried leaves and flowers over Arald's body, serene and slow among the manic dancing, as if she was the only person apart from me who realised he was dead.

All these people were strangers to me. How could they behave like this? Did they not realise they had killed the boy? How could they be so apparently blissful, so full of delight? My eyes were dragged back to the ghastly sight of the grave. That boy had been the closest I had to a friend here. I realised this was a kind of living hell and that I had never been anywhere so dangerous.

I felt a touch on my forearm. The Greatmother was beside me.

'He looks excited, doesn't he?'

'Terrified,' I said.

'No. It was ecstasy. There is no greater honour.'

As if honour could mean anything to him now.

'I have something for you.' She gave me a small cloth pouch. 'You are doing well here. Perhaps one day you too will have earned the role of Nerthus' consort. Keep collecting the amber.'

She passed on around the dancing crowd. I stuffed the pouch into a pocket and turned aside, nausea rising in me. I stepped away. My head was spinning. The drum was too loud, the people too crazy. The day was cold, colder than I could endure. I wanted to go home. I had to get away.

I started walking. A shudder. Shivering. A wailing sound that I realised was my own keening. I was sick into a bush, then pulled myself together, wiping the tears off my face, the snot out of my nose.

Where could I hide? Out there on the open heath, there was nowhere.

I glanced back to see if anyone was following me. What if they set the bear to chase me? I wanted to run away as fast as I could, but forced myself to stroll in case running would make pursuit more likely. I put distance behind me, and eventually reached the river valley that wound through woodland down to the coast. I kept walking, my pace increasing, trying to keep my breathing even. I began to compose myself, to think furiously of a plan, a way to escape.

When I arrived back at the village, it was deserted except for one old woman who smiled vacantly at me as she sat outside her hut, a rug over her legs, spindle whirling. I got my box from my hut, wondering how I might strap it to my back, regretting giving my belt to Arald. The thought of him put me in a panic. I thrust some tools in my writing-box. I thought about going to Don and Uine's place to get some bread but decided that would be stealing. I contrived a way of carrying the box on my back with rope and my fleece and bedding roll. It wasn't perfect but it was comfortable enough. I didn't know how far I would have to walk and this thought drove me to Don and Uine's hut. I could not survive without food. It was winter and I had no weapons for hunting other than my knife, not that I've ever been much of a hunter.

I took what I needed: a leather strap, which made my bundle much more comfortable on my back, their breadloaf, some nuts, dried fish and a chunk of cheese. I wrapped it all in a makeshift bag made with my leather sheet. I left a piece of gold tucked under a pillow to appease my conscience. I hoped they would not begrudge me what I needed to survive.

I thought I heard voices and sudden panic grabbed me. I rushed out. It was all quiet apart from the sea breaking on the beach and my heart hammering in my chest.

I avoided the hut where the old woman was sitting and took the path to the beach, then set off south, walking in the shallows to leave no footprints. I barely knew what lay beyond a half-day's walk but my fear of the unknown was dwarfed by the horror I had witnessed. How could I have stayed so long among people who were capable of such things?

Perhaps you think it's naïve of me to have such scruples when there are deaths in our temples too. Virgins propitiate gods. This is a reality, I know, but there are ways to do it that are civilised. I admit I've never watched how such sacrifice is practiced at Apollo's temple, for example, but that is precisely the point – there is no horde, no gang of drunken dancers singing along. Whatever happens at the temple, even when Dionysus is being offered sacrifices, is sure to be done with dignity. It is not a crazed crowd of barbarians engaged in collective slaughter. Or maybe, to someone who doesn't belong to our world, that is exactly what it would seem to be.

SOUTHWARDS

That was the beginning of the end of my journey, the turning-point. As I walked that morning I was, for the first time, aiming for home. I wanted to return to a land of vineyards and cultivation. I spoke to myself as I walked, relating the horrific event I had witnessed as if to an invisible audience of my peers at home, and I made a plan to keep moving. Once I was well out of danger of recapture by the Greatmother, and had properly understood the geography of this amber land, I would seek a boat to take me back to Albion. There I would go in search of Ussa, reclaim my tin or buy some more.

Perhaps I could also seek out Rian, and stake my claim as father of her baby, if she had in fact brought it to term. What if she had not survived the childbirth? I banished the thought; she was strong. Then, I suddenly came up with the idea of taking the child home with me. That is what I actually meant by 'staking my claim'. I would rescue my son from a barbarian fate and raise him as a Massaliot. I could take them both! I could make her my wife. It was a perfect fantasy. There could be no question that was the right thing to do.

All through the first day I kept looking back to see if I was being followed. I expected dogs, or even bears. I barely stopped, forcing myself onwards, keeping the sea on my right. Fear kept me going. When the path ran out, I pressed on. When I reached the river where we got the best results for amber seeking, I beat upstream to where I knew there was a fordable stretch and waded across the freezing water. I dried out again as I walked on.

The next river was harder; I lost my footing and almost had to abandon my bundle in the flow, but I was lucky and righted myself and found my way across in the end.

By evening, I reached territory that was new to me. I avoided a coastal village and the few houses along the way. I ate only enough to stop hunger from weakening me, and that night I barely slept, although I had to stop through the night hours as it was a new moon and too dark to see my way. I took shelter among dunes close enough to the sea to hear its rhythmic rush and draw. It retreated as the night progressed, the tide ebbing, then creeping back up. I woke to the sound of pebble-shuffling in the early morning when, after hours of worrying, I must eventually have slept.

The second day was grey. Under the low sky, I trudged, but began to recover my spirits. I did not know where I was going, but I was at least going somewhere new. I started to enjoy walking, and felt myself returning to myself as if I had been in a long dream, or under some kind of sleeping spell. I was awake at last, alert to the tracks of animals, the moods of the ocean, the scent of seaweed, the delicious taste of my meagre piece of cheese. And while I walked I dreamed of Rian, and my son.

By the third day I was getting seriously hungry, and my pace slowed. I slept badly.

On the fourth day I came to a large marshy estuary which posed a serious obstacle. I spent a whole day going around the delta, crossing dozens of streams, having to double back when the ground became too treacherous, terrified of bogging down in mud. I was glad the weather was clear. In fog I would have surely perished and I had to reach the far side before darkness, as I knew I would never survive out there on the marsh overnight. It was a land of ghouls and evil spirits, I was sure. I could see woodland and eventually reached a strange alder forest hung with lichens. It spooked me entirely, but I managed to find a dryish patch to spend the night. Fire was not an option. I had no way to light it even if I had been able to gather dry-enough wood.

The next day, the coast veered eastwards and I smelled smoke, then saw that I was approaching a village in a sheltered bay. The cloud was low, visibility poor. I hovered on the edge of an area of fields behind the settlement, then mustered my courage and headed down a muddy path towards where a few boats were hauled up on a beach.

So far I had avoided habitation, keeping out of view of people, but I was soaked and muddy. The cold was making me miserable and I had run out of food. I wanted to sleep somewhere under cover, even a barn would do, but I was longing to sit by a fire.

As I approached the village, two little children came running, stopped under a tree and stared at me, wide-eyed. I said hello and they giggled and ran away. The alien being could speak, they would tell their disbelieving mother. Would she be hospitable?

The first house was a ruin but the second had smoke and the two little faces were gazing out at me from its doorway.

'Hello again,' I said. 'Is your mother or father there?'

A woman appeared behind them. 'Who are you?' Her voice was shrill.

'Is there somewhere I can rest for the night?' I said.

'Who are you?' she insisted.

'My name is Pytheas.'

'What are you doing here?'

'I am journeying. I seek someone who can take me over the ocean. But now I'm cold and wet. I've been walking for days. I can give gold in exchange for hot food and a warm bed.'

These people were not hospitable by culture. She was suspicious of me, but gold works little miracles and I soon found myself steaming beside a fire with hot mead and a stew cooking. I can't describe how like a king I felt, wallowing in luxury. Hardships endured make you appreciate every simple comfort. After days out in the wet, a warm dry blanket is a thing of wonder.

I ate and slept, and in the morning I went down to the shore to ask people about boats and they told me they only took them out in fair weather to fish. One old man said that he had been on the ocean, and from his scratchings in the mud I got a sense of the coastline. We were on a peninsula, and to get further south I would need to walk a long way eastwards first, or get someone to take me across the water. He suggested I might find someone in the next village, where there was a safe harbour, which many ships used as storm shelter. I might find an ocean-going vessel there, perhaps.

FAIR EXCHANGE

Bolstered by this intelligence, full of food, dry and rested, I was in good spirits as I set off again. It was cold but dry, perfect for walking, although out in the open there was a wicked wind, buffeting and bitter. I followed a path along the shore. I was thinking of what I might find in the next village and dreaming of a harbour full of ships, when I was set upon.

There were two of them, big, blond-haired and armed. They blocked my path, and the biggest raised his weapon – an iron cudgel.

'Come now,' I said. 'Don't hurt me please. You can have anything.'

'What?' The thug with raised weapon frowned, as if this was not the response he had expected.

'How much gold is my life worth?'

'Give him the bundle.'

I let my gnomon fall, unslung the fleece-wrapped box from my back. Slowly. Trying not to make any rapid movement.

'I'd be grateful if you would lower your weapon,' I said. 'I'm unarmed. It's hard for me to stay calm with the threat of your cudgel. Please.'

The big man didn't change position. I placed the box on the ground, loosened the leather strap, unwrapped the fleece and stepped back, out of immediate range of injury.

The lesser giant of the two, who seemed to have some authority over the other, bent down and opened the box. He looked at his colleague and grinned. The cudgel was lowered.

'I'm grateful.' I unfastened my leather pouch from my waist and held it out. 'My gold. Help yourself.'

The thug grabbed it and took out a handful of coins for scrutiny. His boss was rummaging in the box, lifting out tools. My case of writing equipment clearly baffled him.

'I need those for writing.' This did not seem to clarify. 'Look at the codex. The square thing.'

He took out my book.

'Open it.'

He did, and wrinkled his brow at the first page, my attempt to create a map of the coastline north from the Garonne.

'This is the coast of Gaul. This is the river Garonne.' I crouched down and reached towards the picture, stroking the lines. 'This is the sea. My journey took me north up there. That is the island of Albion. To the east of there is the North Sea. There is a vast ocean out there. And this is here, whereas that land is many days' sail from here. I need this to find my way home.'

He was looking at me with curiosity. Either because what I was saying was of real interest or because I was confirming myself as a madman, the like of which he had never met before.

I shuffled closer, and reached into the chest for my quill. He tried to stop me touching the tools, as if I was going to arm myself, but could barely repress a grin when he saw that what I was holding was a feather. I mimed dipping it in ink and writing onto the parchment. I think he saw then how I conjured the marks, perhaps only then realised that I had made the diagrams.

I took my courage in both hands, prised the codex from him, laid my quill across it in an act of closure hoping it would protect the contents it had helped me create and set it on the ground beside me. Then I reached into the box, lifted out my sheathed whittling knife and handed it to him, as I would in a ceremony, handle towards him. He could not refuse it, and had to receive it with grace. I pointed out how the safety hasp worked, and he ran his finger appreciatively along the blade. He whistled softly, and said nothing, but when I glanced up into his face, his blue eyes were clear and bright above a provocative smile.

I wasn't quite clear what the next move in the game should be, but a chisel came to hand and he took it with a nod. Then the small adze.

'What's he got?' The thug barely took his eyes from the coins, which he was sorting.

'Carpentry tools.' His boss's voice was deadpan, but his raised eyebrows made it clear we both knew I had handed him three lethal weapons and my act of bravery was a calculated risk that was paying off.

The next objects I removed from the box were my other writing tools. My pen knife was first. 'I need this for preparing the quill,' I said, 'and this is my ink box and block for making the liquid for writing, and I use this needle and thread for sealing parchment sheets.' They were little, delicate objects compared to the weaponry I had given away. My captor lifted his left shoulder in a permissive shrug.

Bread came out next, which he took, tore a bit off to chew, ripped the rest in half, passed one piece to his friend and gave me back the rest. He was genuinely smiling now. The game was on.

A small hammer and some iron nails tied together with twine interested him and I saw, in the neat way he was lining the tools up, that he would take these objects away and make something with them. Anyone passing by would have thought, from our civilised dialogue, that we were friends making an exchange of goods of mutual interest.

My spare shirt? This almost brought the two of them to blows over who should have it, until socks were able to trump it. The boss man took them with glee, leaving the thug with the shirt. Then, lying at the bottom of the box was a tin ingot. My heart sank when I got it out and saw both men realise exactly what it was. Only they could not possibly understand its significance to me.

'I need this,' I said.

They shook their heads.

'Give him back his shirt,' Boss said.

'For that?'

'Yes.'

Thug proffered my shirt and tried to take the ingot from me.

'No, I need it.' It was heavy in my hand. It was all I had to show for my discovery of Belerion and the tin mine. In this ingot was my purpose. It was a symbol that I had reached a certain destination. It was my proof of the metal's origin. I thought of Og's uncle and prayed to the Goddess Artemis to let me keep this ingot. I gave her permission to let Ussa do whatever she would do with the stash I had left on her boat, if only this one last piece could remain in my possession.

She did not listen, or if she did, she either ignored me or had some wiser view. Again, on reflection, it was the latter. She is a goddess. She was sending me to you.

My ingot was prised from my hands by Thug. As soon as Boss started to pull my knife from its scabbard I relented. You may call me a coward if you wish. I don't think it is brave to die in the hands of robbers. It is braver to find a way to live on, knowing what we know.

My box was soon empty. After the ingot, there was nothing of value or interest. The box itself I managed to retain, for which I will be eternally grateful. It is watertight, more or less. It kept my manuscript dry and survived the whole of my journey.

There is a box inside each of us that is similar to this casket. No matter what is looted from it, if we can keep it sound, it is possible for us to journey on. If our inner casket is broken, we are doomed. I know it is possible to break it, and my own came close. The Greatmother tried her best to ruin it, but she failed. I am one of the lucky ones. I carry my inner space intact. I wish to be buried with it.

I tried to put a brave face on my loss. 'Well, at least my luggage is much lighter to carry now,' I said. Especially without that heavy lump of tin. I missed its weight already, its comforting heft of quest fulfilled. I packed the meagre objects I retained back in my box and wrapped my fleece around it as the two men secreted their takings about their persons, in folds and pockets. I refitted the strap and slung my bundle on my back. It weighed nothing.

'I'll continue on my way,' I said.

They seemed abashed now, and it was left to me to try to keep things civil. I was also suddenly more frightened than ever that they might kill me now, even after I had bought my life. They might steal it anyway, because they could, so there would be no witness of their thieving. I could see the thought in Thug's eyes, but Boss was my saviour.

'Fuck off now where you belong,' he said, handing me back my gnomon.

I was grateful for his churlishness and knew if I said anything at all I could be dead.

I fled.

They did not follow.

I don't know why it happened, but I guess the word had got around that I had gold. Perhaps the real surprise is that it didn't happen sooner. I have wondered since then if I colluded in my own robbery, but I know that what they were really giving in exchange for my gold, my tin and my woodwork tools, was clemency. We all three knew that they could, if they wanted, take my life as well as all my possessions, without discretion, but they were choosing not to. Our discussion was one of real fundamentals. What is the value of a life? What is the value of a written story, of the ability of a chronicler to make the marks on a page that, scratch by scratch, amount to a timeless thing, a document that can transcend time? What is the value of a journey, an adventure that needs to be completed in order to achieve its possible worth, a circle that needs to be closed?

For a long time I considered it to be one of the worst experiences of my journey, but I've come to realise that, in a strange way, the mugging led me to discover you, so I look back on it now with something close to fondness. Memory is a strange thing.

THE BOULE

Have I told you yet about the amber bear? I have had it in my pocket for most of today and now it is out again, on my writing desk, catching the sun.

This morning it was the meeting of the Boule, of which I am no longer a member, and I was asked to give my views on their plans for extending the harbour. I was up early and took care dressing, in order to seem the statesman and authority this required me to be. It felt rather like play-acting and yet, once the proceedings began I realised that I do know enough to advise them, and I have strong views on the matter. I have seen a great many ports and harbours over these years.

The local fishermen have been arguing for years that the space given for the triremes is unfair and it is unreasonable that they should be squeezed out of the boatyard at the only time it is feasible for them to take their vessels out of the water for maintenance. Winter is a poor time for fishing but we all expect to eat fish for the spring festivals. We depend on the fisher folk for our sustenance just as much as we do the triremes for our security. So I argued on behalf of the small boats, not for their own sakes but in terms of the year-round business they support around the harbour, the trades they keep alive with their needs for tackle and repairs, the guidance they provide to visiting merchants through their knowledge of the waters, the navigation lore they possess and refine and transmit. I concluded by talking of the role they play in our security by acting as the early warning system of untoward activity in our waters and the ability to help rescue people if a calamity happens at sea. My arguments won the day. I shall be made most welcome down at the harbour next time I go for a stroll around the boats.

I was introduced as Pytheas, the great explorer and seafarer. My father would have been proud, and how I wish there had been someone watching who could carry the story on within my own family, just as the navigation lore is passed down the generations of fisher folk. Instead I set it down here, on this scroll, the periplus of my life.

On the way back from the Boule, I stopped at the Artemis temple to pay my respects to the priestesses, which the amber bear reminded me I should visit. I took them honey and wine, and they were delighted to receive me. One of them is pretty, with an auburn tinge to her hair, and she of course conjured Rian in my mind. But the priestess's eyes were brown, with none of the brightness of those I loved, which were the colour of shallow sun-drenched seawater over silver sand.

The amber bear was in the tiny cloth bag the Greatmother thrust at me when the boy Arald was murdered in that so-called wedding ceremony. I sometimes miss his awkward company even now. How few friends we have in life who make only demands we can meet and who are happy to spend time quietly together with us, not interrupting our thoughts, engaged in some quiet mutual work that is, on the one hand, not too mentally demanding yet, on the other hand, rewarding. Such is the search for amber, and such was Arald's company, also gilded by memory, perhaps. Anyway, the amber bear was the Greatmother's gift to me, the symbol of having been chosen for the great 'honour' of being the next to be slaughtered, and I thank Artemis for my escape, always. It is small enough to perch upon my thumbnail. There, I am doing it now. Can you picture it? Its legs are foreshortened, its head is raised as if it is looking up and out, perpetually attentive. Which I was not.

In my rush to escape the horror, I never opened the cloth pouch until I was hours away from the village. When I saw its contents I almost threw it away because of what I knew it represented, but such workmanship as could create this tiny icon has always fascinated me. Out of respect for its maker, whoever that was, I kept it, but its death-warrant caused me to bury it deep in the inner pocket of my jerkin where I would not bump into it by accident and give myself a fit of the horrors. So it was that my burglars did not find it. I will always be thankful, for three reasons: because it means I could return home with it, as proof, at least to myself, that I had been to the amber land; because the thieves would have stolen it without doubt; and because if they had found it they would most likely have known what destiny had been marked out for me and might well, out of some religious respect or chance for a further reward, have returned me to the murderous crone who gave it to me.

Anyway, there it is, my keepsake now, which I can watch glowing in the sunshine by the window. It symbolises my life, my escape from the clutches of evil, my safe passage home. It marks, perhaps, my transition from youthful adventurer to experienced middle age. It carries my memories, happy and sad. All of this. And if you have read this far, I hope it now explains a little mystery to you, and I hope that the sun will glow through the amber bear to you, because I shall enclose it with this document in my old travel box and direct it to you, once the story I have to tell you is complete.

IVORY

HOMEWARDS

THE DAWN

It is easier than you might imagine to travel across the world with nothing. Perhaps nothing is the wrong word. I had my health, I spoke several languages, I had experience of boats and many different waters. Once I was at the nearest harbour I simply insisted on getting on board the boat going furthest away. I offered myself, my labour, my company, and was accepted. At the next place I did it again. I ate what I was offered. I talked, I asked questions, I was given answers, I pulled on ropes and hauled on anchors with men stronger than me who nonetheless valued my skinny shoulders and my willingness. I learned new words for knots and tackle. I watched keenly. I made myself competent, and each day found a new way to be useful. By these means I travelled south, seeking always a trader heading west across the North Sea to Albion.

I was introduced to him by a pilot who guided the boat I was on through an archipelago full of dangerous shoals and shallows. She wore her knowledge lightly, but all the crew, and the skipper too, were awed by how she understood what was underwater.

She was a small woman, with straight brown hair, a flat round face with big eyes and a broad forehead, a wide mouth with thin lips that didn't smile often. She had a wistful air about her, as if she had known too many drowned souls. One of the crew said that they had heard she had been drowned herself and had returned to earth to prevent others from meeting the same end in the whirlpools and shallows of these dangerous waters. This sea-nymph called herself Cara.

At our destination, a bay with plenty of shallow water for safe mooring, Cara pointed out a ship to me. 'This one will cross the ocean,' she said. When our boat was safe at anchor, Cara whistled to a boy in a coracle who paddled over. She purloined the craft and ferried the two of us over to the ship where she delivered me into the care of an old sea dog named Gurt. Because Cara recommended me, he welcomed me aboard his boat, and made me one of his crew. He slung a rope ladder over the side and I clambered up the wooden rungs onto the big vessel.

Gurt was master of a crew of eighteen men. He would not allow Cara on board because, he said, any female was bad luck, but he spent a long time leaning over the gunnels talking with her down in her bobbing coracle. I guessed they were lovers, if they were ever on land together, but that is only my imagination. How else can I explain his long body hanging half out of the boat and her upturned face, like the sun and moon both in the sky, but never, really, together.

Gurt was a good man. He called his ship *The Dawn* because it rises in the east, crosses the ocean and delivers amber treasures on the western shore. It was a strong boat of pine and lime planking. As well as amber he was carrying a cargo of valuable goods, including animal skins, rolls of fine silk cloth from far to the east, and metalwork.

There were about a dozen other men on board, some whipping ropes onto shackles, others stitching a big sail, everyone busy. I was told all of their names and forgot them immediately because they were sea animals. Most of the crew members were called after a seabird and each had a specific role. This way the master didn't need to know his crew's real names and their lack of history was clearly useful for some of us, for whom anonymity was helpful.

'You will be Tern,' Gurt said to me. 'You're not as strong as Glaucus and Black-back, Eagle and Bonxie, and you have travelled far. You can row with Petrel. He's roughly your build.'

A young man, tall and scrawny, made me realise how thin I had become.

'Is that all you have for clothes?' My wolfskin coat that I had been proud to buy was so shabby these days it no longer counted as good seafaring gear. My boots were still just about functional. My leggings were ripped and filthy. I nodded. 'I have a fleece, and this.' I showed him my hide sheet.

He smiled at me with what I saw as pity, and shouted, 'Dolphin!'

A bald, chubby man appeared out from under the shelter at the bow and strolled towards us. This was a huge boat, I realised, almost as long as a fighting trireme, with a tall mast.

'This is the new Tern. Fit him up for sea if you can.' He turned to me. 'Dolphin will look after you. He's in charge, as far as you're concerned. Mind you do everything he says and Seal will fill your plate well. You look like you could do with some second helpings.' Seal, I gathered from this, was the cook. It was like being part of a child's story.

Gurt ambled away and leaned over the side strakes to talk with Cara, calling Minke over to join him.

'Minke navigates.' Dolphin had a smile of such a relaxed nature I could not help returning it. 'I'd trust him anywhere. Let's get you kitted out.'

From a big chest he pulled out a thick gansey, a fine pair of sealskin trousers, a hat and mittens. 'That coat'll do a few seasons yet. Wolf.' He stroked it, and nodded sagely, as if this told him something important about me. 'You and it have both seen better days, I take it.'

I knew I'd be happy on this boat, and I was. Gurt was a fine leader. He had eighteen crewmembers: Dolphin second-in-command, Minke navigating, and Seal in the galley with Dogfish and Catfish. Octopus kept the boat in order, repairing bust shackles, stuffing caulking between the pine planks of the hull if any leaks appeared, checking the rigging whenever we sailed, fixing tackle, oiling oars. Then there were the twelve seabirds, who rowed and pulled on ropes to hoist the sails and obeyed any other orders we were given. We were paired for rowing: myself, the Tern, with Petrel; Eagle with Bonxie, both bruisers; Black-back and Glaucus, the gulls, who were actually brothers, big gentle giants and almost identically blond, blue-eyed and gormless; Kittiwake and Guillemot, small, dark, endlessly chatty; Gannet and Cormorant, one silently dour, the other argumentative; Puffin and Shearwater, the youngest of us all, with barely a beard between them but plenty of fun. The ship's cat was called Lobster. It sounds like a joke, but in fact it had serious value. In the role of Tern, I had found a place where, at least temporarily, I was welcome. It brought me back to myself and healed me of some of the trauma of life under the Greatmother's tyranny.

After getting me dressed for sea, and giving me a sleeping roll, Dolphin showed me my bench, where I would sleep and row and under which I could stow my few belongings. He was curious about my box; it was his business to know as much about me as he could, and he was nosy in a kindly way so I showed him what it contained. If he was impressed by my writing he did not show it then, but I found out later he made sure Gurt knew about it.

Each of us had our space on board. The tiny area under my bench was my own domain and it was strictly forbidden to go under anyone else's bench without their express permission. This right, and the right to be left in peace (by anyone except Dolphin or Gurt) if you had your back turned or your eyes closed, gave us a freedom, a space to be ourselves, that made the ship a kingdom of consenting adults, despite our childish names. We worked together out of respect. It made me wonder, and I had many hours and days ahead of me to wonder in, whether such harmonious teams of free men are the future, an alternative to slaves and discipline, or whether it was a fluke, an anomaly. Whichever, if emperors and senators were more like the honourable Gurt, I feel sure the world would be a more peaceful place.

Once he had shown me my spot, Dolphin took me to meet Seal – a grey, whiskery, twinkly-eyed man who gave me a floury handshake and a piece of warm, sweet bread. 'Gurt says you must feed him up,' said Dolphin. Seal cut two more slices, one for me and one for my amiable boss.

I was then put in the safekeeping of Petrel, who was carefully whipping a rope, winding a thin sinew around a loop in the bitter end to join it to a shackle. Dolphin's last words were, 'Help him get ready for the Var,' before he went off to join Gurt and Minke in their deliberations with Cara. I presume they were planning our route out through the channels between the islands we had navigated among to get here. I wished I could listen in on their conversation.

'What's the Var?' I asked Petrel.

'Vow of allegiance with the crew, obedience to Gurt, safety on the boat, all of that. Isn't this beautiful rope?' He lifted a length and let it slide through his fingers as if it was a lock of his lover's hair. 'We've all got new sheets for this trip, and this is quality.' He returned to whipping, tugging the sinew tight with each turn around the rope.

'Where are you from?' I asked him.

He looked at me with languid brown eyes. Everything else about him was pale, I realised, except his dark, dark eyes. 'I'm not from anywhere. I'm from everywhere. I've been wandering too long to remember and I no longer care.'

There was something so utterly sad in the thought of this, I was caught off-guard and nearly choked, but before the emotion could take me he said, 'But I'm here now.' It was as if 'here now' was some kind of comforting home, a safe destination.

'It's where we are going to that matters,' a voice said, 'not where we're from.'

I looked up at Gurt. He had taken up a position of observation, feet apart, back against the mast, watching the work of his crew. 'I don't care where you're from, it doesn't matter on board this ship. It's always a new day on *The Dawn*.' It sounded better the way he said it in their tongue, like saying, 'Dawn always brings a new day' or something. Anyway, that was Gurt.

At sunset I swore myself to work with the rest of the crew and, kneeling before Gurt, promised to obey his commands at sea. He handed me the end of a rope, and I wrapped it round my waist and tied a bowline in it, and he gave me a hug and tot of ale and thanked me for the Var.

I loved being on that ship. We were happy together. I travelled on it for two years, and all that I know of the amber trade I learned as part of Gurt's crew. I didn't often get ashore to take measurements with my gnomon, but I kept a record of our movements, and long conversations with Minke enabled me to build up a good sense of the geography of those northern lands. We sailed east from the amber coast into an enclosed sea, Baltica, in which there were many islands, on one of which, Abalus, the amber supplies were truly prodigious, suggesting that this place was perhaps the true origin of all the amber that washed up on beaches around the region. The market there was dominated entirely by the orange gem, as if there was nothing else worth buying in the world. I wished I still had my leather pouch of gold coins. I could have brought back some real treasure.

There was only one occasion – when we had sailed up a wide river that flowed north out of the plains and I met a trader who convinced me he plied a land-route to Athens trading amber for silver – that I was tempted to jump ship and make my way over land to home. But the pull of Albion was stronger. I still had nothing to show for my discoveries of the source of tin there, nor the source of the northern ivory, and there was the ever-tantalising prospect of seeing Rian again, discovering my own son and taking them into my future life, so I remained with Gurt and his promise of a crossing of the North Sea.

At the end of one year, Gurt gave me a piece of walrus tusk as payment for my hard work on his ship. I don't think he realised its significance to me, but perhaps I had once complained while he was listening that I had failed to get any proof of the existence of walrus while I was in the far north. While we travelled, I whittled at the ivory and shaped it into a little dolphin. It was partly a joke, because I had become so fond of the man who had that name, but also partly a serious nod of thanks to Apollo who had kept me safe for so long.

Eventually, we set out on the journey that earned his boat its name. West, following the sun.

SAILING

We embarked in the early morning, of course. There was a light breeze, so we upped anchor and raised *The Dawn*'s sails with a song and were under way without needing to put a hand to our oars. There were so many crew members that once the sails were up it was light work, and I could sit and watch the islands as we slid past them, navigating the complex channels, the tides always in our favour.

The boat pitched and rolled a bit as we approached the open sea, the waves driving in at a different angle from the breeze. At the tiller, Gurt smiled, holding the boat as close to the wind as he could. The further we went the wilder and more barren the islands became, brown heather clinging to the rocks. Gulls soared and swung, and the sea hushed, frothing off the hull. The rhythm of the waves rolling under us lulled me into a trance-like joy.

I was interrupted by Seal proffering a honey-cake. 'Last bite before the open ocean,' he said.

It was delicious.

The wind seemed steady and our course was straight. Once the last island was behind us there was just water, the satin surface ruched and crumpling but not breaking except where it hit our vessel. Bubbles rose to the surface sometimes and I imagined what life might be teeming below. A few optimistic fishing lines were out, but nothing was biting. Our wake hissed and fizzed behind us.

What joy it was to be back on the ocean! I found myself mesmerised by the grey patterns of the sea; an endless complexity of jabbled texture, yet at the same time perfect simplicity. Surface – horizon – sky. There was both nothing to see and everything to look at: my head filled with light and ripples. A breeze sang in the sail and water chuckled past.

I know of nothing better for the soul, no more fulfilling way to fill up a slice of a person's lifetime than a long sea voyage. Have you ever been on one? I am sure you must have. And if you have, do you agree? If you have not, please try to find a way to do so.

On the ocean, time and space redefine themselves forever. The open eye of the sea gazes back as you stare into it, and it is an eye so huge and wise that it leaves the soul blessed by the presence of a bigger life-force than one's own. I do not believe it is a god, though some believe it is. Perhaps I am wrong. I am prepared to believe some deity rules over it and I call him Apollo, perhaps in ignorance, and make libations to him in the hope of safety in return. Whatever it is, god, spirit, living being, or simply water body, it is bigger, so much more enormous, than we can comprehend. We merely skate over it, like a fly on a cow's hide, but far smaller than that. I can conceive of no possible comparison. There is nothing quite like realising what an insignificant little scattering of dust we are in our transit between the womb and the soil, enjoying or wasting our brief moment, our pathetically short burst of being. A sea journey shows us this by its presentation of a spatial scale otherwise beyond imagination. Each moment becomes both valuable and unimportant, precious and beautiful, but not clutchable – a gift given freely to be handed on.

At the start, I always find myself staring out, wanting to witness everything: the passage out from land; the quality of light; the sounds and smells of the waves; the visits by sea creatures, birds and dolphins that seem to take pride in escorting us out into their domain. Then, as the days pass, I reach a dissolution of that desire. I cease to want anything. I stop looking and simply see. Being on watch helps. You must scan the horizon for boats, for life, for land, for anything untoward, anything that provides relief from nothing. When it is over, when the hand on your shoulder allows you to end the search, then eyes and mind can cease striving and let the rolling motion of the surface hypnotise. That is when peace wells up like darkness, oozing up out of an animal core, and with it a kind of bonding happens with the great motherly expanse. Whatever 'I' is ceases to matter.

During a sea voyage the camaraderie of those on board becomes so strong you would not believe it. Jokes become funnier, emotion is honed to its truthful core, dear friendships are made. It is as if the depth of the water below us gives us space to deepen into. I would say it is best to be part of the crew, rather than just a passenger, but even as a passenger, if you have the attitude, you can become one with the boat. The crew will welcome your interest and friendship. Each of us can find our place there, if we will.

There is a warning necessary also, because if you cannot find a place on board, if your will is such that it demands to be loose, or perhaps if in the past there is something that makes constraint a torment to you, then a boat voyage may be a kind of torture, or even dangerous. I would still say try it and discover for yourself whether you can expand into the vastness of the ocean and the sky and revel in their empty and infinite possibilities, while inhabiting the paradox of confinement and close quarters. You will find out if you too can revel in the joy of being small in this enormous universe.

So it is to be upon the ocean. In my book of that title, ironically, I wrote nothing of this, and yet it is what I feel is most fundamental about voyaging on the sea. It was while thinking these things that I completed whittling the dolphin from the piece of walrus ivory. I hope you like it.

ALBION

TRADING

My time as crew with Gurt was the penultimate stage of my voyage. When we landed on the shore of Albion I did not know what would happen next but I was sure I did not want to return to the amber coast on *The Dawn*. I was headed west, then south.

We sailed into a wide river mouth full of boat and ship activity and we hailed a small vessel and asked advice, naming some people Gurt knew. We were directed to a landing beach where our ship's master disembarked, taking Eagle and Bonxie with him, from which I deduced he might not be expecting a completely warm welcome, or simply did not know what kind of reception to expect.

We pulled off from the shore a bit, lounged and enjoyed the sights and sounds of the river traffic, and were soon engaged in banter with people in little boats, curious about our huge vessel. My knowledge of Keltic kept me at the heart of these exchanges and I saw Dolphin's attention on me often. I was being assessed for some role.

Sure enough, when Gurt came back on board a few hours later, I found myself enlisted as a kind of trade broker. Dolphin had the idea that I could draw up a document, listing all the goods they had for barter and noting down the agreed exchanges as they happened. I had little parchment left but readily agreed. The best way of acquiring new writing material is to use what you have in public. Other writers make themselves known and we understand each other's needs.

We slept on board, and the next morning we returned to the beach and began unloading our cargo. I sat on a nearby rock and wrote the list of goods. It was mostly skins, precious stones, mainly amber, and some silver objects, hideous engraved things I wouldn't choose to own even though I am now rich enough to be able to. Dolphin showed me a cup and we both grimaced and laughed.

When Gurt was ready I headed off with him, while Eagle, Bonxie and the Gulls carried bundles and boxes over to a large wooden roundhouse with a wide doorway. Inside, a fire was blazing and there was the smell of freshly baked bread. The floor was made of oak and the wooden benches around the walls shone. The whole place was spotless and welcoming. There were fleeces to sit on and a beautiful young woman in a fine red gown offered us warmed honey-ale from a vat beside the fire. She had dark hair and pale skin and reminded me of Ussa by the way she turned her eyes on men, flicking them away, then looking back, scanning up and down our bodies as if sizing us up for consumption. I wondered what Ussa was doing now that she only had one eye, and what she had done with my tin. I knew it would be long gone, but you always retain a glimmer of hope, don't you?

After we had settled ourselves, the King and Queen made their appearance. I don't suppose they were really monarchs, and no doubt they paid homage to someone, but they were the powerful people of the area. They were both dripping with gold jewellery: she had hoop earrings, a huge and elaborate neckpiece with colourful beads strung among golden chain-work, and bangles and ankle bracelets that tinkled as she walked. Her embroidered dress made the young woman look positively plainly robed, but all the more beautiful by contrast with the wobbling jowls and glassy eyes of her superior. The man was also decked out in style, clothed in fine leather and fur, with a gold torc around his neck and ugly rings on both hands, like weaponry.

Gurt instructed his goods to be laid out and I have to say Eagle did a fine job of making a ceremony of it, unfurling each skin so it glistened in the firelight, highlighting the colours and textures special to each pelt, laying out the smaller goods with reverence and arranging them to complement each other. With this treatment our cargo suddenly seemed like treasure.

Gurt talked about the value of the goods. I followed instructions to record the deal. My presence, with my quill and parchment, which both Eagle and Gurt used to punctuate the performance, seemed to impress the King. Writing was not something he was familiar with, he said, and he came and pored over my work, not daring to touch the parchment, as if it were magical. I wondered what they had been told about this art of mine before I had been brought into this role. The Queen looked on, nodding and smiling.

Then our hosts clicked their fingers and gave instructions to the young woman, who served us biscuits and buttered bread rolls. Meanwhile the Queen opened the hasp of a big wooden chest and began taking out metal work, handing it over to Gurt and Eagle. The King encouraged all of us to look at the pieces. They were mostly weapons: daggers, axes and spikes.

'This is some of the local smith's work,' the King said. 'I know it's nothing much really, compared with the likes of amber, but it's handy enough.' This was a different kind of performance, one of deprecating modesty on the surface. But the weaponry was sharp and cruel, and spoke for itself.

A second chest of objects was presented containing utensils

for cooking and tools for farming. The king lifted one piece out. 'Look here, this is a handy thing, it's a tripod for holding the pot over the fire, lets you get it right where the heat is.' They were well-made of good quality iron, anyone could see that, but it was hard to see why anyone would cross an ocean for such goods.

Gurt showed polite interest but our hosts could see he was not impressed, so they opened a third chest. Everything in it was wrapped in deep green felt and the commentary stopped as the pieces began to circulate.

'Who makes these?' Gurt asked, holding open a silver locket on a fine chain.

'We have some good metal workers,' was all the King offered.

Something about the way he said it made me deduce that it was stolen, and when he made a quiet mention that if we were seeking slaves this also could be arranged, I sensed a frisson of violence and saw that under his gracious exterior there was a warrior who went on raiding parties.

A brooch was passed to me, which had evinced whistles from everyone who looked at it first, and, not for the first time since my mugging, I wished I had my bag of gold coins and could join in the trading. It was an exquisite thing: a silver plait-work decorated with chevrons and dots. I passed it to Gannet next to me, who shook his head with indifference, and passed it nonchalantly back to the young woman. I wanted to grab it back, and kiss or stroke it, to pay it the deference such work deserved.

Just then a noise outside was followed by shouts and a hammering on the door. A hairy man burst in. 'This is the trading house, I take it,' he slurred. 'Show us what you've got, we'll have the lot. We've brung the tin you asked for, and we're leaving as soon as you've given us what it's worth.'

There were two men behind him. Silhouetted in the light, I couldn't make out anything about them except their bulk, but one of them called 'Pytheas', and dodged in front of the hairy man. As he bore down on me, I realised it was Og.

'How are you?' He slung his arm around my shoulder. He was clearly drunk, and his boisterous entrance had put the King on alert. If I were him, I would think he was under attack. Our civilised process of exchange seemed to be degenerating into a skirmish.

'I'm well,' I said as gently as I could. 'Sit down, Og. We were just in the middle of looking at these fine things. This is Gurt.' I pointed to the skipper, who was asking, 'What's going on?' with his eyes. 'I came from the amber coast as part of his crew. This is Og, who I sailed with for many months on a trading ship north from Belerion, up the west coast of Alba.'

'I was a slave then, but I'm a free man now,' Og said.

Everyone's eyes were on us and there was some alarm in most of them. 'I'm sorry we're disturbing everyone,' I said. 'We've not seen each other for a long time. It's unexpected.'

'Where did you sail to?' the King asked, coolly.

'Up to the north of Albion to the Seal Islands, north again to the Cat Isles and north again to Thule, into the frozen sea.'

'In whose boat?'

'Ussa, she is called.'

The King gave the merest lift of his eyebrows. 'The woman with the white bearskin coat?'

'That's the one.'

'Bitch,' said Og. 'Slaving bitch.'

The King stared at him. His hand was on the handle of the short sword slung across his hips, and he had positioned himself so his wife was behind him. The young woman was standing with a fixed smile on her face but she had taken at least one step away towards the King.

'If you've done blethering, I've brought the tin,' the man in the doorway said. 'Do you want it or not?'

'Can you come back later?' the King said.

'I cannot. I've got a tide to catch. I can sail on with it or you can give me what it's worth and we can get on.'

'I'm not used to such haste.' The King smiled at Gurt. 'I do hope you'll excuse this confusion. Perhaps you might also be interested in some tin? Bly, come on in, have a seat, let's do this in a civil manner. And your men, there's a bench here, and here.' He swung around to the young woman. 'Give them some ale. Settle yourselves, gentlemen.' His command was regained and he soon had the newcomers under control and a deal began to be formulated.

'Tin, is it?' Gurt was genuinely interested, weighing an ingot in his hands. He was trying, rather unsuccessfully, to look nonchalant; his desire for the metal betrayed itself in the way his fingers touched the shining surface as if expecting a charge from it. He tried to make the ingot seem light, but the density of tin makes that impossible.

I found an ingot passed to me and I put it to my ear as I'd been taught. It did not crackle. I shook my head. 'Are there others?' I asked.

Og was laughing. 'You can't fool this one, Bly. He's an expert.'

Now Bly was frowning, and Gurt was scratching his head, eyebrows raised. The King was standing back with his hands on his hips, watching us all as if observing a minstrel's play.

The second ingot crackled, as did the third. The fourth did not. I saw Og and Bly exchange looks. Then the fifth, sixth, seventh and eighth sounded true.

'I'll take this up with my supplier,' Bly blustered. It looked as if a ruse to fob the King off with fake or low-grade tin had just failed to come off.

But when it became clear how keen Gurt was to get his hands on the good ingots, and Bly realised what quality of skins we were carrying, the trade became jolly again.

There was a moment when Gurt seemed so enthusiastic about swapping furs for tin that the King realised he was in danger of being left with neither tin nor good quality furs, and he waded in with his silverwork to secure himself some bear and wolverine pelts. Gurt added the silver to his pile of winnings and grinned, rubbing his hands on his thighs. 'Have you got this all written down, Tern?'

I hadn't, but I got to work with my quill, checking off the list of what we'd brought, noting down the deals struck so far. I was kept busy, evaluating tin for Gurt, explaining the wonders and rarities of the amber pieces to Og, Bly and the King and Queen, and making notes of every agreed stage of the exchange. There was a risk of it all breaking down at one point, when Bly wanted more than a bear pelt in exchange for an ingot, when one had been happily swapped for a wolf pelt earlier. I knew there was a real risk that my tidy record would degenerate into crossings-outs, but instead I found myself a surprising ally.

The Queen, who intervened in the dispute, pointed to my record and said, 'A wolf pelt was exchanged earlier for an ingot of tin, isn't that right?'

I nodded. I didn't think she could possibly read my Greek script, but it didn't matter. She knew that the written word had an authority that she could invoke. I put my finger on the note of that transaction and read it out.

'One pelt, wolf, one tin ingot.'

'Therefore…' All eyes were on the woman, magnificent in her embroidered robe. 'A bear skin, both larger and warmer than a wolf skin, cannot be worth less than one ingot as well. It's quite simple. Would you like more ale, gentlemen?'

They ate out of her hands. All the remaining goods were exchanged. Several of the pelts that had gone to Bly ended up with the King, swapped for iron work in which Gurt was so completely uninterested. Our amber pieces were all traded for fine jewellery and weapons. Gurt nodded contentedly as I completed my list and accepted a bronze cup of ale, his first, I noticed. I happily let my cup be refilled.

Bly was no longer in such a hurry to depart. His small chest of tin had been replaced with what, as far as I was concerned, was a large quantity of low-grade ironmongery and a fair few animal skins. It had bulk, for sure. It would take up more of his ship. But that was all I could say for it at that point. I was wrong, of course, as I am so often wrong. He no doubt had a perfectly good reason to think himself lucky in his transaction. There is something in this trade of goods that I have never really mastered, how worthless things gain value and clever people become wealthy and powerful by simply taking something one person does not want and selling it to someone who does. When I set out on my journey my goal was to become rich this way. I was going to turn my gold into amber, tin and ivory and return to make my fortune (while having gained some knowledge and adventures along the way) but after all I had been through I no longer felt that way. Apart from Gurt, all the traders I met were greed-driven zealots. I didn't have it in me to be like that.

Bly's relaxed acceptance of another cup of ale and the completion of our trade gave Og and I a chance to talk. It soon became clear that Og bore bitter grudges against me. I, in turn, still bristled at the memory of being abandoned in the clutches of the Greatmother, who I knew to be a tyrant but whom Og remembered as his saviour, his liberator.

'You left without me.'

'Too right we did. I was all for feeding you to the bears.'

'Why? It was Ussa who enslaved you. It was nothing to do with me.'

'Tell that to Rian.'

'What's Rian got to do with it?' I could feel myself reddening.

'Acting innocent still? You bloody slavers are all the same. You think you can treat a person like a tool, like a toy, nothing more than a pelt to lie on.' He plucked at one of the furs, and let it fall limp.

I felt shame rising, and fought it down. I had paid sufficient penance with the Greatmother and I was not going to be bullied by this man. I did not need to be ashamed. Or did I? To Og, it was as if time had not passed. He had no sense that I had answered for my deeds. Perhaps I never could.

'Where is she? Do you know?'

'Far away from you, thankfully. Except for the brats, she could have put what you did behind her. She's done well, though, I'll give her that.'

My gut froze.

'She has more than one?'

'There you go, feigning innocence again. Yours, of course. Twins, except it's nothing to do with you, is it?' He was shouting and everyone's eyes were on us.

I was blinking very fast, trying to absorb what he had said. Ever since Ussa had fixated on the prophecy told her by that druid, I had imagined Rian bearing my child. It was unknowable, perhaps nothing more than a fantasy, but it had sustained me in dark moments of my journey. This was confirmation and I couldn't disguise the feeling bubbling up. I was proud. I was joyful, even. It was true – I was a father! Is there any greater role a man can play? Twins! If one of them was a boy, he was my son. My son! I wanted to possess that child, I could not help myself. And as there were two, why, one of them surely could travel home with me.

'You know I was very fond of her. I never wished her any harm. She has done well, you say? Are they boys?' I had to work to keep my voice level. I wanted to say, 'Tell me everything you know. I want to know every move she has made.' But of course I could not.

'I don't remember. I just know that Ussa's still chasing after her, just like she's still trying to get the damn stone off the Walrus Mutterer.'

'What's that about the Walrus Mutterer?' the King said.

Og didn't miss a beat. 'He's nothing but trouble.' I wouldn't have thought so fast. He might not have been as drunk as he seemed.

The King said, 'Do you know him? Do you know his whereabouts? I'd like some ivory.'

Og laughed. 'On the ocean, in motion, in a dock, drinking hock.'

The rhyme set Bly to singing and while he sang, I asked Og, 'Does Rian travel with him?'

'How should I know? I saw her on Ictis and he wasn't there then. Why? Are you going after her?'

'No. I'm just interested.' This was a lie. I tried to remain relaxed, and looked him in the eye, but I was trembling with excitement inside. I had offspring! The past three years faded to insignificance. All I could think of was the girl with the amber hair, and my son, maybe even my sons, and how this might transform my future prospects! Now there were two reasons to make my way to Belerion.

BACK TO ICTIS

I travelled with Gurt further southwards to other ports until all his goods were exchanged for things he knew had value back in the amber lands. When he decided it was time to set sail eastwards again across the North Sea, of course I chose to stay in Albion. I was well rewarded for my time with Gurt and I had some skins and amber to help me to travel onwards.

Over the course of late spring and early summer I made my way down to the southern tip of the island and along the coast that fringes the narrow sea channel. I walked most of the way and saw many fascinating sights. I remember a chariot race, which was wild and terrifying – those drivers must have no sense of fear. I ran scared from a palisaded village when the people set their dogs on me, yet further on I was invited to visit a hill fort where I was treated as an honoured guest. I'm still not sure why. Along the south coast I marvelled at cliffs of white chalk, the edges of which are both dramatic and treacherous.

I was always interested to look at boats in harbours and

sometimes was taken on board for a leg of my journey. Like all the shores of Albion, the stretches I sailed taught me great respect for the wayfarers who understand their wild currents and complex tidal flows. I wrote about this at some length in my book, but many of the mariners from our sea mock me for fantasising. They simply do not believe that the seas could be as fickle and dangerous as Homer describes in his great legend of Odysseus. I sometimes wonder if his tale was based on experience of the northern seas. But enough of that. There is plenty of my speculation of such matters in the ocean book, so if you're interested, read that.

I enjoyed my walks, particularly because they gave me time to think about what I had learned from Og, that I was certainly a father. This changed everything, not least my status when I returned home. No longer a childless man, no longer still effectively a boy, as a father I would be entitled to join the Boule, the city council, to become one of the Timouchoi and help to govern the people. With a child of my own, I would be a responsible adult.

And what would the children be like? Twins! How was that possible? Were they boys? Did they, too, have amber hair and sea-green eyes?

I did the final leg of my journey to Belerion on a boat that was heading west to trade wine for tin. It had come from a region of the mainland to the east, the mouth of a big river, and its skipper was a fascinating expert on the tides and currents. I had mentioned Ictis to him and he had agreed to take me in his crew. He was one of my best sources of information about the tides. The diagram in my book of channel currents is based on a detailed chart he kept in a long, thin wooden box. I would have paid considerable gold for such a chart, but it was a possession I was lucky to get a sight of and could never have purchased. He only let me glimpse at it, then hid it away again. Afterwards I drew what I could, in simplified form, from memory. He corrected my mistakes, kindly enough, but would not let me look again at his chart. It was like a sacred object to him and I suppose in a way, because of its ability to save lives and allow him to predict the future behaviour of the water and the shape of land as yet unseen, it did contain a kind of magic. In my whole circuit of Albion, that one chart was the only diagram I saw on parchment. All the other mariners, Gurt included, sail the coasts based on memory, story-telling and songs.

So now I get to the part of this epistle you have been waiting for. I finally made it back to Belerion and I was delighted to reach the place where I had first been with Og and Ussa at the very start of my experiences of Albion, proving to my satisfaction that I had indeed circumnavigated the whole big island, even with three year's diversion across the North Sea and back.

At the island of Ictis, it was a breezy morning. We were greeted by a squadron of oyster catchers dashing back and forth before the waves on the beach, and by one of the Keepers – a calm, graceful woman who seemed to float towards us across the sand, the motion of her feet invisible under her long gown and her body so poised I felt myself in the presence of some goddess. She welcomed us with a warm, honeyed voice. We followed her. I guess some men must have stayed with the boat, but there seemed to be a large gang of us straggling along on our sea legs, looking forward to shedding ourselves of the grime of a long voyage. We were shown inside a large stone building and settled down on benches, taking over the space. Then people brought in food: platters of fresh fruits and warm bread.

The Keepers represent a pinnacle of civilised behaviour among people who are often brutish and ignorant. There was a procedure to go through. Each individual had to talk to a Keeper, one-to-one, about their intentions on the island, and as soon as the meal was over we were told to form a line and wait for our audience. Most of the crew found the whole operation exasperating and sat in a corner playing counters, but the skipper and some others were clearly keen to converse with a Keeper. I do not know what other people's experiences were. Some of the interviews lasted no more than a couple of moments. I suppose they must have answered no to every question. Others talked for long periods.

My interrogation was one of the longer ones. When my turn came I was taken to a small, round, wood and wattle cell. There were flowers in a ceramic vase on an altar-like shelf opposite the doorway, and the floor was strewn with straw and herbs that scented sharp and sweet as we trod on them. My host opened a wicker shutter to let in more light and then offered me a cup of water from an elegant pitcher. She was dressed in a long, pale green robe, like the woman who had greeted us on the beach. Her hair was white. It was like being in the presence of a lily in human form. She addressed me in Keltic.

'Welcome back, Pytheas.'

I was taken off-guard to be known. I wondered if this was going to be the start of an interrogation like the one I had suffered in the amber coast in the clutches of the mad Greatmother.

'Your hospitality is very generous,' I said.

'We like our guests to feel themselves welcome. This is a special place…' She paused and the sound of waves and seabirds filled the room. 'A restful place. What brought you back to Ictis?'

'I am on my way home, but I hope to take some of the smelting metal back with me.' I remembered just in time not to use the word 'tin'. 'I bought some when I was here before. I had gold then, of course. I have lost everything I had, but I need one ingot to take back to Massalia to prove that I have seen what I have seen, to prove I know its origin. If someone can give me some of the metal, I'll strip naked and offer them my skin.'

She grimaced.

I clarified. 'I have a wolf skin coat and leggings. And I have some amber that I can trade.'

'I will see if I can help with the metal. And is there any other reason you are here?'

I shook my head. 'I liked it here last time. I met interesting people. You have a beautiful garden and there is a gentleness about the place. I thought it would be a good place to prepare myself for the final leg of my journey.'

'Yes, we are quiet here. We like serenity.'

'Serenity. Yes, that's it.'

'You didn't come to see anyone in particular?'

She was clearly probing me for something. This was encouraging.

'No.'

'Are you sure?'

'Yes. Unless you know something of the whereabouts of a girl called Rian or a lonely stash of tin.'

'So you know that Rian lives here?'

'Here?'

She nodded. I must have acted surprised enough for her to believe it was news to me.

'She lives here?'

She nodded again.

'I had no idea.'

She said nothing.

'Is her hair still the colour of this?' I pulled out the amber bear.

The Keeper smiled briefly, but there was glinting stone in her eyes. She said nothing. The idea that Rian was here itched at me. I might see her, talk with her. Would she remember any of the Greek words I had tried to teach her?

'Can I see her?'

'Why do you want to see her?'

This person asked too many questions.

'We travelled to the northern ocean together. We had incredible experiences. She's beautiful.'

I am putting off telling you about our meeting, I know this. If I tell you every detail of the build-up to that moment, I may be able to defer it forever. Could I write in that much detail? I doubt it. I do not have the skill and my memory keeps jumping forward, to later, and I have to force myself to dwell on the period just beforehand, to interrogate myself about every nuance and inflection of thought, each phrase I exchanged with this lily-woman.

Why do I not just go on, get it over with? I could state it all so simply, but I want to pause here remembering the agony of believing Rian was close by. And the wondering, the doubt, the fear, the shame; I should admit to you that is what I felt.

Why should I be fearful, you may ask? Isn't it obvious? How was she going to feel? It is so difficult to consider someone else's inner state, especially someone like her, closed creature that she is. To care without knowledge is a curse. I knew she could not feel for me how I felt for her. I knew there was no reciprocation, that there could not be, and yet of course I could not help but hope, or at least wish. I wondered if I would still feel the same about her when I saw her, whether I would still find her lovely, though I couldn't harbour that doubt for long. And I feared the worst: that she would remember me with disgust.

'Does she hate me?'

The Keeper stood up and my eyes followed her so I found myself in a position of pleading, beseeching. It was a foolish question, heartfelt but stupid, and of course she didn't answer.

'When this boat leaves are you remaining with us, or going with them? I gathered that you want to go south across the Channel, is that right?'

I nodded assent and she continued.

'You are welcome to stay with us, if you will work with us, until a boat comes that can take you. Perhaps you would be willing to do a copy of a manuscript for us. I will show you to a room where you can sleep and write. And we will see what can be done about an ingot.'

'You're very kind.' I didn't know if I dared ask, but I had to. 'And Rian? Where will I find her?'

'She is not on the island.'

'Where is she?' Were all my hopes to be dashed?

Scorn crossed her face. I saw that she thought I was completely naive, and then she composed herself. 'I am not at liberty to say.' She closed the shutter. I realised she was waiting for me to get up. 'Are you ready?'

I pressed on. 'My child. She had my child, my children, are they here?'

She hesitated.

'They are, aren't they?'

She would not meet my eye and I felt sure this meant the answer was yes.

'I'm sorry,' I said, rising.

'What are you sorry for?'

'For boring you.'

'Don't be ridiculous.'

I was affronted, but her manner was now more garlic than lily and I wondered what she actually knew about me, what Rian had told people. I followed her out of the hut and around its side, and then up along the path running around the island, spiralling upwards towards the top of the hill. She strode, but not fast, and occasionally stopped to point out details of walling. By a strange piece, she said, 'This was built by the old Keepers of the Moon. See the way it runs.' She drew my attention to distant landmarks that appeared as we got higher, and showed me some flowers newly in bloom. She did all of this without appearing to desire any response and I was not in the mood to say anything to her.

When we stopped, I realised she had brought me to exactly the same place I had stayed the first time I was there, the same cell, with a small bed, two shelves in one corner and a bench outside to sit on and look down on the beach. I put my bundle down on the bed and she picked a pitcher off a shelf and showed me where I could fill it with fresh water from a barrel, and where I should relieve myself. They were fastidious about cleanliness on this island. I remembered it was something I had liked about the place.

She left me alone then and I dithered about, eventually lying on my bed, trying to imagine what I would do if Rian appeared, then realising that of course she wouldn't and instead wondering where my children might be. I had an urge to go looking, but I resisted it.

A blooming honeysuckle smelled delicious near to my cell. Why do I call it a cell? I felt like I was a bee in a hive. It was not possible to have an independent will on Ictis; some Queen sprit ruled there and all the rest of us were drones or workers.

The blossom wafted billows of soft nectar-perfume through the door of my cell, drawing me out to sit on the bench outside, leaning against the wall as the sun idled westwards. A blackbird sang its desirous song, which seemed to contain all the longing there is.

There were many other sounds too: the quiet croaking of frogs in a pond somewhere nearby, part of their clever irrigation or water-holding system no doubt; twittering hidden birds; bees in flowers, humming; the shush-aaah of the breathing waves out on the beach.

Eventually I went to find the sailors, drank enough so that I could sleep, and returned to my cell to wait.

Knowing Rian was hiding somewhere nearby, the guilt that I had been burying for three years finally erupted into my consciousness. I realised I must confess it fully, the deed I had done. Some men would say it is no crime, a mere commonplace, an act of normal nature, even a right. But I now know this cannot be. It would be an excuse, a pretence, to ignore my instinct, my certainty, that my behaviour, if not a crime, had wronged her.

What I did to Rian required a kind of violence in my soul that I have not mustered in any combat with a man, not that I have encountered much of that, I have to admit. I have never been in battle, but the few times I have been attacked and have had to defend myself involved a furious, righteous form of violence that left me feeling breathless and excited. That night on the ocean when I laid Rian down beside me and took her virginity was different. It was more like an act of theft, a stealing away, furtively and full of dread, with something beautiful that was not mine to take. It was like the killing of a small and exquisite creature for its fur. Some men may use euphemisms of seduction, or the language of the marketplace, but I must eventually confess to rape and admit to the true nature of my deed.

She said, 'No.' In that little voice. And then again. 'No.'

I have heard a better man than me describe himself as having made his slave a woman by such an act. All I know is that I unmade myself as a man by it. To this day I have never recovered myself entirely. I meet the broken edges of who I was up until that night, but never again have I known myself whole. I must break off now, finding one of those fractures within, which still hurts as much as it did when it was broken. If this is what it feels like to me, what must it have been like for her? I do not dare to imagine.

ICTIS

THE MEETING

The Keeper came back in the morning. I can't remember her name, so I'll just refer to her as 'the Lily'.

I was sitting outside on my bench looking out at nothing: a thick sea fog was in, and the sea was almost silent, barely whispering over the shingle and sand. She approached from somewhere higher up the hill. My attention was drawn by the sound of children: a squeal, laughter, more squeals. There were the two of you, boy and girl, both fair-haired, being led by a nursemaid, walking alongside the Lily on the wide path. I saw the children around her, like ivy around a tree. I looked again at the honeysuckle clambering over the willow behind my cell.

'Good morning,' I said. My voice quavered.

The maid pushed you two children in front of her, her hands on your shoulders, and you both stared at me.

'This is Pytheas,' the Lily said. 'He just said 'good morning' to you. Are you going to answer him?'

The two of you said absolutely nothing, guarding your voices from this unknown danger, but poking at me with your sharp eyes to make me speak again. I had the sense of what you might do with pointy sticks if you encountered a slow-moving animal.

'How are you?' I said. Four eyes looked down. I sensed some kind of intense communication happening between the two of you. You looked quite different from each other, yet in that moment it was as if you had a single consciousness. Two fair heads, a skinny, narrow-faced boy, a chubby, dimpled girl, one curious but wary soul shared between you. I intuited that immediately, I am sorry to confess, but in what happened from that moment I did not allow my intuition to guide me. I see now, looking back, that all the errors I have made in my life come down to ignoring my instincts, letting my rational mind be fed by greed and allowing it to govern my actions.

Although I don't remember exactly what the Lily and I said to each other that morning, I do remember it was all banal, stilted pleasantries exchanged over the barricade of the two of you.

I asked you, my children, what your names were.

'Soyea and Cleat.' The nursemaid spoke for you.

The Lily explained. 'These are the names of two islands close to Rian's home.' A pause. 'They wanted to meet you.'

I registered all that this remark implied. They must know I was their father. 'They must be a handful.'

'They keep me busy when Rian's away.' The nursemaid chuckled.

'Rian's away,' I repeated.

She looked at the Lily, who nodded and said, 'We have heard Ussa the trader is in the vicinity. I believe you will understand why Rian does not want to encounter her.'

Of course I did. 'So meanwhile you must take care of her children.' I looked sympathetically at the maid. You see, I made sure to establish early on that you were a burden. And then I set about wooing you.

The Lily bowed to me. 'I must return to my work.' She turned away back up the hill, leaving the children in the care of the nursemaid, who looked as if shyness would overcome her now that her protector had gone.

'Come inside.' I gestured in, but she shook her head. I got up from the bench. 'Then sit, please.' She did, if a little reluctantly, the two of you on her left hand side. I crouched, looking up into your faces.

I found myself fascinated by the two of you. I did not know how to win your confidence but I could at least be interested and nod and express approval of all I learned. I asked the maid all manner of questions, which she answered at first in monosyllables, and then, gradually, as if she was relaxing slightly, if only slightly, she began adding a little more in the way of explanation.

I established that you were just past your third birthdays, that you were staying on Ictis only until Rian returned, when you would probably be going somewhere north for the summer, that your favourite food was honey and cakes and that you liked playing on the beach better than anything.

Then I said I wanted to make a note, and I ducked into my cell and fetched out my writing tools. I hoped it might impress you. I explained that I liked to write the name of everyone I met, so I would remember them.

'Have you seen anyone writing?' I asked the two of you. I unrolled a parchment scroll with a flourish, waved my quill close to your noses as if going to tickle you with the feather and then did the same, cheekily, with the maid. There was almost a giggle from you at that. Your grumpy little sibling remained deadpan of course, but I knew I had the interest of both of you by your wide eyes. I set about making some ink, scraping my stick against the block and adding a little water. 'Do you want to stir it?' I proffered the stirrer. You both shook your little heads, but at least you were responding to me.

I stirred vigorously and then dipped my quill into the ink. I lifted it out and threatened to write your names on the ends of your noses. Your hands came up to cover your faces.

'Whose name will I write first? Rian?'

I penned the letters carefully, spelling it out. Then I did the same with Cleat and Soyea, and your eyes were big green pools of wonder.

'Do you want to try?'

'Don't waste your parchment,' the nursemaid said.

'What? It's not waste. A child's first letters? They're as precious as a child's first steps.'

One by one, the two of you took the quill, and tried to scribble with it. You were much the better of two of you. That's why I have some confidence, writing to you, that you'll be able to read what I have laid out here at such length. Not that either of you managed actually to write, but your scrawl at least resulted in a mark on the page that might evolve into a letter, with practice. Still you both seemed to enjoy playing with the feather and making splats with the ink.

'It's a kind of magic, isn't it?' I said. 'Perhaps next time you're on the beach you can write your names with sticks in the sand.'

I could see you liked this idea

'We'd better go,' the nursemaid said, getting to her feet. I got out of the way, so you could slip down from the bench.

'Well, thank you for coming to see me. I've enjoyed meeting you.' I meant it. I was pleased to have been able to make you this gift of writing.

'Say thank you to Pytheas.'

'Thank you,' you both said together, your first words to me. I can't tell you how moving it was, what a sense of achievement it brought. I had given you something worthwhile, sown real seeds.

GREED

I was taking my morning walk after breakfast, before I settled to my scribing duties for the Keepers. As with each day, I walked out to where I could see the sea horizon, scanning for ships. Riding in to the calm water behind the island – the tide was high – was a boat I knew intimately, its white-coated proprietor at the stern. As they approached the wooden jetty, lowering the sail, the boat passed beneath my view. As you can imagine all kinds of emotion arose at the sight of *Rón*, trepidation not the least, but I found myself hurrying down to meet the boat, like a drinker after a period of abstinence.

That woman. She was already on land by the time I reached the shore, shouting instructions to her slaves to unload her goods. I didn't have time to observe her before she recognised me, but the creature who strode towards me, arms outstretched, was, despite the eye-patch, still the same glamorous harpy of my first visit to this island. So the world goes around, and around again. She hailed me as if I were her favourite son. 'Pytheas!' Was there a tinnier note to her voice? Her face was still full, her body strong, her presence utterly in command.

I smiled into the hawk's eye, accepted her embrace and, with a squeeze, said, 'So, Ussa. I'm glad to see you. You owe me some tin.'

I pulled away to see her laughing at me.

'And how's that?' she said.

'There was a sack of my tin in the boat when you abandoned me to the mercy of the Greatmother.'

'You're not feared, are you?'

'Not of you, no.'

'I got a good price for you.' She was still smiling but her eye had narrowed.

I stared straight back.

She glanced behind her. Two of her slaves were approaching, big, brawny men as she always had. Behind them a tall robed man was clambering off the boat. I didn't recognise any of them. But then Ussa was looking beyond me, re-fixing her smile, and I turned. A group of six Keepers was approaching, the Lily at the front.

'You'll get your tin.' Ussa spoke without adjusting her wide, false, smile. Then she stepped aside. 'Greetings, Keepers! I am honoured to be here again. I hope all is well on fair Ictis?'

The obsequious tones of her diplomacy made me squirm, and several of the Keepers couldn't hide their revulsion. The Lily, of course, was a model of composure.

'Ussa. I will not pretend that you are welcome. What is your business here?'

'The druid was wanting a lift here.' She gestured at the tall man. One of the Keepers had run forward to hug him. I guessed he was her father. 'And there's always trade.'

'It is not the season.'

'The season! This is the modern world! Look, this man understands.' She pointed at me. 'It's always the season, everywhere but here, for trade.'

'As you said, not here. You may take your goods elsewhere.'

I had not heard the Lily speak with quite such acid tones before, and to my surprise, Ussa was bristling and talked back.

'People everywhere else flock to me to exchange what they have for what they want.'

'You feed on greed, and greed alone.'

'I nurture desire, that's all.' She tossed her head and allowed her voice to drop in pitch. 'People like to possess things. See Pytheas here, he's travelled half way around the world, and what's the first thing he asks me? Where's his tin? I have exactly what he wants. You have only ideas, and faith, and rituals.'

'Faith is stronger than greed.'

'Oh, you idealist, you!' Ussa chuckled, as if indulging a child. 'I do admire it in you, but you're wrong. Your days are done. Come, Pytheas. Just to be clear,' she addressed the Lily again, 'this is not trade. I have a debt to pay, that's all. I sold his tin ages ago, but I've plenty more where that came from and I'm sure you'll both agree one pure ingot is as good as any other.'

'The most valuable things cannot be so easily interchanged,' the Lily said.

'You sound just like Manigan. Everything has its price. Everything.'

The mention of that man gave me an idea. 'Are you still after him?' I asked, all innocent.

'Sadly yes, he evades me endlessly.'

'I saw him, you know.'

She rounded on me, her smile still wide, her one eye blinking a little too fast. 'Go on.'

'My tin?'

She swivelled to face the slaves standing behind her. 'Fetch Pytheas a hold-sack of smelting metal.'

There were four such sacks on the jetty. The bigger of the two men heaved one onto his back, carried it to me and dropped it at my feet. The metal made a pleasing clatter on the stone paving. I bent, untied the sack, took out an ingot and bent it, listening. It crackled. I tested two more. Both sounded pure.

'I don't deal in rubbish, as you know,' Ussa said.

'Thank you. You're an honourable woman.'

'Do you hear that?' Ussa held her hand out palm up, a cat-like satisfaction on her face, watching the Lily for a reaction. There was none forthcoming. 'And Manigan?' Her eye switched to me. The price of my tin was information, clearly.

'I saw them in Kantion. Manigan and Rian,' I said.

Her eye-brow raised slightly and I feared I might be straining credibility by suggesting they were together.

'He was trading ivory. They said they were going north, up the east coast, once all his ivory stock was gone. He seemed to be getting good value. If I had had this,' I nudged the tin with my toe, 'I'd have offered some of it.'

'You can join me. I'll track him down. And her, my runaway. You'll get what you want.'

I shook my head. 'All I desire now is to see my home again. I'm heading south.'

'Well.' Ussa rolled her eyes.

I knew how little she thought of the idea of home.

'I wish you fair winds. I take it my goods are not required here.'

'No.' The Lily said the word with such force it seemed to propel Ussa round and away. She didn't look back at us.

I picked up my sack. It was enjoyably heavy. 'Now all I need is an Armorican ship,' I said to the Lily as we walked together back up the hill. The other Keepers went on ahead, but she kept my slow pace.

'Why did you tell that lie about Rian?'

'I thought it might be a useful – what do you say – wild goose trail?'

'Why say she is with the Mutterer?'

'Ussa's mad for his stone. It was just a way of making something up that would pique her interest. I know a thing or two about her desires.'

The Lily said nothing, but I sensed I had created an advantage for myself.

'I mean Rian only good.'

The Lily looked at me sideways, and I pressed my point.

'I intend to take my son home with me.'

She lifted her chin and lowered it again. It was like hearing an ingot crackle. I had what I wanted.

DECISION

The next day, the Lily returned with the two of you. I was sitting on the bench in the sunshine. A fresh breeze filled the island with the rustle of vegetation and set the sea rolling across the beach. Waves were breaking on the shore with their regular heave, crash and hush of foam. I watched a big boat that had come in this morning at high tide and now lay at anchor. It looked Armorican: it was solid wood and beamy. I was anxious to be gone and I had a hope that this might be the vessel I could journey with.

I had walked down as soon as they had landed but the Keepers supervising the jetty said that the ship was strictly out of bounds to everyone. They assured me that one of them would visit me later and sent me back to my hut.

The Lily had one of you on each side, holding your hands, and you were both skipping down the track. As you got closer I heard you were singing a silly song, the rhythm of your steps fitting perfectly to the tune. You skidded to a halt just above my cell, panting.

The Lily said, 'You'll be leaving on her, then.'

I wasn't quite sure if it was a question or a demand.

'If she's going south, yes, I hope so.'

She had let go of your hands and you were both flushed and smiling. Cherubs, the pair of you, with an expectant air.

'They want to write again,' she said. 'Ask nicely.'

'Please can we do feather writing?' You asked so sweetly I laughed out loud.

'Of course. I'll get the parchment and quill.' I fetched my writing box and got out my tools, and this time you were keen to stir the ink in the bowl. As we got ready, I said. 'Do you know when they'll sail?'

'Tonight at high tide, probably. It's clear, and the wind is fair. They'll want to be away I'd guess, unless the Keepers' offer of hospitality is too tempting.'

We began by writing your names again. Then we wrote Rian's name and then mine. I stuck to the strange, twiggy little alphabet used for Keltic, even though it felt weird to write my name like that instead of in my usual Greek lettering, but I thought it would only confuse you if I tried to explain that different tongues had different alphabets. As it was, I needn't have worried. Your writing was an indecipherable scribble, a proto-alphabet all of your own. You were the precocious one of the two and demanded to look inside my codex and then asked me to read what it said, and you just accepted that the foreign language I spoke looked different on the page. I taught you to say a few words of Greek: 'boy', 'girl' and 'I love Mother', which made the Lily smile, with a bitter look in her eye.

I was remembering the early days of my acquaintance with Rian, when I watched her writing in sand and taught her some basic Greek vocabulary. Looking back did not make me proud.

Fortunately you were both too excited with your feather writing for my thoughts to linger anywhere but on you. You each drew a picture of yourselves doing your favourite things, unrecognisable to me, but then I wrote, 'Soyea dancing', under one scribble and 'Cleat building a sand fort' under the other and you ruined the rest of the page with your efforts to copy out the letters. Still, I can safely say no piece of parchment has brought me more joy. What are all the fine poems in the world if a child cannot experience the fun of scratching their own name? I have that sheet to this day. As words do, those marks have transcended time and I will carry that happy afternoon in the sun with you to my grave, and perhaps beyond.

It was as you were practising with the quill that I decided to stake my claim.

'When I return to Massalia, I really need to prove I am a father.'

She nodded, clearly waiting for what was coming.

'I shall take Cleat with me.'

'I know he is your son, but you have barely met. His mother

left them in our safekeeping.'

'Just for a little while, of course,' I said.

The Lily turned to Cleat. 'Would you like to go with Pytheas, to where he comes from, on that boat there?' She pointed to the mighty ship.

I watched a little face, all innocence, lift towards mine, look out to the ocean adventure and back to me, and nod. There was trust in that face, a trust I knew in my heart I did not deserve, but what a gift it was. No ingots of precious metal could ever feel more valuable.

'You'd bring him back soon.'

I wasn't sure if it was a question or not, but it seemed impossible to say anything other than, 'Of course, yes.'

Would I return? The idea had only occurred to me in that idle way every traveller has of imagining what a place may be like in another season, if it were actually home. Such fantasies are no more than that, but here, suddenly, I was faced with another thought entirely. This was my children's home. I could not only bring my son up to be a Massaliot, we could frequent this place as well. I could endear myself to your mother by being a doting father, visiting regularly. Of course I would return. I said it with all sincerity and saying it made it sound true, made it a promise.

'When?'

It was already midsummer. By the time I reached home it would be harvest time. And of course, once there, the child would need to settle, to be shaped into a Massaliot. I had no idea how long that might take.

'Your home is only a few days' sail away, you said.'

I had indeed said so, making light of my onward journey. She made me spell out again how far south I would need to travel and how long it would take. I told her it was far closer than Ictis was to the north of Albion, and I showed her my calculations that backed up my argument. She listened with close attention.

'How long would he need to stay? Will you return before Lammas? That's six weeks away.'

I laughed. 'No, no. Not so soon.'

'But by the equinox. After that the weather gets worse.'

I heard myself say, 'Oh yes, I'm sure by then', but I sounded more certain than I was. When I finally reached home, would I really be able to leave again so soon? I knew I should. And it would be good to establish the route between my home and this place as traversable with regularity. 'Yes, by the equinox. And if for some reason it is not possible I will send word somehow and certainly come first thing in spring.'

She frowned at this.

'I'm sure the equinox is more likely,' I added hastily, turning to Cleat and distracting everyone's attention back to the beach. 'We will have a fine time on board that ship, won't we? And then we'll sail back here before the summer's done.'

The sea was gentle and visibility was excellent. We could see far out into the ocean. Any journey seemed possible, nowhere too far or too difficult.

'And I, after all, am Pytheas.' I said. 'I have sailed to the edges of the known world. I have been to Thule and returned. I have been to the Amber Coast and returned. How difficult can it possibly be to return from Massalia?'

PARTING

Some hours later, I had made an arrangement with the skipper of the Armorican ship. I packed up my belongings and vacated my cell, thanked the Keepers for their hospitality and received warmer thanks than my services had really merited – but that reveals everything about those warm and gentle women.

I made my way to the nursemaid's hut. She had begun to pack a bag of children's clothes. You were trying to get her to include some favourite thing of yours, a little piece of blanket. You kept stuffing it in, but each time she patiently took it out and gave it back to you. It wasn't until then, I think, that the dreadful truth finally dawned on you: you were not both coming.

'You'll stay here with me, Soyea,' the maid said. 'Don't you want to stay with me?'

The tantrum you threw then took me aback. You hurled yourself to the ground and screamed with a volume I could not believe possible in one so small. I have to say I was glad you weren't the one coming on my journey. In retrospect, I know that passion like that is sometimes what it takes to get a person through the trials that life throws at us. You must have been feeling torn in two.

Your brother remained quiet through it all, at first appearing a bit smug that he had been singled out for adventure, then merely bewildered as the maid took you off to somewhere else, where you could not witness our departure. Whatever scene of grief you made was out of my hearing and sight. I can only hope it was briefer than the long, drawn-out suffering of your brother.

As your wails faded into the distance, Cleat studied me with a frown. The nursemaid's parting words to him were that she'd be back very soon, and I was impressed that this seemed to be enough to stop him from becoming upset. I tried to engage him in conversation.

'Have you ever been on a ship?' I asked.

He nodded.

I was crouching, to try not to intimidate him. 'When was that?'

He gave the merest shrug.

'Did you come here on it?'

His chin was wrinkling, and the nod was smaller this time.

'Do you like the sea?'

No response at all, just those wide eyes.

'Shall we look if we can see the ship we're going on?'

I stood and gestured out of the open door. He backed into

the corner and shook his head. His mouth was turning down at the edges. I crouched again. 'Now, Cleat. You don't need to be frightened of me. If there's anything you want at all, you can ask me for it. I want us to be friends. Do you understand?'

He stared at me. I wanted to believe he gave a tiny gesture with his head to indicate he did. Perhaps he just blinked.

I wished I had some little sweet thing to give him. I put my hand in my pocket. The little amber bear was there in its pouch. I took it out and showed him, offering it to him. 'Here, you can have this. Do you like it? See how it shines in the sun.' I let the light from the doorway illuminate it.

It seemed to transfix him. He reached out his little hand to touch it.

'It's a bear. Take it,' I said.

He looked up at me and back to the bear, then withdrew his hand.

'Really. You can have it.' I thrust it towards him.

He put his face very close to it and, like a jeweller, scrutinised it intently. His mouth relaxed, I swear it almost became a smile.

'You like it.'

He didn't respond, and we remained like this, my hand out-stretched, waiting, while he gazed at the bear unmoving for what seemed like minutes. It was like trying to get a wild animal to trust enough to take food.

Footsteps broke the silence and the maid returned. She, too, looked at the bear and cooed at it. 'Isn't it lovely?'

Cleat, seeing she was alone, said, 'Soyea?'

'Soyea's at Auntie Bea's.'

Tears began to flow then. The little mouth dipped again and he uttered a phrase that I was to hear more than I could endure in the coming weeks. 'Want Soyea.'

The maid swept him up into a cuddle, which stemmed his weeping. She turned him to face me and pointed at the amber bear. 'Look at the lovely bear.'

'Take it.' I offered it again.

Encouraged by the hug, he reached his chubby hand towards mine and took the little animal into his clutch. I suddenly had a fear that he might eat it, but he seemed to know it was only for looking at. For a while we had a truce. No tears, and I was optimistic the acceptance of the bear might be the start of a friendly relationship. The maid persuaded him to put it safely in its pouch, and the pouch in a pocket and we gathered our luggage and set off for the ship.

What happened next I cannot bear to set down in detail, my dear. It would break my heart again and I have not the strength to endure it over. Suffice to say that when the boat left that evening, both I and your little brother were blinded by crying. I remember affecting a cheery manner that I didn't feel at all, seeing the pain he suffered in parting with you.

HOME

I made my customary libations as our journey ensued, but the Gods are cruel. Cleat and I nursed our separate agonies on the long sea-voyage home. We were together, but in reality we were terribly alone, especially him, poor, desperate, beautiful, sea-sick boy.

I loved him. Please try to believe that. But to him I was a stranger. He would not call me father, even though it was obvious to all who saw us together that he was my son, a small, pale, image of myself.

The Armorican ship took us to the mouth of the Garonne where I met a trader who knew my father. We travelled together up river and through the hills to home. I was glad to have a friendly person to pass the time with because your brother was silent and excruciating to be with.

Once home, I hand-picked a motherly slave to act as Cleat's

nurse, and ordered fine clothes to be made for him. I wanted him to have nothing but the best. I even arranged a partition in my bedroom so he would have his own space.

We were feted in Massalia, of course, and I dressed in finery for my inauguration in the Boule. I decided to take Cleat with me, to show him off to my fellow citizens and to impress him with the grandeur of the ceremony. Though not as tall as a broch, it is a substantial building and more gracefully decorated than anything he would have seen in his homeland.

I ordered his nurse to have him ready to walk immediately after breakfast, but when I went to his room he was lying on his bed, face to the wall, barefooted and still in his nightshirt. I complained and watched as his nurse cajoled and eventually tussled with him to get him into decent clothes. Nothing she could do would persuade him to put the sandals on – he kicked and wriggled until I lost patience. I probably shouted at him and he seemed to admit defeat, limply letting his feet be manhandled into the little leather things, which he looked at with evident disgust. He walked as if dragging a chain behind him, and let me take his hand but didn't hold mine back. His rag doll acquiescence was maddening and I no doubt said things like, 'Show some life, boy.' He displayed no interest in the Bouleterion at all, nor my fellow citizens, several of whom greeted him in a friendly manner, none of which he appeared to register as either welcome or unwelcome. There was no light in his eyes, and during the proceedings he sat slumped in the corner of our family pew, apparently asleep. I assumed he was still tired from the journey. I didn't want to think anything worse than that.

But no matter what love I felt and tried to show him, no matter what the nurse I asked to lavish care on him would do, the wound of his separation from you and your mother was incapable of healing. I told him repeatedly that we would return to Albion. Perhaps he did not believe me.

On my arrival in Massalia, as I had expected, I had much to

do, both family and business matters to attend to, and my book to write. Everyone wanted to know what I had found out about the trade routes for tin and amber, especially, so my calendar was filled with invitations to dine with merchants, politicians and people with maritime interests, even some with genuine understanding of my scientific methods. Summer was soon over, the equinox came and I told him we would have to wait until the spring to make our journey back to Albion.

I fear I neglected him. I thought he would settle in time. I made sure he was offered the best of food: fresh vegetables and good mutton stews, bean soups, good bread, all the things a growing boy needs. He had a nurse and was well provided for with toys, including the ivory dolphin I had carved on *The Dawn*, and my bronze owl, symbol of Athena the wise, but he did not play like other children. I tried to teach him Greek but he said little, and it seemed that whenever he did it was to ask for you. I confess I grew tired of hearing your name, and I must have snapped at him to stop his incessant complaint of 'Want Soyea'.

I have done many things in my life for which I feel remorse and I know it is an endless, pointless waste to feel this way, but still I do, and still there is one thing that I regret more than anything. I fear I silenced him, the poor child. The truth is that without you, he wasted away inside himself.

After a while his nurse told me he was refusing to eat. I hoped it was just the difficulty of settling into a new place, and that hunger would eventually win the day. But in the darkest month of the winter, his nurse came to me one morning and said he had been raving in the night, shouting for his mother, for Soyea, screaming, thrashing, and she thought he was feverish. But when I went in to see him, he was lying in his bed, inert and pale. I sat for a while and he started to squirm and twist himself into odd shapes, making a strange growling, gurgling sound. When I touched his forehead it was clammy but not hot. He didn't seem to know me. I sought out an apothecary and asked his advice.

He said he was attending two other patients that afternoon and would call on us afterwards. I returned to the house, where I had correspondence to attend to and a visiting merchant occupied me for a while. It was this time of year and my brother was away in Athens, as he is now, so I was the acting head of the household.

When I looked in on the boy later, he was lying still, his breath shallow, brow hot to the touch, and I wished the medical man would come more urgently. When he finally arrived he took a cursory look at the patient, pronounced his diagnosis to be 'a chill', and assured me there was nothing to worry about. I had a lingering doubt, but who was I to argue?

Before bedtime I looked in again at the boy. He opened his eyes when I sat down beside him but he seemed to look right through me. I saw his dry lips shape your name, 'Soyea', which I had heard so often from him, but no sound came and his eyes closed at the same time as his mouth. I never saw them open again. I retired, trying to believe the reassurance from the apothecary, but was woken at dawn by the nurse, who simply said, 'come'.

He was dead. Perhaps this was the only way he could escape his pain. Was he too young to believe that spring would ever come? I sat at his bedside and wept.

I realise that in this long epistle I have circled around my feelings and my guilt. I do not want to be a man who lives full of regret, and yet I find myself treating this as a kind of confession. I have, I hope, explained the wrong I did your mother, Rian, when she was in my company. And yet, what I did to your brother, my only son, I can hardly bring myself to write. No words can express my anguish, Soyea. I know no way to say how sorry I am. And yet I am so, so sorry.

I think his silence has affected me. I have images in my head of him in his final days, so frail and so sad, but I don't know where I would find the words to go through all that sorrow again. Let me only say this: my love was not enough. You and your mother were everything to him and he was too young to

220

be taken from you. I should never have done it.

I will not bluster and try to justify it. Nor will I labour on about how heavy I feel. I don't deserve your sympathy nor do I seek it. I simply want to say that I didn't mean this to happen. I know it is no excuse.

I remember once, as a boy, killing a kitten accidently. It was pitiful. I cried and cried. I had murdered it, though I hadn't meant to, of course. I meant it no harm at all. I wanted to love it, to care for it, but it was in the way as I ran down the passage to the courtyard where lunch was being served, just before the door, hidden by the bead curtain put there to stop flies from coming in. I wasn't looking at my feet and trod on it. I must have broken its back. It mewed, and died. I was so ashamed I told nobody. They were calling for me to come and eat. I took it to my bed, floppy in my hands, but after lunch, when I returned, it was cold. I buried it. My father and brother never knew. I couldn't tell them I was crying for a kitten. I never told anyone until now.

And I feel it is the same with Cleat. I wanted to care for him too, but somehow I have killed him. The death of another innocent is on my hands. And yet, I long to believe he would have died anyway, and that where he is now is sweet. But these are excuses. There is nothing more I can say. I am a blank page.

This morning I cut my hair, went to Cleat's grave, and scattered the clippings. I am going grey.

We buried him quietly. The boy's nurse and my old nanny, Danu, sat by his bed and chanted dirges, preparing him for his passage. I encouraged Danu to sing all the Keltic songs she knew. I hope that Hades has been able to restore him to peace. I wonder if our underworld connects with those I visited in Albion. I think often of Seonag in her beautiful cave and pray that her spirits have found my little boy and care for him. I put a bronze token between his lips to pay for his journey to the land of the dead, hoping that the tin in it would return his soul to Mother Earth, as the miners I met believe.

We were a small, sober procession to the graveyard. I placed him in honour in our family tomb, with libations of milk and, after some deliberation, gull feathers, so that Hades might understand his soul belonged over the sea. I had someone come and play a lyre, but it was nothing like Seonag's beautiful playing. I hope my boy has gone where that music can comfort him.

After visiting the grave this morning, I walked down to the vineyard and up onto the hill overlooking the harbour. I had intended to go to the temple, but turned back. A raven flew over, flipped onto its back and then righted itself. I thought of your mother, as I do so often, and of you. I wish you the freedom of a bird and joy in your life, wherever you are, whatever you do.

I am so sorry, my dear, but now I have told you everything there is to know. For thirteen years I have carried the shame of his death. He would have been a young man. You, my dear, if you are reading this, must be a woman. I hope that you and your mother have escaped the clutches of Ussa.

So why do I write this now? Just to unburden myself, and perhaps in the vain hope that this letter can reach you and explain something of the gap that you no doubt feel in your life. I had promised I would return with him, but I was too ashamed to show my face in Albion again. I had no energy for journeying at all. I know your mother must have suffered agonies of uncertainty, wondering what happened to her son. This letter, if she reads it or if you tell her its contents, can offer no consolation.

I know I should expect nothing but your fury, even hatred, but if there is anything I can do to help you in any way, please know that nothing would give me greater comfort. I will not claim the title of my blood, for I have not been a father to you.

Nonetheless, I remain your anguished and loving friend,

Pytheas of Massalia.

ACKNOWLEDGEMENTS

It all began with Clachtoll broch, so my first thanks must be to the Iron Age architectural genius who worked out how to build a 15-metre-high, double-walled dry-stone tower. John Barber, of AOC Archaeology, calls him Ug – so thank you, Ug. You not only left a remarkable legacy on the shore of my home parish, but you sparked in me a fascination with your period and with the people who built, inhabited and visited your implausibly wonderful building. I must also thank Graeme, Andy, Alan, Charlotte and all the other members of the AOC team who have helped to bring the Iron Age (and indeed other periods) to life through their work in Assynt and indulged my wonderings about what Pytheas may have found here when he came, way back in 320BC.

Huge gratitude also to Gordon Sleight, who has repeatedly hired me to hang out with this brilliant team on their various digs, and to pick their brains while ostensibly writing blogs and media releases for them. Gordon has also read these books with a meticulous care and pointed out the many mistakes, anachronisms and pieces of wishful but implausible thinking that I wove into earlier drafts.

Professor Barry Cunliffe was also very helpful in his insights about Pytheas and in encouraging my ideas about what he might have been getting up to in this neck of the woods. Professor Donna Heddle was similarly key in helping me imagine the cultural world Pytheas found here. Staff of the National Museum of Scotland in Edinburgh, and the museums in Kilmartin, Stromness, Kirkwall, Wick, Inverness, Pendeen, Penzance, Copenhagen, Oslo, Krakow and Longyearbyen have helped me in my research over the years. Particular thanks to Neil Burridge for showing me his bronze-smithing magic, to the captains and crews of the Ortelius and the Noorderlicht, for amazing adventures in the pack ice and northern ocean, and to Ian Stephen for sailing wisdom and stories about the sea in times gone by. And thanks to everyone else who has talked to me about the Iron Age and helped me to time-travel back to when Pytheas made his amazing journey. All remaining historical inaccuracy is entirely my fault.

The book could not have been written without the chance to take some time out of the day job, and this was made possible by a generous bursary from Creative Scotland, for which I remain hugely grateful. It came about as a result of urging from staff at Moniack Mhor, who also gave me retreat space and moral support by simply believing in the project.

Margaret Elphinstone was my first reader, critical friend and mentor, and the long conversations and convivial times with her and Mike were priceless waypoints on the journey to the finished books. Jane Alexander and John Bolland were crucial readers of early drafts, so thank you both for the encouragement and helpful suggestions about story and characters. Thanks also to all my other writing buddies: Romany, Jorine, Anna, Maggie, Becks, Anita, Graham, Kate, Alastair, Phil and everyone else who has come to join in writing events in Assynt, not forgetting Ed Group, Helen Sedgwick, Peter Urpeth and Janet Paisley. I'm grateful to Lesley McDowell and Madeleine Pollard for editorial advice, Jei Degenhardt for proofreading, and to all at Saraband, especially Sara Hunt, for bringing it to fruition.

My Mum sadly didn't get to read this book, but her pride in me lives on and I'm grateful for it every day. Thankfully I have my Dad and my uniquely wonderful sister, Alison, offering endless support. Thanks to you both and to all the rest of our far-flung tribe.

This book was largely written at sea, so thanks to the crew of *Each Mara*, the most precious of whom is Bill, my patient mate and co-skipper, to whom I offer buckets of love and hugs, onshore and off.

In the first volume of the Stone Stories trilogy, Rian, a carefree young woman and promising apprentice healer, is enslaved by a spiteful trader and forced aboard a vessel to embark on a perilous sea voyage. They are in search of the fabled hunter known as the Walrus Mutterer, to recover something once stolen.

The limits of Rian's endurance are tested not only by the cruelty of her captor, but their mysterious fellow passenger Pytheas the Greek – and the mercilous sea that constantly endangers both their mission and their lives.

A visceral evocation of ancient folklore and ritual, *The Walrus Mutterer* is an epic tale that introduces an unforgettable cast of characters in an extraordinary, vividly imagined Celtic world.

LOOK OUT FOR

THE LYRE DANCERS

THE THIRD AND FINAL VOLUME OF
THE STONE STORIES TRILOGY

Years have passed, and Rian, still in search of the mystery
of her origins, decides to risk returning to Assynt.

MANDY HAGGITH lives in Assynt in the northwest Highlands of Scotland, where she combines writing with sailing, environmental activism and teaching – she is a lecturer in literature and creative writing at the University of the Highlands and Islands. Her first novel, *The Last Bear*, won the Robin Jenkins Literary Award for environmental writing in 2009. *The Amber Seeker* is her fourth novel. Mandy is also the author of three poetry collections, a non-fiction book and numerous essays, and the editor of a poetry anthology.